# International Praise for the Author

"This tense psychological thriller from Holland's answer to Nicci French utilises a classic trouble-in-paradise set-up . . . What makes it so effective is the broader picture Maier paints of dislocated dreamers out of their depth, obliged to cede control over their lives."

—*The Guardian*

"Maier sketches characters that go beyond the standard thriller stereotypes."

—*Barnes & Noble Review*

"Maier manages to lead us away from the path we thought we were following and constructs an intriguing morality tale that is a bestseller across Europe."

—*Daily Mail*

"A sly, unusual thriller."

—*Felony & Mayhem Press*

"Excellent writing."

—*Literary Review*

"Terrific."

—*Sunday Times*

"Excellent little thriller. If you like your crime fiction suspenseful, erotically romantic, tense and pacy, this is definitely a book for you."

—*Euro Crime*

# MOTHER DEAR

## ALSO BY THE AUTHOR

*Rendezvous*
*Close-Up*

# MOTHER DEAR

## A THRILLER

## NOVA LEE MAIER

TRANSLATED BY JOZEF VAN DER VOORT

Text copyright © 2015 by Esther Verhoef
Translation copyright © 2019 by Jozef van der Voort
All rights reserved.

Previously published as *Lieve mama* by Uitgeverij Prometheus in The Netherlands in 2015. Translated from Dutch by Jozef van der Voort. First published in English by AmazonCrossing in 2019.

Published by AmazonCrossing, Seattle

www.apub.com

Amazon, the Amazon logo, and AmazonCrossing are trademarks of Amazon.com, Inc., or its affiliates.

ISBN-13: 9781542042796
ISBN-10: 1542042798

Cover design by Shasti O'Leary Soudant

Printed in the United States of America

*Mother Dear,*

*Every morning when I wake up, I savor the scent of the sheets, the fall sunshine streaming through the skylight, and the comforting sound of birdsong. I hear thumps and thuds in the hall and the bathroom, and the children bickering as they get ready for school. I stretch out, relish the sensation—and then the crushing darkness falls once again. A voice in my head whispers, You can't feel good—you've done a terrible thing.*

*I often manage to convince myself it's just a small problem. Something that feels awful for a while but surely won't last. I'm getting good at it; you might even say I'm becoming an expert. More and more often, I manage to persuade myself that these horrendous memories have nothing to do with me, as if I'd witnessed a car crash or a robbery. Something life changing and harrowing—but for somebody else.*

*Not for me.*

*I like that last thought best of all.*

*And so, everything goes on like it always has: chores, school, work. But those dark and dreadful memories are anchored in my soul, unseen by the outside world.*

# Three Weeks Earlier

# Friday

# 1

Brian grabbed Ralf's computer and pulled it onto his lap, not noticing his friend's weak protests—or simply ignoring them.

Ralf was used to Brian's pushing him around. And anyway, it was pointless trying to stand up to him when he was using. Ralf took a sip of his Red Bull, laid his head against the worn sofa cushions, and looked up at the ceiling of the shed. The cobwebs had woven themselves like lace around the fluorescent light, and the fiberboard ceiling tiles resembled a tangle of worms. He squeezed his eyes shut. His head was throbbing. Not just because last night had been a long one, but mainly due to his mother's nagging. She'd called him no fewer than thirty times and sent countless messages. Like some kind of stalker. He hadn't seen the messages until this morning—his phone had been off.

He'd stumbled home around six o'clock to find his mother blocking the way to his nice warm bed. She'd been sitting in the kitchen, her eyes hollow and bloodshot, a half-empty bottle of wine on the table. She'd grounded him—*grounded!* Like he was still a baby.

He was eighteen, for Christ's sake.

He had a car.

What gave her the right?

He had to move out, and soon. Maybe rent a place with friends somewhere in Rotterdam or The Hague. If only he had the money.

His mother had yelled and yelled, barely pausing to breathe. His father had appeared when he heard the noise but hadn't gotten involved. He never did. "Your mother knows you better than anyone," he'd said, before heading off to work.

But she didn't know anything about his life. He'd snuck out a thousand times before to drive to The Hague or Antwerp with Brian or other friends. They'd done things she'd only ever seen on the TV shows she always sat gawking at like a zombie. No, she didn't have a clue. But she still thought she knew everything about everything.

And she loathed Brian.

"Why can't he make friends with people his own age?" she would say. Or, "I don't like his attitude."

Ralf would shrug. She didn't have to hang out with him, did she?

Some of his friends had also warned him about Brian. They were just scared of him.

Too bad for them. Whether they liked it or not, Brian was his friend. He was OK. Maybe not for everyone, but he was right for Ralf.

*A friend to everybody is a friend to nobody.*

# 2

"Ugh, typical." Helen felt the first drops as she pushed her bike out of the garage. She turned up her collar, lowered her head, and cycled past the barriers and onto the main road. It had been dry and sunny all day, but as soon as she finished work, the heavens had opened. Cursing under her breath, she veered around a pedestrian who was opening an umbrella in the middle of the bike path. The smell of wet asphalt and damp earth filled her nostrils, and her thoughts wandered to the tattoo on her forearm she'd gotten a few months ago. It was very subtle. From a distance, it looked like a gray stripe, but when viewed up close, it read "Count Your Blessings."

Worse things could happen to a person than a little rain. She saw the proof of that firsthand every day. The anxiousness that had filled her since she became a mother was only amplified by the struggles that so often played out in front of her. Patients would get an injection, close their eyes, and disappear—and where they went, nobody knew. All that was left was a limp, helpless body that the sickness had to be cut out of. But sometimes the sickness couldn't be excised—and very occasionally, the blood pressure would drop, the heart would stop beating, and no amount of effort could bring the patient back from wherever they had gone.

Death didn't discriminate. Not by age, not by gender or race. Whether you were beautiful or ugly, fat or thin, it made no difference. Death took what it wanted, at random.

That was why she still always felt a wave of relief when her daughters and her son got home safely from school or from a party. There was no sound more reassuring than the thud of their heavy wooden gate.

Helen hummed along to a Beatles track on her iPod. She wasn't a Beatles fan except for this song, because her mother used to sing it to cheer her up. The rain might be falling now, but George Harrison's warm tenor assured her that the sun was coming.

She breathed deeply, drinking in the damp air. The tires on her Batavus hissed along the path.

In the distance, she could already see the edge of the forest, the trees and shrubs lining the old railroad embankment. Nearly home.

# 3

Brian entered an address on Google Maps and zoomed in on the aerial photo with rapid, impatient movements. The image froze above a detached house on the outer edge of a well-to-do suburb. This house had the biggest yard of all, plus a light-blue rectangle lined with deck chairs.

"Nice," whispered Ralf.

"Should I tell you a secret?" Brian leaned in closer. His small brown eyes glittered. Brian's left eye was slightly smaller than his right, giving him a permanently angry, defiant look. "Did you know these people keep cash in their house? A lot of cash?"

Ralf didn't stir. He tried to keep his expression neutral. They'd talked about it so often. A robbery. Not a shop or an office, where there would be cameras everywhere and maybe even a gun behind the counter, but somebody's house. That was where the easy money was, ripe for the taking in the form of watches, gold, diamonds, and cash—provided you knew where to look.

"How do you know?" Ralf tried to swallow, but there was a lump in his throat.

"I've got eyes and ears." Brian looked back at the screen. He zoomed the aerial photo out until you could see that the house stood on a dead-end road, partly hemmed in by trees and shrubs. "Perfect," he whispered.

# 4

Wildenbergh was nearly one hundred years old by the time an entire neighborhood sprang up around it during the early nineties. That was why their backyard was so much bigger than those of the other houses. She and Werner had neighbors on only one side: a childless couple— both architects—with whom they didn't have much contact. Woodland, shrubs, and ditches surrounded the yard on the other two sides. Behind that lay an embankment overgrown with bushes and poplars, on top of which there had once been a railroad line. The cart track that ran along it now was rarely used. Total privacy. Nothing but greenery and freedom. Living in a place like this felt like a permanent vacation.

Helen had known about the former farmhouse for a long time. She had biked past it often enough back when the nearby towns and villages hadn't yet swelled into one big sprawl. Even as a child, she had found the house beautiful and imposing, with its big, tall windows and grand front door, and that love had never left her. Werner had been easy to convince when it came up for sale seven years ago. Thom and Sara were in third and fourth grade back then, and Emma was still in first; they had grown up in the house that their mother used to daydream about as a child.

Helen biked under a dark and dense thicket of treetops—oaks, poplars, and birches that had stood for as long as she could remember. After passing the embankment, she left the paved road and joined a narrow, sandy path that led downhill through shrubs and parkland. Many local bikers used this track instead of the main road. It led onto a dead-end street; on the left were full-grown hazels and hawthorns, and opposite them, two large houses. One was the sleek white villa belonging to Otto and Frank, and the other was Wildenbergh, the name immortalized in a mosaic on the façade.

Helen wheeled her bike up the driveway and pushed open the tall wooden gate between the house and the garage.

She parked her bike by the deck. Thom's and Emma's were already there, Emma's schoolbag hanging from the rack by her handlebars. Helen sighed as she picked it up and walked through the back door into the house.

Thom hadn't done much better with his bag—it was lying on the floor in the utility room. A little farther on lay Emma's coat, three and a half pairs of shoes, an energy drink bottle, and a lunch box. The TV in the kitchen was playing Comedy Central, interspersed with the tinny sound of music from a smartphone.

Helen raised her voice. "Hello? Are you going to clean up your things?"

No response.

She hung up her coat and entered the kitchen. "It's not very nice to come home and find it looking like this, guys." She made a show of placing Emma's schoolbag on the dining table. "This was still on your bike."

Emma glanced up from her laptop. She was wearing black eyeliner. "Did anybody die at the hospital today?"

"I expect so, but not in my department."

Emma looked back at her screen. She had begun using makeup when she started junior high, but she wasn't very proficient. There were clumps of mascara on her eyelashes and dark smudges under her eyes.

Helen wanted to mention it but bit her tongue in time. Living in a house full of teenagers was like walking through a minefield. "Where's Thom?"

Emma shrugged.

"Don't you have any homework?"

"Just an exam on Monday." Emma divided her attention between her laptop and her cell phone. Her thumb glided across the cracked screen.

Thom walked into the kitchen. "Hey, Mom," he said, and wrapped his arms around her.

Helen kissed the top of his head and tousled his soft, reddish curls. Her friends' sons had all grown distant overnight, but Thom had remained his old cuddly self, even though he was already fifteen and shaving twice a week.

"Sara stole my charger," said Thom.

"Borrowed," Helen corrected him.

Thom let her go. "If I don't ask for it, I won't get it back. That's called stealing. And now she's probably at Jackie's place again, right?"

Helen nodded. Her elder daughter—who had turned seventeen this summer—had biked straight to her best friend's after school and would spend the night there. Helen assumed she wouldn't see Sara again until Sunday evening; the girl treated Wildenbergh like some kind of all-inclusive resort. She was planning to study in Leiden next year, and then she'd come back only on weekends to have her laundry done. Helen didn't want to think about it too much.

"Mom, I want a tattoo as well," came a voice from behind the laptop.

Helen looked up in surprise.

Emma gestured over the right-hand side of her body. "Around here, a branch with pink and red flowers."

"That sounds great."

Emma's face veered between disbelief and joy. "Oh, Mom, really?"

"Sure, why not? Maybe you could get a snake on your neck too—it'd be so cool, all the way up to here . . ." She drew a line with her index finger from her cleavage to behind her ear.

Emma's face fell. "Don't be stupid, Mom."

"You started it. We'll talk about it again when you're twenty."

Emma pushed her laptop away. "What about Sara? She's getting one tomorrow."

Helen froze. Despite the four-year gap between them, her girls were close.

"Don't look at me like that," continued Emma. "She's going to Antwerp tomorrow with Jackie, and they're going to get matching tattoos."

"Oh, even better." Helen took her cell phone out of her bag and dialed Sara's number.

"You've got a tattoo yourself, you know."

"I'm forty. Your sister is seventeen."

*The number you have called cannot be reached . . .*

Helen tried one more time, against her better judgment. Irritated, she hung up and sent Sara a text, then sent another to Jackie just in case:

Could you tell Sara to call me tonight? Thanks, Helen

Helen rubbed the top of her nose and closed her eyes. She'd been looking forward to this evening. A bubble bath and a nice glass of wine. Peace and quiet. It would have been even better to spend the evening with Werner, but he generally worked late on Fridays, or went back to the Horn of Plenty, his restaurant, after dinner.

Thom looked at the cold oven. "Hey, Mom? What's for dinner? It's almost five o'clock."

# 5

"I'll see you tonight." Brian clapped him on the shoulder and then squinted out through the grimy window of the shed.

Brian did look pretty thuggish, thought Ralf. But his girlfriends were always hot. His latest conquest, Naomi, was one of the prettiest girls Ralf knew. Kindhearted. Big dark eyes. Smooth, golden-brown hair. She was so beautiful, he felt bashful whenever she was around. It was embarrassing. That was why he pretended to have no interest in her whatsoever.

"They aren't back yet," said Ralf. "My father doesn't come home until five thirty, and my mother gets in even later." He opened the door and stepped into the backyard—"the plaza," as Ralf's father called it. That was a more accurate description, anyway, for the big square of bare pavement enclosed by a fence.

"What was all that bullshit about being grounded?"

Ralf shook his head. "Oh, it's nothing."

Brian gave him a probing look. "Are you sure? I need to know I can count on you, remember? I can't do this thing alone."

"Relax. It'll be fine. I'll pick you up at seven fifteen."

# 6

"Can you drive us to tennis, Mom? It's raining."

Helen looked outside. The smooth paving slabs and trimmed boxwoods shone wet, but the surface of the pool was calm and even. "It's stopped now."

"I bet it'll start again soon, though."

Thom watched his sister tackle the subject from behind his laptop.

"Mom?" she continued. "My hair will get frizzy if I go out in that."

Helen regarded Emma in silence. Her daughters had inherited her hair texture, and she knew how much effort it took to keep her blonde fuzz under control. A few drops of rain were enough to undo hours of work. She opened her mouth to agree, but Werner got there before her.

"That's enough nonsense, Em. You can both bike there. Your mother isn't a taxi driver."

"News to me," muttered Helen.

Werner sat down at the table and turned toward Emma. "There's such a thing as rain gear, you know. That's what we used to wear to school or the gym. Man, the places I used to bike."

"Used to, yeah," grumbled Emma.

"The rain was just as wet back then as it is now."

Helen looked inquisitively at her husband. He didn't stand up for her like this very often. Back when the kids were still small, he had been a good and active father, but now that they had begun to develop minds of their own—and opinions that didn't always coincide with his—he had increasingly left the parenting to her. Perhaps it also had to do with his work. Managing four busy restaurants was more than a full-time job. Renovations, PR and advertising, hiring and firing—he had a lot more on his plate than he used to, and he was less playful and lighthearted as a result.

*But aren't we all?*

Helen's work as a recovery room nurse hadn't gotten any easier either. Protocols were constantly changing, and by the time you'd grown accustomed to one state of affairs, you'd already find yourself having to adapt once again. Everything had intensified over the last few years, including at home. The children had seemed to transform overnight from cute, chattering little imps into inexhaustibly belligerent guerilla fighters.

She rubbed her fingers over her tattoo and told herself that she loved her job, and that it was her own decision to work full-time. Things were going well with Werner's restaurants. The children were healthy. So was she. They lived in a dream location inside a dream house.

*Count.*
*Your.*
*Blessings.*

# 7

"It's time," said Brian. The sticker on the brim of his cap gleamed in the moonlight filtering through the windshield of the Volkswagen Polo.

Ralf looked straight ahead and said nothing. They had watched the sun go down from their position in a sandy recess on the old railroad embankment. From up here, they had a good view of the house, but the undergrowth concealed Ralf's matte-black car well.

Brian knew what he was doing.

Ralf's bony fingers squeezed his energy drink. The can popped. "OK."

Brian bent forward next to him. He had casually rolled up a twenty-euro note and now made sniffing noises.

Ralf couldn't watch. He focused on the dashboard clock—7:40. He absolutely loathed the stuff Brian was snorting. It did something to his character. At first, Brian had just done it on the weekend, every now and then. Lately, he was taking that shit at every opportunity. He must be getting addicted. Maybe he already was.

"And what if the police come? What should we tell them?"

Brian lifted his head and rubbed his nose. "The police won't come."

Ralf said nothing. Squeezed the can again.

*Pop.*

"You scared, bro?"

"Of course not." Ralf hated the tremor in his voice, the incessant trembling of his body, his rapid breathing. The more he tried to conceal his fear, the more it forced its way to the surface.

It was at times like these that the differences between them became painfully clear. Brian was capable of anything. And he got away with it too—except last time, when he lost his license for drunk driving. He'd even spent three months behind bars. Some guys in prison had taught him a thing or two.

"Here, have some of this, you pussy." Brian pushed the fold of paper toward him. His eyes gleamed—two dark hollows under the shadow of his cap.

Ralf looked straight ahead, sullenly. "I don't need that crap."

"Suit yourself."

"I have to drive, remember?"

"Sure." Brian stuffed the package into his bag and opened the glove compartment. A pale light shone through the car. He pulled out a pistol and shut the door quickly.

Ralf recognized the gun. Dull metal, covered in scratches. It looked deceptively real, and felt it too. But it wasn't. Instead of lethal bullets, the grip contained a gas cartridge. It was just a BB gun. It wouldn't kill anybody.

Ralf watched Brian weigh the gun in his hand and shuddered. Fake gun or not, this was different from everything they had done before. What if they were going too far?

## 8

Helen stood by the kitchen island with her gym bag over her shoulder and looked at Werner. He was sitting at the kitchen table, absorbed in the newspaper, a frown line between his eyebrows. His soft, red, curly hair gleamed under the kitchen lights. Unlike other men, Werner had grown better looking over the years. More attractive, mature, and just as fit as when they first met almost twenty years ago.

She toyed briefly with the idea of not going to the gym. Thom and Emma were at tennis, so she and Werner would have the house to themselves for the next few hours. That didn't happen very often. But she hated letting Arianne down. Besides, there was a good chance Werner would be called back to work soon, this being Friday. She had long since given up getting annoyed about it.

Helen picked up her phone from the kitchen island and looked at the screen. No reply to her messages.

"Werner? Emma said Sara's planning to get a tattoo tomorrow."

"Out of the question."

"My thoughts exactly. But she's staying with Jackie, and I haven't been able to get ahold of either of them."

He looked up from the paper. "I absolutely won't have it." It sounded like an accusation, and his look gave the same impression.

"What can I do about it?"

He pointed to her arm. "If it weren't for that impulsive decision of yours, then she wouldn't have come up with the idea in the first place. I've never heard her mention tattoos before."

Resistance welled up in her. "Werner, I'm an adult. It's different."

"Bullshit. You should be setting an example."

She tried to remain calm. Looked down at her glass. "What about you, then? With all your beer? Are you setting an example?"

Werner shook his head and folded up his newspaper. "I don't want an argument, Helen. Go to the gym. I'll give her a call."

"But if—"

"We can always head over to Jackie's later if need be."

*We . . .*

*Later?*

He stood up from the table and walked over to her. With his long fingers, he tucked a strand of unruly blonde hair behind her ear. Planted a kiss on her forehead. "Make sure you're back on time."

"Why?"

"It's a surprise." He raised an eyebrow. "However, I can tell you that it might have something to do with your favorite actor, his latest project, and a reservation for two."

She grinned. "That doesn't tell me very much."

"Well, it wouldn't be a surprise, then, would it?" He looked down at her with amusement.

"And the kids?"

"Those two won't do anything crazy, and they can get ahold of us whenever they want. And after that surprise"—he kissed her cheek, her ear—"I have another surprise lined up for you. A very big one . . ." He pulled her hips toward him. His mouth formed a smile, but his eyes didn't join in.

It confused her a little.

"Do you remember when we first met?" he whispered. "You were still living with your mother, and I was in that room in Rotterdam. I used to live on macaroni with ketchup, and I didn't have a penny to take you out to dinner."

She nodded. She could remember it all very well, but it felt like scenes from the life of a different couple.

"When we decided to move in together, we had nothing. But we felt rich, because we only needed each other." He rubbed her shoulders. "Guess what the good news is?"

"Tell me."

"We still have each other. Lately, I haven't appreciated just how special that is." He kissed her tenderly on the lips.

Her fingers stroked the rough fabric of his polo shirt. She breathed in Werner's scent as if discovering it for the first time. How long had it been since they had last stood so close together, actually made contact with each other? Their conversations were always about the children. School. Work. The house.

"I miss it sometimes." Her voice was emotional.

"What?"

"Us."

He held her chin and kissed her on the lips again, then on her nose.

"Should I call Arianne to cancel?"

He let her go. "Of course not. Go and work that beautiful body of yours into a sweat. I'll see you later."

"But . . ."

"I'll take care of Sara."

"Are you sure—"

"It'll be OK. You get going."

# 9

Ralf looked at his friend, who was replacing his cap with a balaclava. All you could see were those glittering brown eyes and part of his mouth.

Ralf had already pulled his own balaclava over his head. It was itchy and smelled new. He followed Brian's gaze toward the house. The yard behind it was dark, with just a pale glow emanating from the swimming pool.

They had seen two children bike away. Shortly afterward, their mother had left the house and driven off in her Fiat.

"What if there are more people inside?"

"There aren't," said Brian. "Just the dude. And the dough."

"What makes you so sure?"

"You leave the thinking to me."

Ralf's phone began to buzz in his pocket. He pulled it out like it was on fire. *Mom* showed on the screen. He dismissed the call and put the phone on silent. "She figured out I'm not there. That'll be yet another drama."

"Stay at my place tonight. We'll have something to celebrate soon, anyway. I'll call up a few girls and—"

"What about Naomi?"

"What she doesn't know won't hurt her."

Ralf tried to run his hand through his hair, but his trembling fingers dug into his balaclava. He had to restrain himself from pulling the thing off his head. It seemed to be getting tighter and tighter. Suffocating him.

Brian jabbed Ralf in his side. "Come on. The only thing you have to do is keep an eye on everything from outside."

"How can you be so sure the guy will do what you say?"

Brian extended his arm. The barrel of the gun pointed toward Ralf. "I'll aim at his head."

"Yeah, but that thing is fake. What if he shoots back?"

"Are you kidding?" Brian turned the gun over in his hand. The metal gleamed in the moonlight. Brian was breathing really fast, Ralf noticed. Those goddamn drugs. His friend was gone, and now he had to put up with a coked-up prick who was convinced of his own genius and invincibility.

Ralf drank the last drops of his energy drink and threw the can into a box on the back seat. He hated getting his car dirty. The Polo meant everything to him. His freedom. That car took him everywhere—Germany, Amsterdam, wherever. But it cost him a fortune in gas—not to mention tax, insurance, maintenance . . .

Freedom was expensive.

That was why he was sitting here.

"OK, listen, dude." Brian grabbed Ralf by the coat, his hands balled into fists. He held his face close to Ralf's. "Look at me." He shook him gently. "The people who live in that house are up to their necks in cash, and soon it'll be ours. OK? Fuck 'em. Say it with me."

"Fuck 'em . . ."

"Exactly." Brian patted him on the cheek. "Look at it this way: we're just making a withdrawal."

# 10

Helen grasped the handles of the machine and pushed them forward. *Four, five.* Her trainer had told her that she needed to keep breathing while she did this exercise, but it was impossible, so she held her breath and got through her reps as quickly as possible. *Nine, ten.* Done. Her arms dropped against her body.

The gym was busier than usual tonight, and there were lines for some of the machines. A dance class was underway next to the fitness area, with a group of twentysomethings being encouraged by a loud instructor. Their soundtrack matched the music playing from the line of TVs that hung over the cardio equipment.

Helen stood up. Enough for today. Arianne was on a cross-trainer on the other side of the room. Her face was red from exertion.

"Are you going already?"

Helen nodded. "Then there'll still be something left of my evening. I won't be at the gym next week, remember—that's when Thom's having his party."

"Do you need any help with that?"

Thom wanted to celebrate his sixteenth birthday in the garage with forty friends and classmates. One of them was Arianne's son; the boys had known each other since elementary school.

"Thom wants to arrange everything himself. I don't think I'll be allowed anywhere near the garage. But you're very welcome to come over for a drink in the kitchen."

"The old folks' club," laughed Arianne.

"I'm afraid that's how the boys see it, yes."

"Do you know what you'll do for drinks yet?"

"We'll get some beer in, and some *tinto de verano*."

"*Tinto de* what?" Arianne's movements were growing slower. Sweat glistened on her cleavage.

"Werner's idea. You fill a glass with ice, then pour in one part red wine and three parts Sprite. Everybody likes it, and it isn't so strong."

Arianne grinned. "No doubt they'll bring the harder stuff from home."

Helen thought back to Sara's sweet sixteen; the following morning, there had been empty whiskey and vodka bottles strewn across the yard. Not one of them had been bought by Helen. But Thom wasn't such a partier; nor were his friends.

Arianne got down from the machine and dabbed her face dry. "You know, Helen . . . I was talking to Jeroen yesterday. He agrees it's a shame we've seen so little of each other recently. Do you remember when the four of us used to spend entire weekends on the road?"

Helen smiled sadly. "Those were the days. But Werner was still a regular employee back then. And the children are older now."

"So you don't have to hold their hands all day anymore."

"No, but now there are other things." Helen's thoughts wandered off to when the children were still small. Sitting on the sofa together watching *Teletubbies*, feeding them yogurt, going on adventures in their own yard . . . Now they could hop on their scooters or get on a train and be exposed to all the dangers she'd protected them from before. Alcohol. Bad company. Crime. Drugs. Sex. Violence. Every generation made the same mistakes, but with new victims each time. She could only hope it wasn't her children who ended up as cautionary tales. On top of that, she had to choose her words carefully these days to avoid alienating them. Their conversations were more inhibited, with deep emotions on both sides. "Parenting is less time-consuming than it used to be, but it takes a lot more energy," she finally said. "I'm often too exhausted to leave the house in the evening."

"But you take on an awful lot too, you know. Three kids, a full-time job, and Werner is never there. Why don't you cut back on your hours a little? I mean . . . for some people, I understand that there's no choice, but you guys really don't need the money."

Helen gave her friend a sharp look. "I love my work."

Arianne took a sip from her water bottle. "I understand that, but it wouldn't be such a bad idea for one of you to take your foot off the gas a little."

"And why should I be the one?"

"Well, it would be trickier for Werner, what with all the people working for him and all the things he's responsible for."

Helen raised her eyebrows. "Since when are financial responsibilities more important than the responsibility for somebody's life? If I don't do my work properly, people might die."

"Jeez, Helen, don't be so dramatic. You get what I mean."

"No—I don't get it at all, actually, especially not coming from you."

Arianne refused to take the bait. "It's just—it'd be easier for you to reduce your hours than it would be for him. That way you could still enjoy your work and also have more time for yourself. For the whole family." She raised her hands in a gesture of submission. "And for your friends, of course."

Helen regarded her in silence.

Arianne shook her head. "Oh, forget it. You're taking it all far too seriously. I just miss you, that's all. We used to have so much fun, the four of us. Man, I always used to ache the following day from laughing so much."

"Those times will come again," Helen heard herself say. "I mean it. But I have to go now. Werner is waiting for me."

"On a Friday night? That's new."

"We're going to the movies. His idea."

"Well, I never. When was the last time that happened?"

"About a thousand years ago."

# 11

Ralf could scarcely keep up with Brian. He was almost running. They'd walked down the side of the yard and scaled the wall, avoiding the loose soil in the flower beds and stepping on paving slabs, lawn borders, and wood chips so as not to leave any tracks.

At the deck, Brian held out his arm to stop Ralf. They peered through the foliage at the back of the house. All the lights inside were on. Through the window, they could see an open-plan kitchen with an island and a large wooden table with leather chairs. There was a broad, open staircase in the corner. The kitchen was as big as the entire ground floor of Ralf's parents' place. A man was sitting at the table, making a phone call. He was slim, with a blue polo shirt and slightly wavy hair, and looked very youthful for somebody old enough to be Ralf's father. A little preppy too—not exactly a man who would offer resistance to an armed and masked intruder. Nonetheless, Ralf's heart skipped a beat at the thought of Brian's going inside.

"Put down the fucking phone," whispered Brian. He kept repeating it, like an incantation. He shifted his weight from one foot to the other and rolled his neck over his shoulders.

Ralf looked at his friend in alarm. Brian was too jittery, too aggressive. Adrenaline and coke were coursing through his veins. It was worse than usual. Slowly, it dawned on Ralf that this could easily go wrong. He had to get out of here while he still could.

Inside the house, the man put his phone down on the table and stood up. Walked over to the kitchen island, took something from the counter, and pointed it at the TV. Flicked from channel to channel.

"See you later," he heard Brian say loudly. No more whispering—was he out of his goddamn mind? Brian stepped out from behind the shrubs and headed toward the house.

Ralf watched him dart toward the back of the house like a thin black shadow, pause for a moment, and then push open the door. Vanish through the gap. Close the door behind him.

The man inside was still channel surfing, oblivious to any danger.

Seconds passed.

It was taking too long.

What was Brian doing?

Ralf's breathing was rapid and shallow. He tried to calm himself. Then he saw Brian enter the kitchen. The man looked up. He said something; Ralf saw his lips move. Whatever it was, it had no effect on Brian. He didn't break his stride, darting fluidly around the kitchen island. The man hesitated for a second before breaking into a run. He dashed up the stairs and disappeared from view. Brian followed hard on his heels, like a panther.

Ralf heard his pulse pounding in his ears like a drum, and his breathing was noisy and gasping, as though somebody had turned up the volume on every sound in his body.

Minutes went by. The kitchen remained empty. Nobody came down. Was the money upstairs?

*What's happening in there?*

Something rustled nearby. Panic-stricken, Ralf swiveled his head. Peered into the darkness. Shadows moved around him, twisting like long arms in a macabre dance. A sudden gust of wind tugged at his jacket. Then he heard a low hum. It grew louder, drew nearer. He listened intently. The noise was coming from the dead-end street leading to the house. A car. *The police?*

Ralf broke away from the cover of the shrubbery and sprinted back to the bottom of the yard. He barely slowed down by the flower beds, racing across the wood chips until he reached the wall. Launched himself over it as though he weighed nothing at all. Panting, he fought his way through the undergrowth, back onto the embankment.

# 12

Helen parked her car next to Werner's Mercedes and got out. The façade of Wildenbergh was dimly lit by a streetlight half-hidden by trees across the way. People said that novelty always wears off, and maybe that was true for them. But every day, Helen felt blessed to live in such a magnificent house. There was a downside, however, which she had come to feel ever more keenly over the last few years. The richer she and Werner had grown materially, the poorer their relationship had become. As though the house, the cars, and the designer clothes were only so much paper over the widening cracks between them. Once upon a time, they had been a team, or at least it had felt that way; lately, however, they had been living parallel lives, Werner always buried in his work. Of course, he could always hire an assistant, but he never did. *That's not my style of management.*

She consoled herself with the thought that they weren't the only couple on autopilot. There were plenty of others who slept in separate beds, had different hobbies and interests, even went on vacation without each other. No arguments, but no passion either. And yet those others had started out as soul mates too, full of shared plans and ideas for the future. Helen's eyes were drawn toward the sky, where a crescent moon was edging the clouds with silver. When she was four, Sara had looked up in awe and whispered, "Mommy, can you see that? That's the *real* moon!" Werner had picked up their daughter and thrown his arm around Helen, and the three of them had stood there, looking up at the sky while Werner told Sara an improvised story about moonmen. It had been a magical moment. Helen had felt connected to her husband and her daughter from the depths of her being.

*We still have each other . . .*

She locked her car and walked toward the gate, her gym bag in hand. Her eyes had to adjust to the darkness behind the house. Aside from the faint glow from the pool, there had been no lights in the yard for a while now. Problems with the fittings, which had short-circuited a few times. Nobody had gotten around to calling an electrician yet.

She heard something rustling and looked up—a hedgehog? Or had she just imagined it? She instinctively drew her bag closer to her, quickened her pace, and entered the house through the back door.

# *13*

Ralf crawled into the driver's seat. He tried to put the key in the ignition, but his fingers were shaking so violently that he only managed it on the third attempt. Panting, he pulled off his balaclava and laid his neck against the cool headrest. Tried to get his breathing under control.

The vehicle on the driveway next to the Mercedes was not a police car but a light-colored Fiat 500. The mother had come home. Too early. And Brian was still inside.

Ralf drew a few deep breaths. He laced his fingers together and pushed his palms out until he heard a cracking sound. Did it again. He felt like a coward for running away, but there wasn't much he could do other than wait. Whatever was happening in there, Brian would find a solution. He was so wired and coked up, not even four grown men would be able to restrain him. Any second now, he'd come storming out and they could get away from here. Then it would all be over. Brian had said he didn't know exactly how much cash there was in the house, but it would be at least five grand. Twenty percent of the haul was for Ralf. Easy money. A hesitant smile played over his lips.

His thoughts went to his father, who had drummed into him the idea that there was no such thing as a quick buck. *Everything has its price, Son. Even when something looks like easy money, the truth is always different. Remember that. Behind every success story, you'll find thousands of failures.* Ralf had taken the lesson with a pinch of salt. His father had spent his entire life working in the same warehouse, starting out as an assistant, before becoming a forklift driver and ultimately ending up in the planning department. That was it, then—his father's glittering career. Not once had he tried to make a success of himself. And he insisted on calling his boss "the big cheese"—like some kind of god-damn rat.

Ralf watched the house. From this distance, it looked calm. Peaceful.

Soon, the place would be crawling with cops, but he and Brian would be long gone.

# 14

Werner wasn't in the kitchen. His newspaper was folded on the counter, and the TV was tuned to National Geographic. Helen put her bag on the dining table and crossed into the living room. It was shadowy and silent. A few spotlights illuminated the white walls and the large modern paintings. Werner sometimes fell asleep on the couch, but the red leather sofa was empty. She opened the door to his office but didn't have to turn on the light to see that nobody was there.

Suddenly, she heard a thud from upstairs. Helen looked at the ceiling. Was Werner taking a shower? No, she couldn't hear any water running. It sounded like something had fallen over up there. Then another thud. As though somebody were moving furniture around.

Helen went back through the kitchen and hurried up the stairs. In her mind's eye, she saw Werner convulsing on the bathroom floor—an epileptic fit, a stroke. She had learned in the hospital that hardworking, apparently healthy men Werner's age could fall victim to a serious attack of that kind without warning.

She sprinted past Sara's and Emma's rooms, leaping over discarded items of clothing and a pile of schoolbooks, and cast a quick glance into the bathroom. It was empty. The noise was coming from the bedroom at the end of the hall. It was the biggest in the house, almost as big as the kitchen, with a high, gabled ceiling lined with exposed beams—when she saw it for the first time, it had reminded her of a chapel.

The bed sat against the right-hand wall, close to the door. A little farther back on the left, directly below the skylight, stood the low bench and the table they had gotten from Werner's parents.

It took a full second for Helen to grasp what she saw. There was a man in a balaclava squatting next to the bench. In front of him was another man lying facedown on the floor. The intruder was tying his wrists together. Helen noticed dark spots on the victim's blue polo shirt. Red splashes on the carpet.

"Not so tough now, are you?" she heard the robber hiss. "Maybe I'll take it all, sucker. Every penny you have."

Air escaped from her throat. "Werner!"

The masked man leapt to his feet and looked straight at her.

Helen stared back paralyzed, powerless to move.

The intruder widened his eyes so much, the whites became visible— the look of a madman. Slowly, his attention shifted toward the bed. There was a pistol lying on the duvet.

But Helen was closer. Instinctively, she dived, grabbed the gun, and took off.

She sprinted back down toward the staircase. Footsteps thumped close behind. Sniffing noises, cursing. She could hardly take it in— it was like she was running through a long tunnel. Her feet scarcely touched the steps; she half fell, half skidded down the stairs and dashed toward her bag—toward her phone.

# 15

If you hadn't heard a gunshot before, you could have easily thought the bang was a firecracker. But Ralf recognized it right away. He pressed his fist against his mouth. There was no mistaking it. After a brief silence came two more shots in quick succession.

That couldn't have been Brian's BB. Had he underestimated the man in the house? Ralf flashed to his friend's response when he'd pointed out that the guy might shoot back. Brian's contempt, convinced as he was of his own superiority. *Are you kidding?* Or had Brian lied and taken a second, real gun with him?

Ralf stared feverishly at the house, wishing that he could look through those goddamn walls. What if Brian had blown the people's brains out? Ralf thumped his steering wheel. "Fuck, fuck, fuck . . ."

Suddenly, he realized that if *he* had heard the shots, then the neighbors would probably be calling the police already. The houses were a fair distance apart, but sound carried a long way.

"Hurry up, bro," he hissed. "Hurry the fuck up." Ralf's legs had started trembling again; his knees tapped against the steering wheel. The muted hip-hop emanating from the speakers suddenly sounded deafeningly loud.

Ralf ripped his flash drive out of the stereo.

He looked back at the house. Not a single door or window opened. No lights went on or off.

No change.

No Brian.

*What the fuck are you doing in there, man?*

# 16

As soon as she reached her bag, Helen realized that she was too late. There was no time to dial the emergency number. There was no time for anything.

She turned around and saw the robber charging toward her. In desperation, she pointed the gun at him and gripped the trigger. "Stop, I'll shoot!" Her voice was high and shrill.

As a nurse, she had learned how to handle mindless aggression. Patients would occasionally become violent out of nowhere, or friends and relatives would suddenly flip out—often due to an underlying medical problem or an adverse reaction to medication, alcohol, or drugs. So far, she had always managed to get through to the attacker and calm them down.

But that was at work.

Not in her own kitchen.

"Shoot, then! Shoot, you dumb bitch!" The robber took a step forward. He was so close to her that she could smell him—sweat, cigarette smoke, and something chemical. His dark eyes were intense; he stared at her like a madman. He paused briefly, then barreled toward her with a yell.

Reflexively, Helen pulled the trigger. Her hand flew upward, as though somebody had kicked it. The bang left her ears whistling.

The intruder wobbled slightly, but recovered and launched himself toward her again, swearing.

"Stay back!" She aimed the gun again, holding it out in front of her with both hands this time. Tears clouded her vision.

He came closer, seeming not to hear.

"Stay *back!*" With a scream, she pulled the trigger again. And again. The ear-shattering noise reverberated through the kitchen. An acrid smell of gunpowder filled her nostrils.

Horror-struck, she watched the man totter, a look of shock in his eyes, before he collapsed on the kitchen floor. Blood spattered the double doors of the fridge behind him. Sullied the bulletin board hanging next to it—free tickets to a musical, a pamphlet from the pharmacy, letters from school.

Her arms dropped. The pistol felt as heavy as an anvil; her whole body was trembling. Yet her hand remained clenched around the grip. Panting, she stared at the robber.

He was lying faceup on the tiles in an unnatural position. His hands—small and slim—clawed around him, as though he were trying not to fall into a chasm. He stretched his mouth open and attempted to suck in air. Each breath was accompanied by a deep rattle from his lungs. His body contracted in spasms. Red bubbles appeared around his mouth, more and more of them, bursting on his skin and on the knitted fabric of his balaclava. He tried to cough. Moisture seeped through his black hoodie. There was a hole there—a wet, glistening hole. The bullets must have penetrated his lungs.

Helen did nothing.

It felt as if this weren't really happening. She stood and watched, frozen to the spot, incapable of moving.

Paralyzed by fear.

# 17

Droplets of sweat ran down Ralf's temples. It was taking way too long down there. Something was definitely wrong.

He was unsure what he should do. Drive away? Wait?

"Where are you, man?" he whispered.

Ralf looked at the clock on the dash. He would wait another ten minutes. If Brian hadn't emerged by then, he was on his own.

# 18

The intruder made increasingly desperate attempts to breathe; his eyes wide open, his gloved fingers grasping at his throat.

Helen didn't stir. She felt as though she had stepped outside her own body and was watching everything from a distance. The man writhed on the floor in front of her, gasping for breath. Scarlet foam around his mouth. His blood on the floor. There was so much, you could smell it. And yet it felt like it had nothing to do with her.

"Helen . . . Helen!"

She looked up.

Werner was sliding down the stairs. Jerkily, without control, and far too quickly. Half on his side, and with his knees tucked up to protect himself, his slim body bounced from step to step. He was holding his head bent forward, and his wrists were still tied together.

"Werner!" She sprang into action. Avoiding the convulsing body, she let the pistol fall from her hands and hurried over to the staircase. She just managed to prevent Werner's head from making contact with the hard kitchen floor. Grabbing his shirt, she pulled him away from the stairs and knelt down next to him. "Werner?"

He said something she couldn't understand. His right eye was swollen, and there was blood on his face. The nurse in her knew that facial wounds almost always looked more serious than they were, but she still couldn't keep the panic out of her voice.

"It'll be OK," she whispered.

She turned him on his side and tried to remove the cable tie from his wrists, but tugging only tightened the rigid material. "Don't move. Stay where you are." She ran over to the cutlery drawer to grab a vegetable knife, and sliced through the tough plastic in a few quick strokes.

Werner winced as he stretched his arms forward and crossed them on his chest, like a pharaoh in his tomb. He balled his fists. "Jesus, Helen," he groaned, his back hunched, his eyes squeezed shut.

Behind them, the robber's movements were growing steadily weaker. His hands clawed again at the air, his mouth wide open in a silent scream. Helen was oblivious.

She anxiously helped Werner to his feet, asking him where it hurt and instructing him to move his limbs. She checked his pulse, shined her cell phone flashlight into his eyes, opened his mouth, and felt his jaw. Strangely, this calmed her. In the midst of a surreal situation, the habitual actions were a source of comfort, though she missed the droning of the monitors, the reassuring bleeps of the equipment, and the intravenous drips that could work miracles on an injured body.

Werner did everything she asked. He was slightly in shock, she established, simultaneously realizing that the same must apply to her. When she stood up to fetch some damp towels, she once again became aware that there was somebody else in the room. It wasn't his physical presence that alerted her, but his scent—the smell that sometimes emanated from a body when surgeries went wrong.

Hesitantly, she approached the robber.

The rattling had stopped. A bright-red layer of blood clung to his mouth. There were no signs of breathing.

She squeezed her eyes shut and opened them again, in the childish hope that the man might disappear and all this would turn out to be a figment of her imagination.

But there he was still, lying motionless on his back, his eyes rolled up in their sockets. He suddenly looked so small, so vulnerable and young.

She knelt down and felt his wrist. No pulse. She took the balaclava off his head. A narrow, angular face. Dark hair, sticky with sweat, close-shaven on the sides. His skin was smooth, with a light outbreak of acne on his chin and along his jaw. She guessed he was about twenty years old.

Against her better judgment, she placed her palms on his chest, straightened her arms, and pushed down hard. And again. The pressure forced more blood out of the body, but no breaths came, and his heart remained still. She pushed down once more with all her might.

*And what then, Helen?* whispered a voice in her head. *What will you do if the patient starts breathing, his heart starts pumping again? He'll just get even more blood in his lungs. He doesn't have a ghost of a chance.*

She lifted his wrist once more. Looked at his fingers. There were black hairs on the backs of them, and his nails had been untidily trimmed. She pursed her lips. It was too late to do anything for him.

Dead and dying people were part of her work. More than once, she had lost patients who had been shot or stabbed. But this time, she was the one who had inflicted the lethal injuries. And instead of saving the patient's life, as she was trained to do, she'd let him expire in agony without lifting a finger to help.

She had let a patient die.

"How is he?" she heard Werner ask.

*I killed him.*

"Helen?" Werner stood next to her, dropped to his knees.

She shook her head.

"How is he?" he repeated.

"Dead."

"Are you sure?"

"He suffocated." She lifted the hoodie. A quick glance at his torso confirmed what she already knew. "I hit his lungs."

Werner looked at her, his lips pursed. A whole host of emotions passed over his face. He took her hand but said nothing.

# *19*

Ten minutes had turned into twelve. Ralf kept thinking he could see somebody—a phantom that approached from the side, hurriedly, before dissolving into the shadows of the trees.

Fifteen minutes.

Just a little longer, a little longer . . .

To his surprise, the dead-end street still wasn't full of emergency vehicles. He'd expected sirens and flashing lights, but it had remained eerily quiet.

He began to doubt his own ears. Had there really been shots? He had been absolutely sure of it before, but now everything seemed uncertain.

Eighteen minutes.

No police.

No Brian.

Nothing.

Maybe Brian had run away from the other side of the house, and there was a good reason why he hadn't come to the car. Was his friend currently making his way home on foot? Brian had left his cell phone in the car, so Ralf couldn't call him to check.

Ralf looked at the house again. Thought carefully. Maybe Brian had assumed he would come to help him if it took too long.

He looked at the clock.

Twenty minutes.

# 20

"How did he get in?" Helen tried to manage her breathing. Her hands were shaking uncontrollably.

"Through the back door. He just appeared in the kitchen. I—" He rubbed his face with both hands. Breathed in deeply. His shoulders were shaking. "My God, tell me this isn't happening . . . Is he really dead?"

Helen looked at him in silence. Yes, the robber was dead. Even if a team of specialists were to come running in now with the most advanced equipment available, they still wouldn't be able to bring him back.

"Did he want money?" she asked softly.

"Yes. He obviously thought I kept the daily takings at home."

"Do you know him?"

Werner hesitated for a moment. "I think he used to work for us in the kitchen. One of the temps."

"This is exactly what you were worried about. You were talking about it just the other day."

He nodded. Stared at the boy in silence.

Helen followed his gaze. The mingled odor of gunpowder, blood, and urine made her want to vomit. She held a trembling hand over her nose and mouth and walked over to the table.

"What are you doing?" Werner asked sharply.

She pulled her cell phone from her bag. "Calling the police."

"Don't!" He leapt to his feet and pushed her hand down.

"Don't?"

"We aren't making any phone calls. To anybody."

Perturbed, she shook her head and tapped the telephone icon with her thumb.

Werner gripped her wrist and wrenched the device from her hand. Slid it into his pocket.

"Hey! What—"

"Listen. Look at me. No police. The media will have a field day."

"Media? It was a break-in! We could have been killed, both of us."

"You aren't thinking clearly, Helen."

"It's not our fault, is it?" She pointed at the lifeless body. Her voice cracked. "*He* was the one who came into our house with a gun!"

"Listen. That gun—" Werner's breath caught. He ran his fingers through his hair. Paused for a moment. "That gun—belongs to me." He looked down regretfully at the robber. "You killed that boy with our pistol. He came in here with a BB gun. I managed to get it off him upstairs. It was fake."

She felt herself go cold. "You have a gun?"

He looked at her guiltily. Said nothing.

"We have a gun in the house, and you didn't think to tell me? Have you lost your mind? There are three teenagers living here; this is absurd, you know—"

"Shh . . ." He held her arms and tried to pull her toward him.

She acquiesced briefly, before putting her hands on his chest and pushing away.

He kept hold of her. "I didn't want an argument," he whispered. "It was my decision, OK?"

"Somebody just died because of your decision."

"But we're still alive! Do you understand what I'm trying to say? *We* are still alive!"

She pursed her lips and stared at the man she had been married to for nearly eighteen years. Where had he gotten it into his head to buy a gun? More than once over the last few months he had told her that he was afraid of becoming a target. He had even implied he wanted to take countermeasures. But she had no idea it had gone so far.

Her voice sounded a good deal calmer than she felt. "Werner, we need to hand this over to the police."

"Hand it over? Do you think you'll be off the hook, then? The police won't take anything off our hands; they'll be all over us like a rash. This isn't just a break-in; this is news. This"—he made a broad gesture—"will be the talk of the whole country before you know it." He glanced fearfully at the clock hanging over the counter. "We can discuss it later. Emma and Thom will be home in half an hour. We need to get him out of here."

She looked at him in confusion. This was moving too fast.

"Now, Helen! We can't let them see this."

"OK. I'll meet them outside and take them to your mother's." She tried to get through to him, but there was a wild expression in his eyes. She'd never seen him like this before. As calmly as possible, she continued. "If I hadn't done anything, he would have killed me. You too, probably. It was a life-or-death situation. *Life or death.* The police will understand; everyone will understand. We haven't done anything wrong."

"But will they believe that in court? What about my customers, the guys in the kitchen? Your boss? Your colleagues? The neighborhood? The teachers at school?"

"Who cares if they believe it? It's the truth."

"There's no such thing as truth, Helen, only perception. And that's different for everybody. If we report this—everything will change."

"Everything already *has* changed." Helen looked from Werner to the blood spattered on the counter and the white tiles above it. She had chosen those tiles herself shortly after they had bought the house. "Traditional Dutch white"—now stained with the blood of a stranger.

A dead stranger.

She began to feel nauseated. She'd gunned him down and left him for dead. Literally. She had watched in a trance while he succumbed to his injuries. She, Helen Möhring, recovery nurse, had let someone die before her very eyes. It was her job to do everything she could to keep people alive. Yet she had done nothing.

Would the judge believe her if she explained that she'd been in shock? How seriously would the prosecutor take the postmortem report, which would reveal that the robber had suffered for several agonizing minutes before finally expiring?

Werner's fingers dug hard into her arms. "Helen, listen to me now. Think of us—think of Emma, Thom, and Sara. We have three wonderful children who we can't keep locked away in a golden cage."

"What does that have to do with—"

"How do you know that boy doesn't have friends who will want to settle the score? Brothers, a father, or an uncle out for revenge? An eye for an eye?"

Helen froze. The fear penetrated her physically, like a sharp, icy hand that reached through her back and seized her heart.

Werner stroked her hair, sought her eyes. "Look at me, Helen. Trust me. I think it's horrible, I'm scared to death, just like you, but I can see very clearly how we should resolve this."

"I don't know if—"

"Have I ever made a bad decision?"

Slowly, she shook her head. "What do you want to do? Bu—bury him? But where?" There was desperation in her voice. "In the yard? In the flower beds by the swimming pool, or farther back, where the swing used to be? I don't think I can handle that. I can't—"

"Shh." He placed a finger on her lips. "Trust me. I know exactly what we need to do. Help me."

## 21

Ralf shot upright behind the wheel and stared intently at the two bikers weaving toward the house and talking loudly. A rattling bike chain, the constant, quiet jingle of a bell that hadn't been fitted properly. The boy and the girl were coming home, each with a tennis racquet on their back.

They disappeared from view behind the garage. Shortly afterward, he saw two black shadows move across the deck behind the house and go inside.

His heart throbbed in his throat. He kept watching, expecting at any moment to hear screaming, commotion.

*Something.*

The seconds ticked by, drawing out into minutes.

Ralf looked at the clock again. Nearly fifty minutes had now passed since he had heard the shots. If Brian had killed those people, their kids would have raised the alarm by now. But nothing happened. Everything was quiet.

Maybe Brian was already home?

Ralf started the engine. With his headlights off, he rolled out of the sheltered bay, turned onto the cart track, and slowly headed toward the road.

# 22

"It smells funny in here."

"Yeah, like a dog-rescue center or something." Thom wrinkled his nose.

"No, more like Maros."

Maros was a local butcher shop. Helen froze momentarily, then dropped her cleaning cloth in a bucket of cold water and wrung it out. Continued mopping down the white tiles above the counter. "Come on, it's not that bad, is it?"

"Er, Mom, since when do you clean the kitchen at night?"

Helen did her best to make her voice sound as normal as possible, but was unable to prevent a slight tremor. "Since when are you guys interested in your mother's cleaning schedule? Do you want to do it for me?"

"No way."

Thom and Emma remained by the kitchen island and looked around. Emma lifted her nose. "It smells really weird, Mom."

"Blood," said Helen.

The children looked at her in alarm.

If the situation hadn't been so bewildering and horrifying, she could have laughed. Instead, she carried on scrubbing. "Your father slipped and hit his head on the kitchen island."

Werner came down the stairs. He was wearing clean clothes—a dark shirt and jeans, with a pair of leather flip-flops on his feet. The lump by his eye had begun to turn blue, and his lip was swollen—there was a jagged black cut in it.

Emma gaped at her father. "Jeez, Dad."

"I know—it looks bad, huh?" He laughed.

"Looks like you were in a fight," said Thom. There was a note of admiration in his voice.

"If only—that way at least I might have gotten a good story out of it." Werner looked at Helen. "Do you need any help?"

Helen looked around, wiping her forehead with her sleeve. "I think it's all clean now."

Emma walked over to the bulletin board. "Holy crap. There's blood on the theater tickets."

"They'll still let you in even if your ticket has a few stains on it." Helen hurried over, wrapped the cloth around her index finger, and quickly wiped off the spatters. Then repeated the action for the stains on the wooden frame. Her heart pounded behind her ribs.

Thom looked at his father. "Did all that come from your lip?"

"Yeah—crazy, huh? I can hardly believe it myself."

"Wounds on the head and face always bleed really badly," said Helen. She poured the bucket out into the ceramic sink and rinsed the towel. It stank of iron.

"What are you guys up to this evening?" asked Werner.

"Yorick and Stijn are coming over in a while to hang out," answered Thom.

Emma took off her jacket. "I'm going to stay at Sophie's tomorrow, so I want to get my studying out of the way for the exam on Monday. Why are you asking?"

Werner's eyes sought out Helen's. "Well, your mother and I were planning to go to the movies, but—"

"I think it'd be better if we stayed home tonight. You look shot to pieces." Her hand flew to her mouth in shock, but she recovered and quickly added, "Want me to make you some coffee?"

# 23

Brian lived as a property guardian in a former Asian restaurant that stood by a lake in the park. The enormous building resembled a farmhouse and was in a state of complete neglect, with damp walls and a leaky roof. The red-and-gold awning over the entrance had once given an impression of grandeur, but it was now covered in black stains and hung askew. A developer had bought the property with the intention of erecting a chic apartment building on this idyllic spot, surrounded by old chestnut trees and close to town. Until that happened, fifteen or so rooms in the old structure were being rented to people who paid very little on the understanding that they might be evicted at any moment. Ralf thought there was something spooky about the place. Especially at night. It stood a considerable distance from the road and was barely lit. The front door was seldom locked; anybody could come in or out. Ralf and Brian had once come across a vagrant camping out in the former restaurant kitchen with his shopping cart and sleeping bag.

The odor of cigarette smoke and cooking fat penetrated Ralf's nostrils as he entered the building. A few dim lamps were lit in the hall. Pots of bedraggled artificial plants cast a blur of shadows. He walked through the kitchen, still lined with stainless-steel counters and shelves. A narrow staircase at the end led upstairs. The smell grew stronger now, mingling with mold and damp. The staff had slept up here; their mattresses had still been on the floor and their posters and calendars on the walls when Brian moved in.

Ralf stopped at the third door on the right. He pushed down the handle, but it refused to open. Ralf knocked. "Brian?"

Nothing.

He banged the door with the palm of his hand. "Brian? Hey, dude?"

The next door along swung open. Brian's neighbor had his arm thrown over the shoulders of a girl who regarded Ralf with curiosity.

"Maybe he's asleep?" The guy closed the door behind him and walked past Ralf, toward the staircase. The girl giggled.

Ralf waited until they were out of sight, then fished his keys out of his pocket and opened the door.

Brian's room was small and packed with furniture. A double bed with a glossy black duvet, a wardrobe, a sideboard, a coffee table with a tinted glass top, and a few chairs. The dusky-pink curtains were drawn—Brian never opened the window. Next to the bed stood a half-full glass of Coke with a plastic bottle next to it. On the coffee table lay a crumpled Marlboro pack and an overflowing ashtray.

Brian was nowhere to be seen.

# 24

Werner and Helen had once gone in together with some friends to buy bulk meat from a cow that had grazed on the field close to their house. The chest freezer had been specially acquired for that purpose. For months on end, there had been nothing but beef on the menu, until the whole family was sick of it. Helen had no idea what to do with all the extra meat and bones. "Make soup," the farmer had said. But it was much quicker and easier to use bouillon cubes nowadays. Last year, Helen had regretfully thrown away the dried-out, ice-encrusted remnants, then cleaned and switched off the freezer.

Now it was running once more at full capacity. All of the lights were on—green, yellow, and red—and every now and then, it made a quiet gurgling noise. Werner had set it to "quick freeze." A few old cardboard boxes were piled on top of the lid, and a faded parasol leaned against it.

Helen stood, looking at the freezer, arms folded. "This is insane," she whispered.

"It's for the best," said Werner softly. "If anyone finds out, the story will take on a life of its own. We'll lose everything."

Helen turned her head and looked at him questioningly. He went on talking. From his demeanor and his movements, she could see he was trying to persuade her that this was the only choice, but his words didn't really reach her. All she could think of was what he had said to her earlier that evening: *We have three wonderful children who we can't keep locked away in a golden cage.*

*An eye for an eye.*

"What if I go mad?" she whispered.

He put his arm around her and drew her to his chest. Kissed the top of her head. "You won't. We'll get through this. He's OK in there for now, and I'll come up with something."

"Mom, Dad?"

Helen froze at the sound of Emma's voice.

"Yes?" called Werner.

"Can I have a bag of potato chips?" Emma stood in the doorway at the top of the basement stairs.

"Of course, honey," Helen heard herself reply. "It's the weekend."

"OK!" A moment's silence. Then, hesitantly, "What are you doing down there, anyway?"

"Cleaning up!" Werner yelled back.

"Oh, right, have fun, then."

Once the footsteps had died away, Helen laid a trembling hand over her mouth.

"It's all right," whispered Werner. He produced a half smile and drew her closer against him. "The kids are so self-absorbed these days, they won't notice any of this. Nothing at all."

"Do you think so?"

"I'm sure of it."

*Saturday*

# 1

The patient was thirty-four, a mother of two. Her eyes shone. "I'm sorry, Nurse. I know it'll all turn out fine like you say. I'm just scared."

Helen laid her hand on the woman's arm. "Everybody gets a little bit scared just before an operation. That's completely normal." She hoped the smile that cost her so much effort came across as sincere.

She had scarcely been able to control her nerves while opening the recovery room with her colleagues this morning. In the changing room, she had forgotten to put her phone and her rings in the locker, and shortly after that, she had run into the wall with a cart and dropped a basket of cannulas. "Rough night?" Paula, one of her older colleagues, had asked as she helped her pick up the needles from the floor.

"I st—stayed up until the kids came home."

Paula understood. "The teenage years are all blood, sweat, and tears, aren't they? I'm glad my kids have left home, for what it's worth. Means I can sleep again at night."

"Nurse?"

Helen awoke from her reverie with a start.

"I guess it's for the best," said the patient.

She had forgotten what operation the woman was due to undergo, and cast a quick glance at the monitor. *Appendectomy*, it said. "Oh yes, absolutely. It'll relieve all your pain straightaway."

From the corner of her eye, she saw Lex Melo approaching—one of the nurse anesthetists. Like everybody in the unit, he was wearing blue scrubs with short sleeves and plastic clogs.

"Look, my colleague is here already," said Helen. "He'll take you through to the OR, and I'll see you again very soon in the recovery room." She leaned forward confidentially. "They've got a superb team working in there—the very best people we have."

"And if Helen says it, then it must be true." Lex winked at Helen from behind the patient. "You haven't had surgery before, if I understand correctly?"

The woman looked a good deal more cheerful when he directed his attention toward her. No doubt because of his eyes, thought Helen—big and brown, the most beautiful eyes in the whole hospital. He had once told her that he'd inherited them from his Brazilian grandfather.

"No, that's right. This is my first time."

"We're always extra careful when that's the case," he joked.

Helen watched as he wheeled the bed toward the operating room. Lex was tall and not exactly slim; yet from the way he moved, you could see he was fit and comfortable in his own skin. When he'd joined the team three years ago, he had sent a lot of the female staff into a tizzy for weeks on end. Some of the men too, for that matter. Helen had been amused by all the commotion, as had Lex himself. They soon established that they shared a sense of humor and were irritated by the same things. Helen considered herself lucky that she could now regard him as a good friend, but she took care not to spend time with him outside work.

There were limits to what a friendship between a man and a woman could bear, especially when the attraction wasn't exclusively platonic.

## 2

"Still in bed?"

Ralf woke with a start, blinking in the bright sunlight. His mother was standing by his bed, hands on her hips. Her short, bleached hair was dark at the roots.

"Mom, it's Saturday."

"It's two in the afternoon. You'll sleep your life away at this rate." She grabbed the covers and pulled them back.

Ralf sat up, avoiding her eyes. He could draw them from memory by now—those piercing, light-blue eyes that had regarded him with nothing but reproach for the last few years.

"Look at this mess. Really, Ralf, you need to . . ."

She continued ranting at him. Any second now, she'd start going on about his future, telling him he needed to find work. A Saturday job, at the very least—though more than anything, she'd like to see him finish his education so she could pack him off for a full workweek at some boring company with a bunch of even more boring colleagues. Her idea of a bright future. She wouldn't rest until she'd achieved it. He didn't dare imagine how she would react if she found out he'd stopped going to school weeks ago.

"I don't understand how you can sleep in here," she continued, picking up dirty clothing from the carpet and dumping it at the foot of his bed. "It stinks. Your father and I—"

"Give it a rest, Mom."

"Don't you take that tone with me!"

"Oh, fuck off, would you?" Ralf leapt out of bed, strode past his mother to the bathroom, slammed the door behind him, and locked it.

He took off his T-shirt and boxer shorts and stood under the shower.

As the warm water flowed over him, he thought back to when he was still in elementary school. Whenever he had a problem or felt sad, he would crawl onto his mother's lap, and she would stroke his hair and hug him, tell him that everything would be OK and that she was proud of him.

She hadn't been proud of him for a long time.

His eyes prickled with tears.

A hand pounded on the bathroom door. "Ralf? Don't spend too long in the shower! Money doesn't grow on trees, you know. And make sure you clean up your room!"

## 3

Helen sat at the large, round table in the break room with Lex and Anouk, a younger colleague from the recovery room. The team members never took their breaks all at the same time. There always had to be nurses available to monitor the patients. The first few hours after surgery were critical, especially for patients who were already weak before their operations—those who had heart and lung problems, for example.

"Have you guys ever noticed how often we use the word 'just' over the course of a workday?" asked Anouk. Her sturdy legs were crossed, and she was dangling one of her plastic clogs from her toe.

"How do you mean?" replied Helen.

Anouk stirred her coffee. "Could I 'just' borrow the doctor for a moment? I'll 'just' put in a drip . . ."

"I've never thought about it before," murmured Helen.

Lex's chair teetered on two legs. He was preoccupied with his cell phone and didn't join in on the conversation. He'd probably decided that Anouk's "we" didn't include him. His work as an anesthesiologist's assistant was highly technical, and he had much less frequent and briefer contact with patients than the recovery nurses did.

"You'll be shocked when you start looking out for it," continued Anouk. "It's a real filler word, that 'just.'"

A colleague entered the room, placed a cup under the coffee machine, and pushed the On button. "Maybe it's because we're always being told to 'just get it done.' You end up rushing from one patient to the next."

"It's not as bad as all that on our ward, though, is it?" replied Anouk, turning to face the newcomer.

Helen retreated gratefully into her cocoon and began playing a game on her phone. She wanted to get back to work as quickly as possible. There was nobody to watch her when she was with patients, and she could simply ask her standard questions and administer her standard treatments. That was already complicated enough.

She wished she could turn back the clock. In her mind's eye, she had already pictured herself running out of the house and down the street with the gun a hundred times, screaming bloody murder and shooting in the air. In that version of events, the robber stayed alive and wound up in a jail cell—where he belonged.

"What did you get up to last night?"

Helen looked up in alarm, straight into Anouk's big green eyes. The question was aimed squarely at her. "Er—why do you ask?"

Anouk grinned. "Jeez, Helen, the way you reacted. Is there something you aren't allowed to tell us?"

The other colleague chimed in. "You're blushing!"

Lex looked up from his phone.

"I didn't do anything at all," she said, and got up from her seat. "I'm going back to work."

The chair fell to the floor with a bang.

# 4

The black duvet still lay rumpled in the same position at the foot of Brian's bed, and the half-full glass of Coke still stood on the floor with the plastic bottle next to it. Ralf picked up a car magazine and flipped through the pages without really looking at them. He took a bottle from the sideboard, set it upright, and examined himself in the mirror. A charging cable lay on the shelf by the sink. He uncoiled it, found the socket by the bed, and plugged in Brian's phone.

It felt strange to be poking around in Brian's stuff when he wasn't around. Brian had such a strong personality that he imbued everything around him with a strange charge. In his absence, the room actually felt rather mundane. Shabby, almost. For somebody who was so successful, Brian didn't have many nice things. Apart from his clothes and his Golf GTI, anyway. Though the car was currently gathering dust at a garage until Brian got his license back.

Ralf opened a few cupboards, peered inside, and closed the doors again. He spotted a bag of potato chips and tore it open. Began devouring them where he stood. He hadn't had any breakfast that morning; immediately after showering, he'd jumped in his car and driven away.

"What are you doing here?"

Ralf spun round in alarm. Potato chips crunched between his teeth, and crumbs fell to the floor.

# 5

Helen guided a cannula into the vein of a twenty-two-year-old motor-cyclist. The man had been brought in by ambulance. He had internal injuries in addition to several visible wounds that had caused a good deal of blood loss. His body was covered in bruises and hematomas. She taped down the cannula and pulled back the covers to apply stick-ers to his chest. A large gray tattoo revealed itself, depicting two hands holding a rosary. *Guess it didn't protect you,* she thought cynically. She worked swiftly.

Seeing the tattoo, she was suddenly reminded of Sara. Were she and Jackie currently getting tattoos of their own in Antwerp? Or had Werner gotten hold of her in time? They hadn't discussed it any further. It had completely slipped her mind. Sara's plan suddenly seemed so insignificant compared to everything that had happened.

# 6

Ralf knew the guy. He was called Mikey, though Ralf didn't know whether that was his real name.

He strutted into the room and nudged a whiskey bottle to one side with his Air Jordan. Ralf recognized the model and color. A limited edition that cost four hundred dollars. Mikey also wore a red cap that looked just as exclusive as his shoes, but otherwise, Brian's dealer was dressed unobtrusively in a dark pair of chinos and a shirt in a similar color.

Mikey stopped in the center of the room. "Where's Brian?"

"I don't know."

Mikey looked at him, sizing him up. Said nothing.

"Hey, buddy, I'm looking for him too, you know. He—he isn't answering his phone."

"I'm not your buddy," replied Mikey. "He was supposed to come around yesterday and pay back some money he borrowed from me."

"Well, that's got nothing to do with me."

Mikey walked forward, stopping within arm's length of Ralf. Stared at him aggressively.

Ralf shifted uneasily. Brian's dealer had unhealthily pale skin, and his eyes sat close together and were slightly crossed. The combination gave him a bit of an alien appearance. Ralf had thought Mikey was a creep from the very first time Brian took him to Mikey's room. He was a wackjob. Someone to steer clear of, instead of living in the same house and buying drugs from him on a regular basis, as Brian did.

"I'll give him one more day," said Mikey. "If he doesn't pay by tomorrow night, then I'm charging one hundred percent interest. If he thinks he can take me for a ride, he's wrong. You tell him that."

Ralf opened his mouth to repeat that he didn't know where Brian was, but Mikey had already spun on his heel and left the room.

# 7

The sun shone pale as Helen left through the staff exit. A thin veil of clouds was drifting high in the sky.

"You seemed a little off today." Lex appeared beside her and tried to make eye contact.

Helen focused on the fork in the footpath up ahead; the bike shed was on the right, while Lex would have to turn left toward the parking lot.

"I didn't sleep well," she said tersely.

"Is something wrong with the kids, or with Werner?"

Just eight steps to go.

"Helen?"

She wanted to say something so badly, but it was impossible.

She couldn't tell him anything.

Out of the question.

"I don't want to talk about it." She went to follow the path to the right, but he put a hand on her arm to hold her back.

He did it very gently, not too insistently.

His eyes locked with hers. "Helen . . ."

"Thank you" was all she said. She looked down at the ground and hurried to the bike shed.

## 8

It was six o'clock. Ralf had called a few of Brian's friends, but nobody had had any contact with him since yesterday afternoon. There was no one home at his mother's house. He'd tried Naomi too; like everyone else, she had no idea where Brian was. She said he hadn't replied to her messages. That wasn't unusual—Brian wasn't exactly the type to bombard his girlfriend with declarations of love, or to provide her with any information at all, for that matter.

Brian worked for a transportation company on a casual basis. Sometimes on the weekend, sometimes during the week. Ralf looked up the number, then thought better of it. Would he call Brian's workplace if he couldn't get ahold of him under normal circumstances? *No way.* So why should he do it now? His friends had all been surprised to hear Ralf on the line, and rightly so. It wasn't the first time Brian had gone AWOL for a day. Or longer.

Ralf thought carefully. What would he do in this situation if there was nothing wrong? Certainly not start a manhunt.

But there definitely was something wrong.

Ralf put his phone away and started his car. He wanted to go back—to the place where he'd seen Brian for the last time.

# 9

"I'm going to bury him," murmured Werner. Shouts emanated from the living room—Thom was playing video games with a friend.

Helen pushed her empty coffee cup back and forth on the table. "Where?"

"Maybe some remote spot in Limburg or the Veluwe. Not around here, anyway."

Through the kitchen window, Helen could see Emma wandering in the yard with a plastic bag, gathering leaves for a biology project at school.

"I don't know," she said.

"We have to do something." Werner picked up their cups. He carried them over to the counter and set them under the stainless-steel coffee machine. Silently, he focused on making two cappuccinos, sprinkling cocoa on top, as usual. The topping seemed inappropriate at a moment like this. "It'll be OK as long as nobody finds him."

She accepted one of the cups. "But if somebody does find him, there'll probably be fibers on his clothes that can be traced to us. Our DNA too." Helen recalled how she and Werner had dragged the boy into the hall and then carried him down the basement stairs. She'd held his knees, and Werner his armpits. She often had to lift patients at the hospital, including some who had passed away. On those occasions, she had always managed to switch off her emotions and do what needed to be done—but this time she had experienced an overwhelming sense of revulsion.

"No doubt," said Werner. "But those fibers and that DNA aren't linked to our names in the system. The police would need to suspect he'd been in our house if they wanted to do anything with that information." He took a sip of his cappuccino.

The lump around his eye had grown, Helen saw. A dark crescent was developing on the outer edge of his eye socket. His lip was so swollen that it interfered with his speech.

After a brief silence, she said, "He might have told somebody that he was planning to rob us." She gave him a probing look. "That's a possibility, right?"

"Of course. But then the other person would be an accomplice, so they wouldn't exactly rush off to tell the police." His eyes wandered over to the flat-screen TV hanging on the wall, which was playing a recap of a tennis match.

Now that the worst of the shock had passed, the manager in him was beginning to take over. Werner was acting as if he had a business problem to solve. And she had been assigned the role of insubordinate employee.

"You aren't at work, Werner," she said softly. "We have to do this together."

"Not necessarily."

"I think you're underestimating how much work it is to dig a deep grave. It'll take you hours, maybe even a whole day. And I presume you won't be able to get all the way out to a genuinely remote spot like that in your car, will you?"

He nodded thoughtfully.

"So he'll need to be dragged there. And then you'll need to cover the tracks made by his body. Assuming you haven't been caught by that point." She shook her head. "It's too risky."

"We could do it together. It'd be quicker that way. And not during the day, but at night."

"That would look even more suspicious if somebody saw us."

Werner stood up and looked down at her with irritation. "Do you have a better idea, then? You were the one who shot the boy, not me."

"What should I have done?" she asked sharply. "Talk to him? He was completely crazed—probably on drugs." A shiver ran down her back at the memory.

"He didn't have to die, Helen."

"That's not what I—"

"What I mean is *I* wasn't the one who created this problem."

She leapt to her feet and struck the table with her palm. "*You're* the one who brought a gun into this house without thinking to discuss it with me. And *you're* the one who didn't want to call the police."

"You shot him three times, Helen. Three times."

"I was panicking."

"And yet you still managed to hit him three times, even though you've never fired anything more than an air rifle in your entire life."

"I don't know why—"

A loud bang resounded against the wall. Both of them looked up in alarm. *The gate,* realized Helen. At the same time, they heard the high-pitched whine of a scooter.

"Sara," said Werner.

# 10

Ralf wasn't sure what he expected to find here. He knew Brian wouldn't be lying somewhere nearby, licking his wounds like an injured animal. But still. That house was the last place he had seen his friend. Right there in that big kitchen, chasing the man up the stairs with his gun in his hand.

He placed his hands on the wall and used a tree stump as a step. The yard was long, with shrubs, trees, and flower beds, a substantial lawn, and a swimming pool in the middle with a wooden cabin and a hedge around it. It was so big, it felt more like a park than a yard. And the house itself looked more like a hotel, or the office of some law firm.

Ralf was startled by a sudden movement and crouched down. A girl was walking across the lawn. Around twelve or thirteen. Jeans, a red hoodie, and light-blonde, curly, almost frizzy hair. She had a plastic bag in her hand. The only reason she hadn't noticed him was probably because she was busy looking at the ground, as though she'd lost something. Ralf wondered whether this was the same girl he had seen coming home last night. It was possible; she was around the same size. As he watched, he heard a scooter—the noise rapidly drawing nearer. The scooter slowed down, and he heard the gate open and then close with a bang. He couldn't see who it was; the hedge between the deck and the swimming pool blocked his view.

The girl gave up her search and stood upright. She called something to whoever had just arrived, and the newcomer greeted her back— another girl, by the sound of it. Now he could see her too as she walked along the side of the house and went inside. He couldn't make out her face from this distance, but she was slim, wore a tailored coat, and had the same color hair as the first girl. Her sister?

## 11

"Hi, Mom. Hi, Dad." Sara hung up her coat in the utility room and walked into the kitchen.

She had the same stubborn, frizzy hair as Helen and Emma, though she'd been hiding it under straighteners for years now. Today, she wore her hair up. A layer of powder covered her pale skin, and sleek black lines ran along her eyelashes before ticking upward from the outer corners. She looked older and more mature than seventeen. That was partly due to her clothing. Even in elementary school, Sara had longed for the day when she could finally stop shopping in the kids' section. She had expensive taste: ever since she had started receiving her clothing allowance, she had preferred secondhand designer clothes to new outfits from H&M. Werner called her "our little lady of leisure," in a tone that suggested he didn't consider it a bad thing.

"Did you have fun with Jackie in Antwerp?" asked Helen.

"I guess." Sara took a glass out of the cupboard and poured herself some Coke. She remained standing next to the kitchen island. "Mom, Dad? Could you go out next Saturday night?"

"Go out?" Werner leaned his elbow on the back of the leather dining chair. "Why?"

"It's my turn to host movie night."

"That's a little inconvenient," said Werner. "Thom is turning sixteen on Friday, and I think two parties in one weekend would be too much of a good thing."

"But that's perfect, isn't it? We can use up the leftovers from Thom's party. You always buy too much." She looked brightly at her mother. "And then you two can go and do something fun on Saturday."

"We'll see," said Helen.

"Aw, please? I already talked to Emma. She's going to stay at Linde's on Saturday."

"And I'm going to Yorick's," said Thom as he entered the kitchen. He opened the fridge and studied the contents intensely, as if his life depended on it, before finally selecting a bottle of Fanta and wandering back to the living room.

"Let me sleep on it," said Helen.

"Aw . . ."

"Sorry. Your father and I have a lot on our plates at the moment."

Sara rolled her eyes and sighed. "Work, admin . . ."

"Less of that, young lady," Helen heard Werner say. "And isn't there something you should be telling us?"

"I don't know what you mean."

"Maybe something about what you did in Antwerp—or rather, what you had done?"

"Oh, you mean *that*."

"Yes, that," said Werner sardonically.

"Well, we didn't go through with it. The guy was ridiculously expensive, and he's booked for the next two months. Jackie wanted to try somewhere else, but it was some dirty biker with a beer belly. So gross."

"I bet he was a lot cheaper," remarked Werner in a considerably more cheerful tone.

"I'm not an idiot, Dad. I want it to be a nice one."

Helen looked her daughter in the eye. "I think you're too young to get a tattoo, Sara. And you need to discuss things like that with us first."

"What difference does it make? You'll never see it." Sara's cell phone began to buzz. She took it out of her bag and looked at the screen.

"It's not about us; it's about you. You're still too young to—"

"Yes, yes, I know already: I'm too young to understand the consequences of my actions," Sara shot back. "What do you think I'm going to do? Get a tattoo right here saying 'Boner Garage'?" She drew an imaginary line above her pelvis with her phone.

"Who knows?" grunted Werner.

Her perfectly made-up eyes burned with indignation. "Come on! I'm not stupid."

"You aren't an adult yet either."

"Well, who is? Sorry, but I need to take this. Oh yeah, Jackie's on her way over. She's staying the night." Sara held the phone to her ear and disappeared down the corridor.

# *12*

The blue sky was growing darker and darker. Bats had emerged from their hiding places and were swooping noiselessly over the swimming pool, which emitted a blue-green glow.

Ralf squinted at the back of the house. There were lights on inside, both downstairs and behind a dormer window on the top floor. From time to time, he saw silhouettes moving around.

Brian hadn't named any names. In fact, he'd told him nothing about the people who lived here; however, based on what he'd seen today, Ralf thought it was probably a husband and wife with three children. An average family, but rich. Maybe they owned a jewelry store or a car dealership. It didn't look like a mafia hideout, anyway. All the same, three shots had been fired in there yesterday, and nobody had called the police. And Brian had been missing ever since.

The woodland soil was springy beneath his sneakers as he walked around to the front of the house. The garden wall merged almost seamlessly into the garage, and the short driveway was bordered by a neatly trimmed, waist-high conifer hedge. There were two cars: a dark-colored Mercedes and a light-blue Fiat 500. Ralf crawled to the corner and peered at the road.

He noticed that his heart had started beating faster. The road seemed quiet. Across the way, an electrical substation was hemmed in on both sides by dense, rustling undergrowth. Behind it, he knew, lay a shallow moat that ran all the way around the affluent neighborhood. He crossed the driveway and walked up to the mailbox, a green plastic container on a pole. There was no name on it, just a number: 23. He opened the door and peered inside. Nothing. Then he looked at the house. The curtains were closed, but he could hear vague sounds—voices, a TV. Hesitantly, he walked up the path that led to the front door. It was straight and narrow, laid out in paving stones. There was no nameplate here either—nothing.

*Who are these people?*

*Sunday*

# 1

In many respects, Sara took after Werner's mother, Helen realized as she placed a cappuccino on the table in front of her mother-in-law.

Ria retrieved a silver dispenser from her handbag and dropped a tablet of sweetener onto the thick layer of foam. Her pearl bracelets clacked together softly.

Werner's parents came to visit every Sunday around midday, for what had somehow become a set date since Sara was born. There was no way of avoiding it—though, fortunately, they had purchased a houseboat that spring and had taken to going on weekend trips. Helen had so far managed to fend off the occasional invitations to join them, as Werner's brothers and their families had already done, but she had been less successful in dodging joint vacations in the Gers in France. The family had a tiny, ancient farmhouse down there, located in a remote spot with views of the snowcapped Pyrenees. When the kids were younger, they had spent countless vacations camping out both in and around this "witch's house," where leaky air mattresses, heavily chlorinated tap water, and a complete lack of privacy were the order of the day. It was also a place where Ria would exhibit an alarming character shift and "let her hair down" under the influence of the cheap wine she procured in jerricans from the local vintner. Another trait Sara had inherited from her grandma, thought Helen.

"You've got a stain here," whispered Ria, as if imparting a weighty secret. She ran her finger along the neck of her own immaculate white blouse.

Helen pulled her top forward a little and examined the collar. A tiny mark. "I see it, thank you. I'll wash it tonight."

Ria explained to her in a lowered voice that she should soak the stain first. She did so very patiently. To Ria, Helen would forever be young and ignorant. It never occurred to the woman that her daughter-in-law had already managed to remove thousands of stains from all manner of blouses, pants, and shirts, all by herself.

Ernst sat next to Ria on the red sofa. He was wearing a pair of turned-up gray pants, a shirt, and a dark-red sweater. Ernst didn't talk much. He had moved here from Germany in the seventies to work for a division of a German company. It was meant to be a temporary posting, but the company extended his contract, and Ernst met Ria and started a family. Their three sons all had children of their own now. And so, Ernst had never gone back. In all that time, he had made little effort to master the Dutch language. Helen had the impression that Ernst viewed that as a shortcoming, and that he compensated for it with a rather distant and reserved attitude.

All in all, Werner's parents weren't the sort of people you would voluntarily choose to spend your Sunday afternoons with.

"Helen, could you fetch my father a glass of cognac?" she heard Werner ask.

She stood up and walked through to the kitchen. In the hallway, she passed the basement door. It had never been locked before, but it was now.

Helen took her time in the kitchen. She washed her hands, then put the cups and plates on the counter into the dishwasher. Checked the soil in the herb pots on the windowsill—basil, curly-leaf parsley, and chives. Watered them. She examined the mark on her top and dabbed at it halfheartedly with a damp dishcloth. That only made it worse.

Suddenly, another stain swam into view on the wall immediately in front of her. She had found a constant succession of new ones since last night. Brown spots on the table leg, on the side of the kitchen island, on the handle of a rarely used drawer. She wiped the wall clean and threw the dishcloth into the trash can.

# 2

It had rained again overnight, and the dense shrubs were slowly releasing moisture onto Ralf's clothing. A drop of water ran down his neck, and a thick branch scraped persistently down his back. Ralf's hiding place wasn't comfortable, but it offered a perfect view of the front of the house.

A gray BMW 5 Series had pulled up half an hour ago. Two stylish retirees had gotten out—the husband wearing a red windbreaker, and his wife a long beige coat. The red-haired husband had welcomed them in. There was a black shadow down the side of his right eye, which was half-closed from swelling, and he also had something wrong with his lip. That face had looked better before Brian had gone into the house.

The girl who had been wandering around outside yesterday had kissed the old-timers on the cheeks three times and called them "Grandma and Grandpa." The man's parents, Ralf guessed—"Grandpa" was also a ginger. After that, they had gone inside.

# 3

"Did you get up to anything exciting last week?" asked Ria.

Helen opened her mouth. "Well, no, we—"

"Business as usual," she heard Werner say.

"And school? How are the children doing?"

"Great. Outstandingly, even." Werner shifted forward to the edge of his seat and began to describe a new program at Thom's school where the students could study languages such as Russian and Chinese. That led to a conversation about the future of international trade with Asia and the decline of the Western European economy.

Helen looked at Werner and his parents. She watched them talking and moving as if through thick glass. The sounds were muted, deadened, and a hysterical, tormenting voice welled up in her mind with increasing insistence: *Hey, did you two know there's a dead body in our freezer?*

*A dead body!*

*In. The. Freezer.*

"Helen? What on earth is the matter with you?" asked Ria, looking at her in astonishment. "You have the strangest expression on your face!"

Werner jabbed her with his elbow. A silent reproach.

"I don't think I'm feeling very well," she said.

Just as she was about to stand up, Sara entered the room, with Jackie trailing behind. Although they were fully dressed and made up, they gave the impression that they had only just gotten out of bed.

"Grandma, Grandpa!" Sara hugged Ria and gave Ernst a kiss on the cheek. He handed her a five-euro note and winked, just like every week. That was the real reason for Sara's over-the-top enthusiasm. She, Thom, and Emma were impossible to drag out of bed on a Sunday without financial reward.

Helen took advantage of the commotion to slip out of the room. Once in the hall, she stepped into the bathroom and locked the door. Her breath caught. It felt as though a raging swarm of bees were in her stomach, the insects fighting their way out and blocking her airway. She stood in the dark, with her back against the cool tiles—her eyes squeezed shut, her mouth wide open in a silent scream.

# 4

The gate next to the house swung open. Ralf heard laughter, chattering. Two girls: one with a brown braid running halfway down her back; the other slimmer and more elegant, her blonde hair worn up. They were riding a white scooter, with the blonde in front.

The door to the house opened as they wheeled down the driveway, and the man came running out. "Sara?" he called. "Remember, you're eating at home tonight, OK? No messing around."

"Yes, Dad, I know. See you later," answered the girl in front. Her friend waved at the man halfheartedly.

Ralf felt a rush of adrenaline flood through his veins as the scooter zoomed past.

*Sara . . .*

He knew that girl.

# 5

"What the hell was all that about?" Werner looked at Helen angrily.

"I don't know."

"Honestly. How difficult is it to control yourself for an hour or so?" Werner shoved glasses into the dishwasher. "You should have seen your face. My parents must be wondering what's going on."

She raised her hands helplessly. "We should have called to tell them they couldn't come today. The same goes for Thom's party on Friday. Can't we postpone it? I mean, we—"

"Absolutely not, Helen. Everything needs to carry on as usual. We have to look normal."

She dropped her hands. "What if I can't?"

"Jesus, Helen. Just look at yourself. I thought the recovery room was where you found the toughest people in the hospital? Nurses with balls, because they have to spend all day dealing with life, and death, and macho doctors, right? Or so I've always been told."

"That's completely different," she said. "That's work."

Helen retreated from his tense glare. She was just as disappointed in her own panicky behavior as he was, though at the same time, she realized that she had already been a little overworked even before the dreadful event had taken place. Her difficult relationship with Werner was eating away at her, and when she got home from work, the children consumed the last remnants of her energy. "I didn't sleep a wink last night. Or the night before. I can't get any rest while there's a corpse in the house."

"We're going to sort it out, as soon as we can."

She didn't hear him. "Do you know what I was thinking about this morning?"

"What?"

She looked at Werner. "What if he wasn't alone?"

"What do you mean?"

"Well, robbers normally operate in pairs, or in a group."

"Maybe. I'm no expert in that area."

She frowned. "But you've watched those police reenactment shows, right? Sometimes you get lone criminals robbing gas stations or mugging old people in the street, but nobody ever robs a house on their own."

"This guy was alone." He almost snarled the words. "You were there yourself. And it doesn't make any difference, anyway." He walked up to her and took her face between his hands. "Stop fretting, Helen. Things are complicated enough as it is. We have a problem, and in the next few days, we're going to solve it. The important thing right now"—his voice grew milder, and his expression softened—"is that we act like nothing has happened. OK?" He raised an eyebrow. "Whether you think you can do that or not."

"Yes, but . . ."

"No buts."

Helen looked at Werner in astonishment. The manager in him had completely taken over. He had always been cooler and more distant than other men, but she and the children also knew his other side—a fun, dedicated father who genuinely cared about his family. She had watched that version of him recede further and further in recent years. *People don't really change,* her mother had said to her once. *Some character traits just grow stronger over the years, while others fade away.*

It would make all the difference if he were to throw his arms around her now and make her feel that they had a connection—but he didn't. Instead, he turned away and rested his hands on his neck, his eyes closed.

# 6

Naomi and Sara knew each other. The longer Ralf thought about it, the more certain he was. Brian had invited a group of people over to drink at his place not too long ago, and that girl had been there. She had caught his attention—not just because she was good-looking, but because there was something unusual about her. She seemed older than everyone else, more sensible. Maybe even smarter too. More and more details bubbled up in Ralf's memory. She had a German-sounding surname. Muller, Mahler, something like that.

On a whim, he pulled his phone out and looked up Naomi's number. She responded enthusiastically when she heard his voice. That felt good, somehow.

"I haven't spoken to him," she said. "He isn't answering his phone. I guess you haven't seen him either?"

"No. We'd agreed to meet today, but he didn't show up." He paused for a moment. "So, I wanted to call a few of his other friends, but I don't have their numbers." He gave the names of some guys that Brian vaguely knew.

"Oh, I think I have those," he heard her say cheerfully.

Ralf ran his index finger along the inside of the steering wheel. "How about I come over to your place?" he ventured.

"OK."

*OK?*

Ralf grinned broadly. "Great, see you soon."

# 7

"I could drive to the Czech Republic. Remember when we went skiing there? Completely isolated—all tiny villages and roads that don't go anywhere. I could push him into a ravine somewhere and come straight back home." Werner spread a layer of tapenade over a piece of toast. "My parents' house in the Gers never gets any visitors either, for that matter."

Helen picked at some loose skin on her cuticle. "You'd be away from home for the night."

He shrugged. "I do that fairly often anyway, when I go away for trade fairs."

"But there aren't any trade fairs at the moment."

He paused briefly. "I could leave early in the morning, then. I'd be back around midnight. If we planned it right, the kids wouldn't even notice I went away. I wouldn't need to spend the night anywhere either."

Helen took a moment to process this. She did her utmost to not think about how bizarre and gruesome their topic of conversation was, and focused instead on how feasible Werner's ideas were. His pragmatic approach disturbed and unsettled her, but she also knew he was right. Emotions wouldn't get them anywhere. Deep down, she wondered how long she would be able to stand this. "You'd leave a digital trail—gas stations, toll roads. And somebody might notice your license plate. A foreign car would be particularly noticeable in a remote area. If someone finds the body, the first thing the police will do is check whether anyone has seen anything unusual."

Werner tapped his bent index finger against his chin.

"What's the matter?"

"I was just thinking that I might have an accident. Or get stopped by customs."

Helen covered her face with her hands. "I feel like I'm going crazy. Maybe—maybe it would be better to bury him in the garden." She looked up, sought Werner's eyes. "But I don't know if I can cope with it—just the idea that there's somebody lying out there. I'd never . . . It's so horrible."

"I wouldn't want that either." Werner grinned mirthlessly. "Not in my backyard."

"I sometimes think—" She shook her head. "If we were to call the police right now, then—"

"Then we would be a couple who shot dead an intruder with an illegal firearm and hid his body in the freezer for two days."

"For Christ's sake, Werner!" Helen slammed her palm on the table-top. She hardly felt the pain. Leaping to her feet, she kicked the unyielding oak of the kitchen island in frustration, and kicked it again. Then she stood still, breathing rapidly, her whole body trembling. She wanted to scream as loud as she could, pull her hair out by the roots, hurl plates and knives at the wall, physically attack Werner. For two days, she had done her level best to act as normal as possible—to negate and suppress all the emotions she felt—but she could do it no longer. She suddenly felt completely drained. "We've made a terrible mistake." Her voice sounded hoarse. "There's no way out. We should have called the police right away."

Werner said something in reply, but she didn't take it in. She raised her head and looked outside, her eyes filling with tears. It was growing dark. The swimming pool would soon need to be covered to protect it from falling leaves, and the pump would have to be cleaned for the winter. The rest of the garden lights were still broken. She could hardly imagine that not even forty-eight hours ago she had still been worried about all that—about such trivialities.

She wiped the tears from her cheeks with her sleeves and continued to gaze through the window, at the neatly trimmed boxwoods and the roof-shaped plane trees. Their branches were entwined with the bars of a trellis, on which she would hang garlands of peanuts and suet balls every winter. It was wonderful to watch the birds coming and going. Balm for the soul.

"I've heard that pigs will eat anything," she suddenly heard Werner say.

She turned to face him abruptly. His blue eyes had a glassy look to them.

"Werner . . . that's going too far. Seriously. You don't know what you're saying."

# 8

The last rays of the sun fell through the windows of the restaurant and flooded the room with an ochre-yellow glow.

Naomi was sitting opposite Ralf at a table, stirring her raspberry milkshake with a straw. Her brown hair glittered with spots of golden light.

"Hey, buddy," Ralf said into his phone, his eyes fixed on Naomi. "I'm looking for Brian. Have you seen him at all?"

"He'll probably be at Naomi's place."

"Nope, he isn't there."

"Well, he must be somewhere."

"I guess so. Thanks." Ralf hung up. He'd called just about all their mutual friends. None of them had seen or spoken to Brian since Friday.

"No?" Naomi looked at him inquiringly. Her lips gleamed in a soft pink.

"No." Ralf picked up the last piece of the burger from the box in front of him and used it to mop up the remnants of lettuce and sauce before eating it. Stress made him hungry.

He didn't give anything away to Naomi, but with that last phone call, he had abandoned any hope that Brian was still alive. In truth, he'd known it since the evening it all happened—but knowing and accepting were two different things. He simply found it hard to believe that somebody had gotten the better of his friend. Brian seemed invincible, totally in charge of any situation. Then again, Biggie hadn't been able to believe it either when he'd heard that Tupac had been shot dead in Vegas.

"Maybe he's at his mother's place," said Naomi.

"I don't have her number. Do you?"

Naomi shook her head. "I don't know her very well. But I know where she lives. We could drive over there now?"

Ralf had already tried Brian's mother's house yesterday, but he didn't tell Naomi that. He had known Emily for a while now. The first time he met her, he had taken her for Brian's sister, or a neighbor. She didn't look like anybody's mother, let alone Brian's. He must have inherited those mean, beady eyes from his father, as Emily had brown, Bambi eyes.

"Should we go?" Naomi urged.

Ralf folded his hamburger box in half, then folded it again. Said nothing. In hindsight, he was glad Emily hadn't been home. Brian didn't see much of his mother, and anyway, he had disappeared only two days ago. Emily wasn't stupid. She'd understand instantly that if Ralf was looking so soon, something was wrong. And that he knew more than he was letting on.

"I have to go to the restroom." Naomi got up and walked away.

Ralf watched her walk across the room: tight jeans, high heels. He'd been so jealous when Brian had introduced him to Naomi, and he found it even more surprising that she had unhesitatingly gotten into his car just now and let him drive her to McDonald's. She'd sat so close to him that he could smell her chewing gum, as well as a hint of her shampoo, or whatever it was that smelled so wonderful. He had deliberately driven the wrong way so that he could sit next to her in the car for a little longer. Brian would tear Ralf a new one if he knew about all the things he'd done with Naomi in his imagination.

When she came back, she'd freshened up her lipstick; her mouth was a darker pink. There was also something different about her hair.

He stood up. "Come on; let's go."

"To Emily's?"

"No. No point worrying her." He gave her a sidelong look. "Should we try visiting some of your friends?" *Friends called Sara, for example,* he added mentally.

It was worth a try. There hadn't been a good opportunity to ask her about Sara yet, since there was no obvious reason why he would be interested in her.

Once outside, Naomi said, "Maybe it'd be better if you took me home. I need to study for my exam tomorrow. My mother will kill me if I fail history again."

He walked beside her in silence. She was giving him the slip, just when he really needed her.

Her face brightened when they reached his Polo. "Your car is really nice, you know. I can't wait until I get my driver's license. But that's still two years away. You won't catch me dead on a bike once I get a car."

As he unlocked the door, he said as nonchalantly as possible, "I could give you a driving lesson sometime if you like."

Her eyes flew wide open. "Really? Are you serious? Oh, that would be amazing!" Then her face fell. "This is a joke, right?"

"No joke. Brian must have let you drive his car a couple of times already, I bet?"

She raised one of her thin eyebrows. "Brian won't even let me hold the steering wheel."

"Well, I don't mind you holding mine," he heard himself say.

# Monday

*Mother Dear,*

*Do you remember the conversation we had in that old coffee shop in town? We spent the whole afternoon there. I'm sure you remember the time I'm talking about, even though it was nearly eighteen years ago. I don't think we'd ever had such an open and honest discussion before. I was twenty-two, and in my eyes, you were beginning to change from a mother who stood far above me to a woman who walked by my side.*

*You told me you were very happy with me, but that you regretted ever meeting Father. You wished you'd chosen a different partner for yourself, and a different father for me. One who was less selfish. Two years earlier, we'd gotten word from Aruba that he drowned while diving— but by that point, we hadn't seen or heard anything from him for six years. His absence had shadowed my entire youth. My tough, handsome father—why did he choose another woman over us? Didn't he think we were good enough? I often blamed myself, and sometimes I blamed you. So unfair, but I didn't know any better.*

*Because you had made the wrong choices when it came to men, you thought it was your duty to protect* me. "Children should do better than their parents, not repeat their mistakes," you said. You were talking about my choosing Werner.

You didn't think he was a bad person, and you said as much. Those were the exact words you used, and only then did I understand the situation—that you actually couldn't stand him.

"There's a lack of warmth in his character; it's as though nothing really touches him," you said that afternoon. When I told you that you'd gotten it all wrong—that when we were together, he was really very kind and loving, and that I would rather be with a tough guy than a tree hugger anyway—all you did was shake your head.

What neither of us knew on that day was that I was already a month pregnant with Sara. You never said anything negative about Werner again, though you made your point very clear in a different way further down the line. Fortunately, you never let the children see any sign of your aversion to him. We went on to have many more conversations, but I never forgot that afternoon. Usually, the memory roused feelings of anger and frustration. Didn't I make better choices than you when it came to men? Only now, over the last few years, have the things you said back then finally sunk in. A little late, right? I always was a slow learner. But I think I now fully understand what you meant that afternoon. You were wise; I was young and in love. And pregnant.

The reason I've come to think so differently about all this is because I've met Lex. By now, I know him well enough to see that he would have been a much more suitable partner for me than Werner. I feel like I'm a better person when I'm around Lex.

*But, Mother, what good does that do me? What good does that do the children? Things turned out differently. Werner has his faults, but he's there for the kids, and he never lets us down.*

*I don't want to be one of those parents who turns her back on her family when things get tough and flounces off to seek her own happiness. Because at the end of the day, Mother, I'd just be doing exactly what Father did all those years ago. I'd be putting myself first—ahead of Sara, Thom, and Emma. This family gives the kids stability, certainty, strength. It's their foundation.*

*And yet, after Friday, I'm not so sure about that anymore. I thought I knew Werner—but do I really? He bought a gun without telling me. What possessed him? And how do you even get hold of a gun? I wouldn't know where to start.*

*But Werner knew. And then he kept that awful thing in our bedroom. Mother, it's true that he'd been afraid of a robbery for a long time. But a lot of people worry about that—do they all go out and buy guns? Is there something I don't know? Does it have anything to do with all that time he spends at work? Do Werner's actions really add up?*

# 1

"Good afternoon. I'm Helen. What's your name?"

"Piet van Drunen," replied the patient—a man with thick gray hair and a piercing glare.

"And your date of birth?"

"March twenty-seventh, 1950."

Helen typed the first letters of his surname on the touchscreen. His data promptly appeared on the display, *below-the-knee amputation*.

"I'll just put in a drip for you," she said, and disinfected a spot on his forearm. She doubted that the man was still working full-time, given his age, but she asked him nonetheless.

"I'm a dairy farmer."

"That's hard, physical work," she said.

"It's not as bad as it used to be."

"Do you have anyone to help you?"

The man explained that his son was going to take over the business, but that he was still very active himself. His expression hovered somewhere between anger and suspicion.

"How are you feeling?"

"I'm worried they're going to cut off my good leg. You hear about things like that happening from time to time."

She smiled. "Not in this hospital."

"People make mistakes, though, don't they? Left for the audience is right for the actors, if you know what I mean?"

She knew what he meant all too well.

"Nurse, it'd set my mind at ease if you could write something on my bad leg with a marker."

"Didn't they do that on the ward already?"

"No—look." The man yanked back the blanket as if he'd had an argument with it and displayed his leg. Dark patches, the toes black and blue. She lifted the blanket farther to examine the other leg. It was pale and lined with thick veins, but she could see no discoloration. This was a clear-cut case even without labeling—maybe that was why they hadn't bothered. "I assume your left leg is the bad one?" She touched it with her hand.

The man nodded.

"Good." She took a pen from the drawer and drew a large arrow on the affected leg, pointing toward the man's foot. "There we are—nothing can go wrong now. The doctor will be here in a minute to talk you through what he's going to do, so there's no need to worry." She put the blanket back and checked the drip.

When she looked at the clock, she realized a whole hour had gone by in which she had been entirely preoccupied with her work. Werner had gone to oversee the morning shift at the Horn of Plenty, as usual. He'd dropped the pig idea, for now. Until they came up with something better, anyway. *Something we can both get behind*—those were the exact words he had used.

Madness.

Petra, one of her colleagues, sought her eyes. "Hey, Helen? You look so pale all of a sudden. Are you OK?"

"Yes—yes, I'm fine. I think I just haven't eaten enough today," she said quickly, and turned back to her screen.

## 2

Ralf descended the stairs as quietly as possible. The fourth tread from the bottom was creaky, so he stepped over it. Almost there.

"Where are you going?"

*Shit.*

That woman had unbelievably acute senses. It was as if she'd woven an invisible spider's web over the entire house and could detect the slightest vibrations.

"I'm going out," he said.

His mother blocked his way. She was wearing a black T-shirt with some positive slogan or other on it; she wore that kind of shirt a lot and had a wardrobe full of them upstairs. "Happy Life!" "Kiss Me, I'm Famous." "Follow Your Dreams!" It was a shame the words contrasted so jarringly with the sour expression above them.

"No, Ralf. You're staying at home. We need to talk."

"Do we really?" He looked at his cell phone. Naomi was waiting for him to take her for her first driving lesson.

"You're in big trouble," she said.

He looked at her in alarm. Was this about Brian? Had the police paid a visit? Nervously, he followed his mother into the kitchen.

She sat down at the table and pushed aside a stack of pamphlets and magazines.

Once he had sat down opposite her, she announced, "I got a letter from the truancy officer."

Ralf relaxed. Exhaled.

"He wants us to go in for a meeting," she continued.

"That's ridiculous. I'm eighteen—I don't even have to go to school anymore."

"This is about last year. They say you were absent for three months without permission. They take that very seriously. The man was even talking about a fine."

"He can do what he wants. I'm not going. I've got better things to do."

"Oh really?" she asked warily. "Like what?"

"All kinds of things. Class. Work."

"That's interesting. Because I didn't just get a letter from the truancy officer—I also got a phone call from the administration at your new course. It seems you've only been in twice. And then I rang up Dennis Faro—you know, the man at the market you told me you do some work for." She paused for a moment. "He hasn't seen you since the start of the summer."

Ralf shrugged. "That fat fuck can kiss my ass. He always gave me the crappiest jobs."

His mother continued to look him directly in the eye. She scarcely moved. Normally, this was the point where she would leap to her feet and point at him, yelling and calling him a liar. This time, she remained calm, composed. He didn't know which was worse.

"You aren't going to school, you aren't working, yet you have a car, and I always see you wearing new clothes. It doesn't add up, Ralf. Anyone can see that."

His phone buzzed. It was Naomi.

You weren't joking about the driving lesson, were you?

He stuffed it away again. "Well, Mom, thanks for the chat. Sorry for ruining your lives and everything, but I really have to go."

"No, you're staying here. I want to know what's going on."

He stood up abruptly. The chair wobbled. "That course is shit; they don't teach you anything there. Half the students don't show up, so I really don't know why I should have to." He walked toward the door, fishing his car keys out of his pocket on the way.

"Yet you still let me buy you hundreds of euros' worth of goddamn textbooks for the new year!" she hollered after him.

## 3

The dairy farmer hadn't come out of surgery yet. There were two other patients in the recovery room. One was a Surinamese woman with short gray hair who was complaining of double vision.

Helen tried to reassure her. "It's because of the anesthetic, ma'am. Your eyesight will go back to normal, but it sometimes takes a little while."

"How long?"

"Maybe fifteen minutes. Just try to relax a little."

She scribbled down a note.

"Hey, could you come and help me, please?" The question came from Jurgen Heemstra, one of the younger specialists at the hospital. He caught her eye briefly before walking over to the other side of the room, where the patients were prepared for surgery.

The specialist didn't look back. He blithely assumed that she would drop everything she was working on to run after him.

Helen turned back to her patient and continued checking her vital signs. She couldn't see anything unusual, but that didn't necessarily mean everything was OK.

"I think it's getting better already," said the woman after a short while. She covered one eye with her palm. "It seems like it's only on one side . . ."

"That's very possible, you know. It's nothing to worry about; everything looks normal. Some people just need a little more time." She tucked the woman in. "Are you comfortable? Warm enough?"

"Yes, thank you," whispered the woman.

Somebody quietly cleared their throat behind Helen. She turned around: Heemstra.

"So . . . do you think you'd have time to help me now?" His head was slightly cocked.

She smiled inwardly, but took care not to show it on her face.

"Of course."

She followed him through the glass swing doors that led to the operating rooms. From the corner of her eye, she saw a surgical assistant coming out of one of them. Her arms were wrapped around a rectangular container, the kind that was used throughout the hospital. Made of blue plastic, they had yellow lids and distinctive white stickers on the sides displaying a code and a warning sign. They came in different sizes. Some were specially designed for needles, some for blood and bandages. And some were for human remains.

This one probably held the dairy farmer's leg. Helen stopped in her tracks. Watched the assistant walk past.

Somebody stopped and spoke to her, but she didn't hear what they said.

She hurried over to a side door and peered down the hall, where the assistant was walking at the same brisk pace through the sliding doors and into another area. Helen focused on the container. It was as if everything around it blurred. Those things had a unique feature: once they were closed, it was impossible to remove the lid. That was for hygienic reasons. The containers were collected by a waste-processing company that put them straight into an incinerator, where they were destroyed. Unopened.

"Hello, are you in there?"

A whistling sound filled her ears.

"Earth to Helen?" Anouk moved into her field of view and placed a hand on her.

Helen blinked. "Sorry, Anouk, I didn't see you there."

"What's up with you? Are you sick or something?"

"I couldn't sleep," she said quietly. Her voice wavered, and her stomach contracted, as though somebody were squeezing it.

"Go and sit down for a little while."

She shook her head. "No, I'll be OK. Could you give Jurgen a hand for me?" She evaded Anouk's inquiring eyes, hurried down the corridor, and retreated into a restroom. It was empty. She turned on the faucet and held her hands and wrists under the cold water. Splashed water on her face and neck. Stood there for several minutes, her chin on her chest.

# 4

Naomi moistened her lips by quickly running her tongue over them. Ralf found it an endlessly captivating spectacle. The sun played on her sleek hair as it hung over her shoulders. Brown, but glittering in the light. He had to restrain himself from running his fingers through it.

The car drifted too close to a bush. Branches scraped audibly over the paintwork. Ralf reached out and gave the steering wheel a nudge to send the car rolling back toward the center of the parking lot.

Naomi let go of the wheel.

"Keep your hands on it," he instructed her.

She obeyed, with flushed cheeks, but took her foot off the accelerator and made a show of lifting her knees. "I can't go any farther. Seriously."

"You're doing well. Now, push down the clutch."

She didn't react.

"The pedal on the left."

She lowered her left leg and pushed down. Ralf put the car into neutral and pulled up the hand brake. "That's enough for today."

"I did everything wrong."

"No, you didn't. You did really well for somebody who's never driven before."

"Really?"

He nodded.

They swapped places. Ralf felt relieved to be back behind the wheel. Nobody had been run over, the police hadn't shown up, and his car was still in one piece—aside from a few scratches, but they'd be easy enough to repair.

"How was your exam?" he asked.

Her face brightened. "That's sweet of you to remember. It went really well. I think I passed." She told him enthusiastically about various answers that she had managed to correct at the last minute. "By the way, I still haven't heard from Brian. Have you?"

He shook his head.

"Don't you think we should go and see his mother? I mean, three days is a long time."

"Nah. It's just Brian being Brian, right?"

She looked at him in surprise. "But you're worried about him, aren't you? You were yesterday, anyway. Or did you call all of his friends for nothing?"

Ralf nodded. Thought carefully.

"Well then."

He broke eye contact and stared at a point in the distance. Tapped the steering wheel with his thumb. It was ridiculously unlikely, but nonetheless, suppose . . . suppose that Brian had been shot and yet still managed to get out of the house—bleeding, seriously injured. Where would he have gone? Not to his place, and not to a friend's either.

"OK," he heard himself say. "Let's head over there now."

## 5

Helen's shift was over. She was walking to the changing room, following her colleagues at a distance. Her surgical mask dangled around her neck. She took off her cap and crumpled it up. Shook her hair loose. Near the operating rooms, she passed a small corridor with a wheeled metal cabinet. It wasn't parked against the wall but stood in the middle of the hall, as though the person pushing it had been called away in a hurry. One of the doors was still open, and there were medical devices and instruments on the shelves. Some still with blood on them. Instruments were put in cabinets like this after use and then taken to the sterile-processing department, where they would be washed, sterilized, and packaged under two layers of paper—spotlessly clean and ready for the next operation.

Helen stood still. Among the items in the cabinet was an electrical device that resembled a cordless drill—except that where you would expect to see a drill bit, there was a small saw blade instead. Helen had seen the device in action many times, back when she used to work in the OR. It sliced through bone and tissue like a knife through butter. Hesitantly, she approached the cabinet. She reached out her hand, gripped the device by its handle, and lifted it up. Examined the cutting blade. It was covered with tissue and minuscule splinters of bone. Bits of Mr. Van Drunen, she realized.

# 6

"Hello?" Naomi bent forward and pushed the mail slot open, peering through into the hallway.

Ralf watched her, observing how her buttocks moved inside her jeans and her blouse rode up over her lower back. The bare skin it exposed was smooth and tanned. He turned his head to one side and concentrated on a car down the street.

"I can't see anybody," she said.

Ralf pulled his phone out of his pocket. It was half past five. "Maybe we should come back this evening. Or tomorrow morning."

"Tomorrow morning I'll be at school." Naomi stood upright. She was touching his chest slightly. "Hey. What if he's just in his room?"

"I went there on Saturday. His bed hadn't been slept in."

"Maybe he's there now, though?"

Ralf didn't like the idea of going back. There was nobody there apart from Mikey, whom Brian still owed money to, and Ralf would prefer not to run into him.

"Aw, come on!" She grabbed his forearm and rubbed it. "Pretty please?"

His skin tingled where Naomi touched his jacket, and he felt mild shocks run through his body. He stared at her lips. If Brian was somehow still alive, then he needed to let them know about it pretty damn fast.

"OK," he murmured. "We'll go and take a look." Some part of him that he couldn't quite control took her by the hand and led her back to his car.

# 7

Werner and Helen were walking arm in arm through the neighborhood. They couldn't talk in peace at home. The entire house was full of kids: some friends of Thom's had come over after dinner to play video games, Sara and Jackie had locked themselves in the bathroom with a makeup bag, and Emma was working on a school presentation in the kitchen along with two classmates.

"I regret not paying more attention to all those cop shows," said Werner.

"They're probably just as full of nonsense as the hospital dramas."

"But it would help me come up with ideas."

*Ideas like those pigs of yours, no doubt.* "This isn't a movie, Werner. In real life, you don't have any control. You can't rule out the possibility that somebody might notice you and call the police."

"It must be doable somehow." Werner's hair blew across his temple. "There are still plenty of murders the police don't manage to solve. Corpses with traces of DNA on them, but nobody to link them to. Or sometimes they can't even identify the body in the first place. And then all those missing persons." He looked at her. "I really think it would be better if I tried to get rid of him somewhere abroad. In a river, or a lake."

"I might have an idea," she said hesitantly. Her voice was quiet. "But it's—really, it's too gruesome for words. Complete madness."

He looked at her. "Tell me."

She told Werner about the protocols around clinical waste. "Nobody checks what's inside the containers once they've been closed. The lids are permanently sealed."

"But surely the contents are taken out again at some point?"

She shook her head. "No, the containers are destroyed as they are. They go straight into the incinerator."

"Are you sure?"

"Yes. It just means that we—" She couldn't bring herself to say the words.

"I understand what it means."

Nausea welled up in her again. "Never mind," she whispered. "Forget it. I never said anything. I—I must be going mad."

Werner grabbed her by the shoulders. His inquiring eyes ran over her face. They were bigger than usual—they even seemed to protrude slightly, and they looked at her with a sudden fervor that made her recoil. "On the contrary, Helen. I think it's a brilliant idea. Truly brilliant."

## 8

"I've never understood why Brian was so into living here," remarked Naomi softly.

They were walking through the huge kitchen. Ralf could see extractor fans, ovens, and cutlery trays, but also a lot of gaps; the best goods had been ripped out and sold.

"It's cheap," said Ralf. "Nobody complains if you make too much noise, and you can always park right in front of the door."

"But it stinks." She wrinkled her nose. "And you can be evicted at any moment. I couldn't live here."

"Me neither."

They went up the stairs. The hall was empty, to Ralf's relief. Mikey had to be at home, as they had just seen his dark-purple BMW parked next to the entrance. Ralf opened the door with Brian's key and stepped inside. Locked it again behind them.

Nothing had changed. The sheets still lay rumpled in the same way at the foot of the bed, as if Brian had kicked them off when he woke up. His iPhone was connected to the charger, exactly where Ralf had left it.

Naomi saw it too. "Hey. There's his phone."

Ralf froze for a second. "Oh yeah. Maybe he has another one with him?"

Naomi busied herself with the device for a moment, but couldn't get past the security screen and put it back down. "So everything looks the same as it did on Saturday? He hasn't been here?"

Ralf nodded.

She picked up an empty bottle from the floor and placed it on top of a cabinet. "Where is he, then?"

Ralf evaded her questioning look—those gorgeous dark-blue eyes of hers, framed by thin, black lines. Cracks were starting to appear in the shell of lies that he had constructed around himself. But he couldn't confide in Naomi. That would be incredibly stupid. She'd tell the whole story to a friend, who would tell it to somebody else in turn. That was just what girls did, and then it would only be a matter of time before the police came knocking on his door. It had already happened to plenty of guys he knew.

"No idea." He shrugged.

She opened the curtains and looked outside. The window was dirty, with thin cobwebs in the corners. "Ralf . . . I don't think I should be telling you this—I mean, you're his best friend and all—but . . .." She blew a strand of hair out of her face. "I sometimes have my doubts about Brian. Whether I really want to go out with him."

This was just about the last thing he had expected her to say.

"Take all this, for example." She spread her arms. "We go to visit his mother, we call everybody he knows, we make ourselves sick with worry—and he's probably just crashing with friends in Amsterdam or Rotterdam, or who knows where, and not for one second thinking about me. Or about you."

Naomi continued talking, but Ralf was unable to follow exactly what she was saying. The expansive gestures she made with her arms served to push her breasts forward, and those small, round forms were scarcely covered by the blouse she was wearing. They were about the size of Ralf's hands, maybe a little smaller. He had to restrain himself from reaching out to touch them.

Pulling that blouse over her head.

Undoing her bra.

Laying her faceup on the bed . . .

"What are the odds he'll end up laughing in our faces any day now?" She let out a cry of frustration and kicked the cabinet. "Oh, I'm so over it!" Her breasts jogged up and down with the effort. Two perfectly round hemispheres that trembled as she repeated the action.

His body began to respond.

He turned around. "Come on," he snarled. "We're going."

# 9

*"La maison?"*

"The house."

*"Le jardin?"*

"The garden."

Helen turned the page of the French textbook. "Great, Emma—I think you already know it all by heart!"

Emma looked different this evening. After dinner, she had retreated into the bathroom to clean her face, exfoliate it, and apply a mask. The hard, black lines and clumpy mascara had disappeared, and her freckles were no longer concealed under a layer of foundation. Her frizzy blonde mop was tied up in a rough ponytail on the back of her head, and stray, unruly hairs formed a transparent diadem. Sitting there, under the soft light at the kitchen table, she once again resembled the little girl who had skipped hand in hand beside Helen until so recently.

"It works well, doesn't it? Writing down all the words next to each other a few times," continued Helen. "That's how I always used to memorize things too."

Emma nodded obediently.

"OK, once more from the top . . . *le toit?*"

"The roof."

"And how do you spell *toit*?"

A faint trilling noise sounded, muted by the soft leather of Helen's bag. She always used to ignore her phone when she was busy with something—*they'll call back if it's important*—but that had come to an end once the kids had grown old enough to begin moving through the world independently of her and Werner. Sara wasn't at home; she had gone to visit a friend after dinner.

Helen unzipped her bag and took out her phone. *Lex* showed on the screen. Surprised, she answered.

"Is this a good time?" he asked.

"Er—yes, sorry. Of course." She stood up from the table and looked out through the kitchen window. The garage door was open, and the lights were on—Werner was busy fixing the light on Thom's bike. She turned around, expecting to see Emma looking at her inquisitively, but she was using the unexpected break to answer text messages on her phone.

"Helen?"

"Er—just a second." She waved to get Emma's attention. "Sorry, I have to take this," she mouthed, pointing to her phone, and then quickly walked into the hall. Closed the kitchen door behind her. "I was just helping my daughter with her studying."

"Sara?"

"No, Emma. French vocabulary." She was annoyed that her voice sounded higher than usual.

"Should I call back later?"

"There's no need. I—" She stopped in the middle of the hall. Her eyes were drawn toward the basement door. Could she hear something rustling down there? Anxiously, she tried the handle. The door was still locked. Her relief immediately gave way to the horrible image of the robber lying in the freezer at the bottom of the stairs. She could remember exactly how they had left him there—dressed in his black sweatpants and hoodie, his head turned to one side, his arms folded over his chest, and his knees raised. They had put a plastic bag containing the two guns and his balaclava in the gap between his shoulder and his head.

"Helen?"

She stumbled into the living room and sat down on the sofa. Her legs were trembling. "OK," she said with simulated cheerfulness. "What's on your mind?"

"I was going to ask you the very same question. I spoke to Anouk this evening about that staff trip to Rome. She said you were acting very strangely today. More than one person on the team noticed it."

"You and Anouk talk about me?"

"It just came up in conversation, Helen; come on."

Helen pursed her lips. At times, the hospital felt like one big incestuous village. A walled stronghold whose inhabitants were constantly watching one another, and where nothing remained hidden for long. That had never been a problem before; in fact, she had always found it amusing—reassuring, even. But then, she had never had anything to hide before.

"That reminded me of our conversation yesterday, and I thought I'd just give you a call. I hardly recognize you."

She searched for the right words, biting her lip.

"Is it something to do with Sara?" he continued. "Have you had more problems on that front?"

"No, no. Things are going great with Sara. Thank goodness."

"Are you sure? She's pulled the wool over your eyes before."

She closed her eyes and took a deep breath. "I stopped checking up on her a few weeks ago. She hasn't told any more lies, not about anything important, anyway. And it looks like she's stopped hanging out with that boy as well."

"That's wonderful. Things like that can really eat away at you. I used to lie awake at night worrying about Sanne, and I can imagine the feeling is even worse when it's your own child."

"How are things with her?" asked Helen, attempting to steer the conversation in a different direction.

Sanne was Lex's younger sister. His mother was forty-six when she was born; Lex had been twenty-four and his twin brothers four years younger. Nobody had been expecting any further additions to the family, and the surprise had been greatest of all for Lex's parents. Lex had once brought his sister along on a staff outing: a sullen goth in pale makeup who was difficult to relate to and hardly resembled her older brother. She had already run away from home a few times.

Lex told her that Sanne had discovered an interest in Japanese art and music. In the hope of getting closer to their daughter and her world, his parents had booked a trip to Japan for the three of them next spring. "I just hope for my parents' sake that she's still interested in it by then," said Lex.

"I hope so too."

There was a brief silence.

"Helen, I've known you for a while now, and—"

"There's really nothing the matter." She tried to give her voice a note of authority. "Please believe me. You guys are all worrying about nothing."

"Er—'you guys'? Just to be clear, *I'm* the one who's worried." His voice took on a mild, confidential tone. "We're friends, aren't we?"

Helen swallowed. She had always confided in him, over all kinds of private matters. The only thing she didn't discuss with him was her marriage with Werner. That was off-limits. Over time, she had come to value Lex's opinions over those of her friends, and sometimes his judgment even carried more weight than Werner's. Maybe that was because Lex truly listened to her and took a genuine interest. He loved people, whereas Werner tended to use people for his own ends. Werner was the ultimate manager, a leader who moved purposefully toward his goals. Even in love and parenting. It was a characteristic of his that she used to find exciting. Opposites attract.

"Mom?" Emma stood in the doorway. "Are you coming to help me again?"

"Of course, honey," she said. "Uh—"

"I heard," he said. "Sorry for bothering you."

"You never bother me," she answered impulsively. "Thanks, Lex."

She hung up.

# 10

"Thanks for dinner. It was tasty."

"I'll pass on your compliments to Colonel Sanders."

Naomi smiled. "You really never eat at home, do you?"

"Sure I do. I go there for seconds."

She laughed out loud.

At her request, Ralf dropped her off at the corner of her block. "Otherwise, my brothers will give me another grilling."

As they said goodbye, she unexpectedly put a hand on his leg. Ralf covered it with his own as nonchalantly as possible.

"Someone I know is having a movie night on Saturday," she said. "I don't know whether Brian will be back by then or not, but either way—do you want to come with me?"

Ralf didn't respond right away.

This wasn't a casual invitation. When a girl invited a boy to go to a movie night, that meant she liked him. Not all movie nights involved sex, but there was sure to be some kissing. Ralf knew very well that she was angry with Brian and felt he had let her down, but Brian was still his friend. On the other hand, Brian had never taken care of Naomi. If the robbery on Friday night had gone according to plan, they would have celebrated by hiring a couple of girls.

She gave him a deadly serious look. His silence had made her nervous.

Just as he was about to say that he would like to spend Saturday night with her, but preferably not with her friends, she added, "It's at Sara Möhring's place. Their house is an absolute mansion, and they have so much alcohol, her parents don't even notice if a couple of bottles go missing. So we won't need to bring anything with us."

# 11

Helen opened the wine cabinet and looked inside. On the pale wooden shelves lay more than a hundred bottles of wine, just waiting to be drunk. Wines from France, Italy, Portugal, and Greece. Some of them were rare and expensive—gifts from suppliers to the Horn of Plenty. She hadn't drunk a drop since the incident. Although she would give anything to feel that languid sense of satisfaction flow through her body once again—to feel her tense muscles relax—she was afraid that the alcohol would affect her in the wrong way, and that she would say or do things that couldn't be undone. Inconsolable weeping, for instance. Shattering plates out of pure impotent rage, or arguing with Werner in front of the children. Or all three at once.

She closed the door and turned around. Werner was watching her from the kitchen island. She had the impression he'd been there awhile. "Better not," he said.

"I know."

"Later."

She nodded. "Later" sounded good. It was a hopeful word. "Later" implied that one day all this would be over, and she would be able to go back to her normal life. Helen felt a need to embrace Werner, to get close to him, but his wild, almost vacant expression deterred her.

His jaw was clenched. "OK," he said to nobody in particular, before walking past her and into the utility room. She heard the back door open and close, and saw that he was heading toward the garage.

# 12

Ralf was sitting up in bed, his computer buzzing on his lap. The name "Sara Möhring" didn't produce many hits. Sara had made her social media accounts private, but her name regularly popped up on lists of tennis tournament results. He found her in some group photos on the tennis club website, but no other information was available.

Next, he typed in the address: "Kraaienveld 23." One of the top results led to a website with a photo of the house. The accompanying text told him that it had been sold seven years ago for nearly seven hundred grand. Ralf whistled through his teeth. A company now appeared to be registered there: the Horn of Plenty Ltd. Ralf sat up straighter. The Horn of Plenty was a chain of four big, popular, all-you-can-eat restaurants. Whichever one you went to, they were always packed. Ralf had never eaten there, but he knew people who worked in the kitchen or as waiters.

Brian had also worked there for a while, in the kitchen. Ralf even had to pick him up there once, about four or five months ago, because Brian's car wouldn't start. He navigated to the Horn of Plenty's website and clicked on the *Who are we?* tab. Next to a generic marketing spiel about *an enthusiastic team who are always ready to provide you with a delicious lunch or dinner* stood photos of smiling people in uniforms. One of them featured a red-haired man looking into the camera with a satisfied grin. *Werner Möhring*, said the caption.

That jackass had tried to rob his old boss!

# 13

Werner was wearing a set of blue hospital scrubs, plastic overshoes, and rubber gloves. A surgical mask covered the lower half of his face. It was spattered with blood.

"This is your fault, Helen," he growled. "I should make you do it."

His eyes nearly popped out of their sockets as he wielded the saw, dragging it steadily back and forth. Rivulets of perspiration ran down his cheekbones. Strands of hair sticking out from under his operating cap were plastered against his forehead.

He worked like a man possessed, emitting rhythmic gasps as he applied extra force to the saw and pushed it away from himself. Soft, sticky tissue dripped from the blade.

Helen watched with revulsion as she sat against the concrete wall of the basement, which felt warm and damp under her back. She was unable to move.

"I'll never forgive you for this," she heard him whisper, panting from behind his surgical mask.

She wanted to tell him how dreadfully sorry she was—that she would turn back the clock if she could—but a lump in her throat stopped her from speaking. Feverishly, she gazed around at her surroundings.

The basement looked different. The white paint on the walls had faded to an indistinct gray covered in stains and patches of exposed concrete. A buzzing, flickering light bulb dangled from the ceiling.

Werner suddenly stopped sawing. He swung the soiled tool onto his shoulder and slowly turned to face her. "Your turn!"

Helen woke with a start. Drops of sweat were running down her neck. She tried to scrape her sopping hair off her face, but her right arm was numb. The sheet had come loose from the mattress and wrapped itself around her upper body and her neck. Panicking, she fought her way free. The thin cotton was damp with her sweat.

It was dark and silent in the bedroom. She switched on the bedside lamp and looked at the space alongside her. No Werner. She ran her hand over the mattress: his side was cool and dry.

Helen slipped out of bed, breathing rapidly. Her heart felt like it was beating high in her chest. She hurriedly pulled on her dressing gown and slippers and walked down the hall.

Werner wasn't in the bathroom. The doors of the kids' bedrooms stood ajar. She stopped to listen at each doorway but heard only the calm, regular breathing of her children as they lay in deep sleep.

Nervously, she went down to the kitchen. The light under the exhaust fan was on, but nobody was there. With mounting unease, she walked on into the hall. It was dark, but not entirely: a faint glow emanated from the gap between the locked basement door and its frame. She heard muffled noises from below.

Trembling now, she placed her ear against the door. The noise grew clearer and sharper. It sounded like a file running over a hard surface—a nutmeg seed, perhaps. Helen stood and listened, breathing through her mouth. *Back and forth. Back and forth.*

She hadn't been dreaming.

Werner was down in the basement.

# Tuesday

# 1

"Look at this. Late-payment penalty."

Ralf snatched the envelope from his mother's hand and stuffed it into his back pocket. "Haven't you ever heard of privacy?"

"I don't understand you, Ralf. Why don't you pay your fines right away? Now it'll cost you even more."

"I'll take care of it," he muttered.

"Take care of it? And how exactly are you planning to do that? You don't have a penny in your bank account."

She knew that too, then. "I said I'll take care of it, didn't I?"

He had sixty euros in his wallet. Not even enough for a tank of gas. A solution had to come along soon. A job, for example—and ideally one that paid more than minimum wage. It was just a pity that nobody was looking for an eighteen-year-old boy with no qualifications. They'd made that much clear to him at the temp agencies. The best-paid job they'd been able to find for him was in an industrial laundry. "Most of your colleagues will be Polish. You have to pull your weight and be physically strong, but by the looks of you, that won't be a problem." Ralf had decided to pass on that offer.

Maybe Jeffrey was still looking for somebody. He had been talking lately about a job at a cannabis farm inside a shipping container. It was tougher than the laundry: you had to work nonstop for twelve-hour shifts in the heat and the stench, under the constant risk of a robbery or a police raid—but it also paid a few hundred euros per day. If he could stick it out for three or four days, he'd be in the clear for next month.

He grabbed his jacket from the coatrack and headed for the door.

"Where are you going?"

"To find a job," he answered.

His mother's face brightened, but her smile vanished again almost instantly. "Nothing illegal, I hope?"

So, she could read his mind as well as his mail.

"Mom . . . I'll see you later."

"Ralf, wait. Do you remember that youth project I told you about the other day? I've spoken to a few people there and explained your situation to them. You can start next week."

He stared at her blankly.

"You get assigned a sort of coach," she continued, "who sits down with you to look at your positive qualities and help you get your life back on track."

"Amazing," he said dully. "That's just amazing, Mom." He walked out the house and slammed the door behind him. Did she really think he was suitable material for a useless, hippie, socks-and-sandals project like that?

In his car, he grabbed his phone and sent a message to Jeffrey— Where are you, dude?—before starting the engine and driving down the street. Only then did he see in his rearview mirror that a purple BMW was following close behind.

## 2

"Sorry. This won't get us anywhere."

Werner's voice sounded like he had stumbled out of a smoky karaoke bar in the early hours of the morning. His skin looked gray, and the swelling by his eye had begun to change color from purple to yellow.

But it wasn't his appearance that Helen found alarming. Werner had a new kind of energy. Nervous, jittery. It felt like she was sitting at the kitchen table with a stranger.

"You should have woken me up," she said. "We could have done it together."

He shook his head. "That wouldn't have made any difference. It just can't be done with a handsaw. I spent half an hour sawing away at one—" His eyes roved restlessly across the kitchen. "It'll take weeks. Months." He raised his palms, spreading his fingers. Werner's piano-playing hands had never been suited to heavy labor, and they were now covered with broken blisters and grazes. "It was quite a job just getting him out of the freezer—he was completely frozen to the sides."

Helen clenched her jaw and silently looked past Werner and out of the window. A man on the other side of the street was walking two huge Rottweilers and obviously struggling to control them. One of the dogs dragged him over to the bushes next to the substation and started sniffing all around it.

She scratched her neck. "I had a nightmare last night that seemed so real. It woke me up. I went downstairs to look for you, and I heard you in the basement."

Werner fixed her with a glassy look. "Oh?"

Helen rubbed her forehead. Her fingers were shaking. "I couldn't bring myself to set foot in there; I'm sorry. It's so horrible, Werner. I—I don't know what to do."

He regarded her in silence, his eyes narrowed to slits. For a moment, his expression felt accusatory, but she must have imagined it.

"We can only do this once, Helen," he said softly. "There's no second chance. We have to get it right the first time."

Very occasionally, and especially when she was tired, Helen would look at her husband and—in a flash—see him as he might appear to a random passerby. A stylish man around forty, with slightly graying hair, a high forehead, and fine, aristocratic features. A lot of people would call him handsome. Helen hadn't fallen so much for his looks; rather, it had been his inner strength that attracted her. Werner was the kind of man who was ten steps ahead of everyone else, who always thought things through and knew what needed to happen. But this morning, for the first time, she saw desperation in his eyes.

"There must be saws out there that you can use to cut through frozen flesh and bone. A hacksaw, maybe?" he wondered out loud. He picked up the iPad from the table, but his fingers hovered motionless above the screen.

"What's the matter?"

He pushed the device away in frustration. "Suppose—suppose we get linked to all this one day. They'll definitely go through our browser history if that happens."

"I think they would, yes. But maybe we don't need to look it up online." She told him about the cordless drill the orthopedic surgeon used at the hospital. "Of course, I don't know how well it works on frozen body parts. Nor do I have any idea how to bring something like that home unnoticed. It won't fit in my handbag. But it might go in a—"

"What sort of blade would something like that have?"

Helen held her thumb and index finger apart. "About that big. Pretty thin. Like an electric bread knife."

He leapt to his feet. "Get your coat."

## 3

Ralf had driven through a red light and abruptly changed direction a few times in an attempt to lose Mikey, but the BMW continued to pop up in his rearview mirror. By the time Ralf turned onto Jeffrey's street, there were only two cars between them.

He thought about the can of pepper spray in his glove compartment. Very effective, but he didn't dare use it on Mikey. Brian's dealer knew where he lived and would at the very least break his arm or leg in revenge. Ralf could think of only two ways to get rid of him, aside from killing him: talking to him and hoping that he would listen, or paying him what Brian owed.

He drove slowly past the apartment where Jeffrey lived with his girlfriend, Denise, and their infant twins. The curtains were open, and he could see movement inside. Jeffrey was usually at home in the morning, and he was also quick-tempered and strong—maybe he could get him involved in this?

Hunting for a parking space, he drove to a small shopping area at the end of the street. It was quiet here. The fast-food place was still closed at this time of day, and the door to the Turkish shop was shut.

He parked and got out. The BMW's tires squealed as it hurtled across the parking lot and came to a stop. Mikey leapt out. Before Ralf had a chance to say anything, Mikey grabbed him by the throat and forcefully pushed him back against his car.

# 4

"Can I help you at all?" A boy with a freckled face approached Werner and Helen. "Jan-Willem," said his name tag.

"Um, well . . ."

Jan-Willem pointed to the wall display of electric saws. "There's a twenty percent discount on all Black and Decker products this week. It's a great offer, and on a good brand too. We don't get many complaints." His eyes met Werner's. Jan-Willem's eyebrows and eyelashes were so light, they seemed almost transparent. "As long as you don't have any really big jobs on your to-do list."

"Well, I—" Werner clenched his fist and started coughing, turning his back on the boy.

Helen forced a smile. "We're looking for a really good one, actually. One that doesn't overheat too quickly, you know? So you can work with it for an hour or so without stopping."

"They're all capable of that, but it depends on what you use them for. What will you be cutting?"

Helen looked to Werner for help, but he was still coughing.

"Ma'am?"

"It's for meat. Meat and bones," she said quickly.

"Excuse me?"

Werner had stopped coughing and was staring at her with a bewildered expression. His eyes watered.

"We feed our Rottweilers frozen meat and bones. We want to saw it into smaller portions, but it takes much too long with a handsaw."

Werner had scarcely moved.

"This isn't the first time I've heard that," the young man said with a grin. "BARF, they call it, right? Bones and"—he thought for a second—"raw food."

Helen nodded gratefully.

"My sister feeds her Labradors that way too," he continued. "It's more natural. Kibble was just invented by manufacturers to make money, of course."

Werner joined the conversation. "What kind of equipment does your sister use?"

"For frozen meat? The one at the top." He pointed to an electric saw costing around one hundred euros. "But it isn't part of the special offer, I'm afraid."

"We'll take it anyway," said Werner.

"An excellent choice." Jan-Willem bent down and searched through a pile of boxes for the right model. "If you've been messing around with inadequate equipment, then you'll know it's worth the investment. Having the right tools is half the battle."

# 5

"I don't know where he is!" Ralf pushed his chin down toward his chest to relieve the pressure on his neck.

Mikey's fingers encircled his throat like iron hooks. He was smaller and thinner than Ralf, but quick and unexpectedly strong. His other hand was also pressing a butterfly knife into Ralf's side. "I see you at Brian's place all the time, and now you turn up on Jeffrey's street. What does he know about this? What are you all up to?"

"Nothing, man. Jeffrey is just a friend of mine. Can't I visit my friends?"

Mikey moved his face up close to Ralf's, narrowing his crossed eyes into slits. "OK. One more time . . ."

"I'm looking for him just as much as you are!"

Maybe Mikey believed him, or maybe he had just made him uncertain. Either way, he let go of his throat.

"How much does he owe you?" Ralf's voice was high and hoarse.

"Three grand. He took over a batch of blow from me that he'd found some customers for, and he was supposed to bring me the money the same evening."

Ralf's jaw dropped. Had Brian been planning to start dealing? "When was that?"

"Friday."

Something started to dawn on Ralf. Brian had assumed he would be at least five thousand euros richer on Friday night after paying a visit to Werner Möhring.

"I'll tell you what." Mikey waved the knife at him. "I'll give you until Sunday. Twelve o'clock, Brian's room. If neither you nor that dirty thief shows up, then you'll have a serious problem on your hands. Both of you." He brought his lips up to Ralf's ear and whispered, "I wouldn't get too attached to that bitch of his either. She's first on my list."

## 6

Werner and Helen had purchased a large plastic tarp and a few rolls of duct tape from another hardware store, and while buying their regular groceries from the supermarket, they had also picked up four packs of extra-large freezer bags and a roll of gray garbage bags. All paid for in cash. They had spread the plastic-smelling tarp over the basement floor before coming back up to the kitchen.

Werner looked at the clock. It was ten past eleven. "What time are the kids getting home?"

"The girls get back at three thirty, and Thom will be here an hour before that."

"Good." Werner drew a deep breath. His eyes were pensive. "I need a drink."

"You don't have to do this on your own."

He glanced at her with an expression that she couldn't quite put her finger on, before walking over to the cabinet where he kept his liquor.

Helen realized that it had been a long time since she and Werner had spent a weekday morning or afternoon together. They used to do that regularly—back when Werner was still an employee at the Horn of Plenty and she worked more evening shifts than she did now.

"Somebody's been in here again, for Christ's sake," she heard him say.

After noticing on a few occasions that some of his alcohol had gone missing, Werner had taken to unobtrusively marking the level by scratching a line on the label with his thumb. If the level in the bottle was lower than the last marker, that meant somebody else had taken a drink from it. Helen found that sort of monitoring distasteful. She preferred to assume her children were honest—at least with her and Werner. The outside world could be hard and unfair enough as it was, so she felt everybody in the family ought to be able to rely on one another. Sara's recent deceit had shown her the naiveté of that—and on top of it, now she had to deal with children who were developing their own identities and pushing the boundaries.

Was there a teenager anywhere in the world who left their parents' liquor cabinet alone?

"What have they been drinking?" she asked.

"My Aultmore Adelphi," he replied. "That bottle cost me a hundred fifty goddamn euros."

"Our kids have good taste," she said softly, unable to suppress a faint smile.

Werner came back with a glass of whiskey. He leaned his back against the counter and took a sip. Closed his eyes briefly. "Man, I needed this."

On the counter behind him lay the new electric saw, gleaming in the fall sunshine.

# 7

The day had gotten off to a bad start, what with his mother's nagging and that run-in with Mikey so soon afterward. Then, at Jeffrey's place, he'd learned that the jobs with his weed-growing friends were spoken for already. "You're too late, man. There's a lot of people looking for that kind of work."

Naomi was sitting next to him in the passenger seat, unaware of the threat hanging over her head. They'd just had another driving lesson. She was getting better.

"I don't know," she said. "At first, I thought Brian was just being a jerk, but now I think—"

"What do you think?"

"I don't know." She looked at him. "It's just so weird, isn't it? It's already Tuesday afternoon. Don't you think we should talk to the police?"

"No. That's up to his mother. We're just his friends."

"But Brian sees her so rarely that she probably doesn't even know. She might not report him missing for a few weeks."

He took off his cap, examined the shiny sticker on the brim, and gently ran his thumb over it. "What do you say we wait one more night? If he hasn't turned up by tomorrow, we'll go and see her. You and me. OK?"

## 8

The high, whining noise reached as far as the kitchen—the same pitch for minutes on end, then back to a stuttering staccato.

At times, it would suddenly fall silent.

Helen paced in circles around the kitchen island, her arms folded. She felt guilty.

Cowardly.

Of course, Werner had wanted to do it all on his own. "What's the good if both of us go crazy?" he'd asked, and she had been only too happy to concede the point. But she would never forget the look in his eyes before he disappeared into the basement. Such coldness, such resolve. And yet, behind that tough exterior lay uncertainty and fear too. It was unavoidable. He was just as afraid as she was, only he didn't want to let it show.

"My part will soon be over," he had said. "After that, it's your turn. I can't help you at the hospital."

The noise from the basement died away.

Silence.

Helen listened intently. How much progress had he made? Was it even working? She tried not to picture the scene too vividly, but her subconscious fed her a stream of horrific images. The blue tarp spread out on the cold floor; the boy who—

She felt a wave of nausea and pressed a fist against her mouth. At the hospital, there was nothing gruesome about somebody who had just passed away; it was simply sad. But the bodies of deceased patients were treated with respect, while in the world of murder and manslaughter, things were very different. Until recently, she had only known about that world from TV shows and books, violent fictions that scarcely affected her. That scene in *Breaking Bad*, for example, where the corpse gets dissolved in acid and has to be more or less mopped up afterward—she had found it ingenious and fascinating rather than horrifying or repugnant. Only now did she realize that even the best fiction was nothing like the raw, dirty reality.

Helen rubbed her upper arms. The temperature seemed to have dropped—as if the piercing cold from the freezer had gradually seeped through the rest of the house.

When she turned around, she saw a police car pulling up by the front door.

# 9

"Thanks for the lesson. It was really great." Naomi leaned toward him and, before he knew what was happening, planted a kiss on his cheek. It was slightly moist, dangerously close to his mouth, and a little too long to be just friendly.

"I'm looking forward to Saturday." His voice sounded a bit hoarse. He held her gaze.

"Me too." Her hand moved hesitantly toward the door handle.

"That Sara, how do you know her, anyway?"

"From tennis camp last summer." Naomi shifted her hand from the door handle to the zipper on her tight-fitting cardigan. She played with it as she told Ralf about the bottles of expensive liquor that Sara had brought with her from home. That supply of alcohol had made her endlessly popular.

Ralf did his best to listen attentively. He glanced at Naomi's lips—soft and strong at the same time—and her tongue, which occasionally came into view between her teeth whenever she pronounced a word beginning with *th*. With all his might, he tried not to stare too much at her breasts. Occasionally, he looked away, feigning indifference, and breathed in her scent. When he was with Naomi, he almost forgot about Mikey and the disaster that awaited them both. He had long since stopped thinking about his mother and her tiresome "get my son back on track" projects.

"Sara is the reason I know Brian."

"Really?"

"Yeah. Brian and Sara were together at one point. Only very briefly, though."

"Weird." Sara was stunningly beautiful, but with her cool, calculating attitude, she didn't seem like Brian's type at all. He tended to go for more obedient girls. Uncritical ones, ideally. Brian's ego was easily wounded. "He never mentioned her to me."

"No, she made him swear not to tell anyone about it. She lost her virginity to him, at the start of summer vacation." Naomi looked at him with alarm. "Shit, you won't tell anybody else, will you?"

He raised two fingers. "Scout's honor."

She looked at him inquiringly, then leaned closer. "It was in the kitchen at the Horn of Plenty, when nobody else was around. If her father had found out, Brian would have lost his job."

"Probably his balls too," remarked Ralf. He experienced a sudden fervent hope that he would never have any daughters of his own.

"Even before that, her father couldn't stand her dating somebody beneath her. I mean, she's still in high school, but the boys she fell for were quite a bit older and had jobs already." She picked something from under her nail. "I can see where she's coming from, though. High school guys are—well, they're just boys, really. They're happy if you let them hold your hand or whatever. They aren't real men."

*What did she mean by that?*

She touched his forearm. "I really need to go inside now. My little sister is home alone this afternoon, and I have to look after her."

"Do you need any help?"

She shook her head. "Better not."

He paused. "What time do you get out tomorrow?"

"Twelve ten."

"Then I'll pick you up from school."

"OK," she said, and hurriedly got out of the car.

He watched her walk down the path behind the houses. The leather schoolbag hanging over her shoulder was the same shade of blue as her sneakers. She turned around briefly at the corner, smiled, and lifted her hand. Then she disappeared from view.

"Sorry, Brian," he whispered out loud. He put his hand under his belt and adjusted his boxer shorts.

# 10

The doorbell rang—a deep, loud gong that Helen had always found rather theatrical, but which somehow suited Wildenbergh's high ceilings and gleaming stone floors, and for that reason had never been replaced. Right now, she wanted nothing more than to ignore it, but it was too late for that.

There were two police officers at the door, and they must have been there for a reason. She fought the impulse to flee through the back and reluctantly walked into the hall. One of the officers, a black woman around thirty, made eye contact with her through the side window.

There was no way to warn Werner.

With a trembling hand, she opened the front door. She tried to act as normal as possible—surprised and curious, a little anxious—but she wasn't sure whether it would come across that way.

"Good afternoon. Is this a bad time?" It was the man who spoke. He was around fifty, balding, and had a round, friendly face. A baton, handcuffs, and a gun hung from the belt around his waist.

She closed her eyes briefly. "Er—no, of course not."

"We're currently making inquiries in the neighborhood. Have you heard anything unusual over the last few days?"

"No, I don't think so," she replied quickly.

The noise from the basement had stopped. Werner had hopefully heard the bell and was keeping quiet, but she couldn't be sure. She broke into a sweat. What if the reason for the silence was that he had finished his gruesome task, and was about to step into the hallway in his filthy scrubs—dazed, wild-eyed, with a bloody saw in his hands? Helen could scarcely resist the temptation to look over her shoulder.

"So, you haven't seen anything strange either? Anything out of the ordinary?"

"Out of the ordinary," she whispered. A shiver ran through her body. She quickly recovered and glanced at the police officers. "I don't think so. Why do you ask?"

"There's been a break-in at your neighbors' house."

She exhaled almost imperceptibly.

"The thieves forced the back door open; they probably got into the garden through the woods. The cat sitter noticed this morning that some of their possessions were missing."

"How terrible. What did they take?"

"Unfortunately, we can't share any details."

The woman adopted the same line as her colleague. "We haven't managed to get ahold of your neighbors yet. The cat sitter told us they're due back tomorrow from their vacation."

"Vacation," Helen echoed. She raised her hands and produced an apologetic smile. "Sorry, I didn't know they were gone. Otto and Frank often go away for a few days, but they don't always tell us. We don't actually have very much contact with them."

Suddenly, the house was filled with a high-pitched, piercing noise that was slightly muted by the basement door. The sharp screech of toothed metal grinding its way through solid material. The sound stopped briefly, and then the appliance squealed to life once again.

The policewoman peered into the house. "Doing some home improvement?"

Helen looked behind her. Her whole body was shaking. She feared that the tremor was audible in her voice too. "Oh, you know, there's always something that needs fixing in an old house like this."

The male officer coughed. "So, you didn't notice anything last night? Or early this morning? We're trying to establish what time the break-in took place."

"I'm sorry I can't help you. I didn't notice anything. My husband and I have a lot on our plate at the moment."

"Oh?" asked the woman.

Helen gave a start. *Why am I talking so much?* She made a dismissive gesture. "Nothing in particular. Work. And stuff with the kids . . ."

"Teenagers?" asked the policeman.

She nodded. "Thirteen, fifteen, and seventeen."

He shot her a sympathetic look, then handed her a card. "Perhaps your husband or somebody else saw or heard something. It'd be very useful if you could give us a call to let us know."

"OK, I will."

"Oh, and Mrs. Möhring?"

Helen looked at the female officer.

"The days are getting shorter. Neighborhoods like this one are unfortunately popular with criminals, and thieves are getting more ruthless all the time." She gestured at Werner's Mercedes and looked up at the façade of the house. "You might want to think about getting some cameras. They aren't so expensive these days."

"Oh yes. Good idea. Thanks for the tip."

The policewoman gave her a friendly nod. "Have a nice day."

"And good luck with it all!" the man said with a wink.

# 11

It was already growing dark by the time Ralf drove home. He had spent the entire afternoon with friends and had eaten at their place too—frozen pizza and leftover spaghetti. Thanks to the idle conversations and loud music, he had managed not to think about anything the whole time he was there—but that wasn't possible now that he was back in his car.

He parked around the corner from his parents' house underneath a few large chestnut trees, their leaves already changing color, and turned off the engine. As the interior lighting slowly dimmed, he remained motionless behind the wheel. Bikers trundled past, scooters and cars too. Now and then, people let their dogs out onto the patch of grass next to the car. Nobody noticed him.

Ralf tried to imagine what Sara could have seen in somebody like Brian. His looks? Brian looked like a thug who was always spoiling for a fight. His personality wasn't much to speak of either. Everybody thought Brian was a scumbag—apart from all the girls who were impressed by his car. But Sara's father was rich. His Mercedes was way newer and more expensive than Brian's Golf GTI. What was it Naomi had said? *High school guys are just boys. They're happy if you let them hold your hand.* Brian was no boy; that much was true. It seemed he'd made that clear enough to Sara when he'd taken her virginity in her father's restaurant.

Brian had quit not long after that—he'd stopped working at the Horn of Plenty in July, and then waited a few months before trying to rob his former boss in his own home.

How had he come up with that idea? Ralf could only guess. Brian had kept him completely in the dark. He hadn't even told him that the robbery was at Sara Möhring's. Ralf barely knew Sara, but still, Brian should have shared that information. Had he deliberately neglected to do so? Now that Ralf thought about it, Brian had known an awful lot about the family's movements. He'd known exactly where everybody would be that evening, as if he'd been watching the house for weeks. But he hadn't. Brian was definitely too lazy for something like that.

In hindsight, Ralf wasn't sure why he hadn't asked more questions.

What *had* Brian told him about? he wondered now. Taking Sara's virginity? Nope. Not a word. On the other hand, Brian had had so many girlfriends. Maybe he didn't think it was even worth mentioning.

And yet . . . Friends talked about things like that, and Ralf had thought Brian was his friend. Was the reverse also true? Or had Brian only viewed him as a useful helper and—since losing his license and his car—a chauffeur?

# 12

"Do you want a piece, Dad?"

Werner shook his head. "You guys finish it. I've had enough to eat."

"Yeah, we've noticed—barely anything," said Sara. She rolled her eyes, but covered the chocolate cake and put it in the fridge. "You're starting to act like Mom with all her diets. It's like you two are encouraging each other. You won't get fat from one piece of cake, you know."

Werner rested his forearm on the back of the chair. "Perhaps I need to remind you that your father runs four restaurants. I get offered food all day long."

She pouted. "But not by your own daughter."

"No. By real chefs."

She made a face and left the kitchen.

Werner took a deep breath and looked blankly through the window.

Helen could tell that it was costing him enormous effort to hide everything from the children. He was at his limit. And the job still wasn't done. He'd had to stop working abruptly this afternoon at two thirty when Sara unexpectedly came home early from school, bringing three friends with her. The four of them had occupied the kitchen all afternoon. They'd baked a cake and taken photos of every step in the process—a project for school.

"I can sneak off for a few hours tomorrow morning," said Werner. "But I need to go to the restaurant in the afternoon—there's no avoiding it. I didn't go in at all today."

Thom stuck his head through the door. The older he got, the more he resembled Werner, with his refined, bony features and slim figure. It was as if she'd had nothing to do with the creation of her own son. Amazing how genetics worked sometimes.

"Have you gone shopping for my party yet?" he asked.

Helen and Werner both turned to face Thom.

"Party?"

Thom's eyes widened. "Jesus, what are you two drinking there? I'm having a party on Friday, remember?"

"Yes, of course I remember," answered Helen.

Thom stared at his parents incredulously. "Are you sure? Normally there'd be boxes from the cash-and-carry in the garage by now."

"It's all taken care of," Werner snapped. "Your mother and I are trying to have a conversation here. Could we have a little peace?"

"Well, excuse me!"

"Now that's enough!" Werner stood up from his dining chair and pointed at Thom. "I'll cancel that party of yours altogether if you don't shut your mouth."

Helen kicked Werner under the table.

Thom was about to speak but thought better of it. He spun around and strode into the hall.

"And close that goddamn door behind you properly!"

"It was already open!" yelled Thom, pulling it shut behind him—a little too hard.

The kitchen was silent for a few seconds. Then Werner turned to face Helen. "What did you kick me for?"

"You don't have to take your frustration out on him. Thom's right— we haven't thought about his birthday for a second."

"Do I need to remind you why?"

"He doesn't know that, though, does he? It's his sixteenth birthday—it's really important to him."

Werner stared at the tabletop, gripping his glass. His entire demeanor radiated frustration and resentment.

"Goddamnit," she heard him mutter. "The house will be packed yet again on Friday. Perfect timing."

"Maybe there won't be anything left by then."

Deep lines appeared on his forehead. "Can you smuggle half a torso in your purse every day?"

She looked at him in alarm.

"Because that's what we're talking about here. We still have an awful lot of work to do." He stood up and left the kitchen.

# Wednesday

*1*

She had never used it before: a tall, narrow, dark-red leather tote bag with a hard, rectangular base, a zipper on top, and two floppy handles. When she'd spotted it in a shop window in Rome four years ago, she'd thought it looked both chic and sturdy; back home, however, it had proven too big to use as a handbag and too small for going shopping. Helen had now retrieved her poor purchase from the linen closet in the hall and dusted it off a little. It leered up at her from the floor next to the kitchen table. There were two unusually heavy packages inside it, carefully wrapped in gray garbage bags and sealed with duct tape. The rest of her things were stored in the front compartment. She bent down to zip the bag up, and felt the chill rising from it.

"Give it your best shot," she heard Werner say.

She nodded almost imperceptibly.

"You can do it."

She nodded again.

He touched her shoulder. "I'll see you tonight. Good luck."

She turned around and sought his eyes. "You too."

He gave her a slightly distracted look. For a moment, she thought he was going to kiss her, but he simply squeezed her shoulder.

# 2

On the breakfast table lay a stack of forms along with an envelope, a pen, and a note in his mother's neat, curly handwriting.

*Could you fill these in for me, Ralf? I'll be home at five thirty tonight.*

He set down his breakfast plate and cup. These were the best mornings, when both his parents were at work. No nagging about his eating habits, and nobody to say anything when he spent an entire hour in the shower, wandered around in his boxer shorts, and played Comedy Central on high volume.

Ralf cut his toast and fried eggs into small pieces and covered his breakfast in a layer of mayonnaise. He ate quickly, washing his food down with Coke. At the same time, he scanned ads on Craigslist. A few people in a neighboring town had put some promising motor scooters up for sale. Nearly new, no exterior damage. The asking prices were correspondingly steep. Two of the scooters were kept outside, to judge from the photos, and one of them even came with a matching rain cover. He pushed his plate aside and called the number on the first ad.

A woman—*Jantine or Janine?*—picked up.

"Hi, my name's Mike Jansen. Is the scooter still available?"

It was. He asked a few questions for the sake of form.

The woman enthusiastically supplied him with information. "That's right, we always keep it outdoors, but there isn't a spot of rust on it, and the seat is dry too—no rips or tears."

"When could I come over and take a look?"

"This evening would be best—my daughter will be home then. It's her scooter."

"Evenings are awkward for me." Ralf doodled triangles on his sheet of paper. "I work in a restaurant. Could I drop by during the day? Maybe tomorrow or the day after?"

"Um—could you come right now? I happen to be free today, but I'm back at work tomorrow and the day after. Otherwise, I could do the weekend?"

Ralf pulled one of his mother's forms toward him and wrote on the back: *Thu + Fri daytime.* "Hmm, that'd be tricky. What about tomorrow evening?"

"No, there won't be anybody here then."

He scribbled down another note and said, "You know what? I'll come tonight after all."

Ten minutes later, he had made four phone calls and written down two addresses. The first option looked like the better one. He would go and take a look tomorrow night.

# 3

Helen walked into the hospital via the staff entrance, but instead of turning right toward the changing rooms and the recovery ward, she continued straight down a wide corridor that led to the central hall. She walked hurriedly. The bag was heavy—much heavier than a handbag ought to be—and every time it brushed against her leg, she felt the chill. Two nurses were standing in conversation by the escalators. They nodded at her, and she endeavored to return their greeting as casually as possible. *Nothing to see here,* she impressed upon herself. Nobody could possibly know what she was carrying.

Her heart throbbed in her throat as she entered a small hallway and used her pass to open a door. She found herself in a narrow side corridor. Nervously, she took in her surroundings. She had never actually checked whether there were any security cameras in the hospital, but there had to be some. At the main entrance and in the central hall at the very least. She scanned the walls and the ceilings but didn't spot anything.

She had to get rid of the packages before she started work; otherwise, she would have to leave them in her locker all day along with her clothes, phone, keys, and wedding ring. She quickly pushed a door open and slipped inside.

The room was dimly lit and not much bigger than a typical bedroom. The walls were lined with wheeled trolleys, each about the height of a man. One was filled with plastic bags of general waste, while the second held laundry bags with white bedding inside them. The third had a stack of around a dozen blue plastic containers on it, with their bright-yellow plastic lids lying next to them. The fourth and fifth were empty. By the end of the day, they too would be full to the brim with all kinds of waste and refuse, ready for collection by Transport.

Stiffly, Helen separated the topmost container from the rest of the pile and placed it on one of the empty trolleys. She unzipped the bag and stared inside. A layer of condensation had already formed on the packages; their contents were starting to thaw. Fighting her repulsion, she removed them from her Italian bag one by one and placed them in the container. Then wiped her damp hands on her jeans and lifted the tub to check the weight. It felt heavy. Heavier than something like this ought to weigh?

*Heavier than the people from Transport are used to handling?*

Footsteps echoed in the corridor, the squeak of shoe soles.

She peered fearfully at the door. Her heart hammered behind her ribs as she hurriedly put the lid on the container, pressing down until it caught with a loud click. At the same moment, she saw the handle on the door move downward.

# 4

Directly in front of the red-painted door of number 8 stood a dark-gray Mercedes. The gleaming sports car looked out of place on this street— in this whole neighborhood, even.

Out of habit, Ralf scanned the license plate. "That's Werner Möhring's car."

"You mean Sara's father?"

He nodded.

"Do you know him?"

"No, but I know his car." His eyes were focused on the Mercedes. "Brian once pointed it out to me when I picked him up at the Horn of Plenty. Or maybe I was dropping him off."

Naomi made as if to get out, but Ralf grabbed her arm. "Wait a second."

The red door swung open, and Werner Möhring stepped out of the house. The swelling by his right eye had gone down since Sunday, Ralf saw, but there was still a dark shadow around it. Werner zipped his jacket up to his chin and got into his car.

"That's him," said Ralf softly.

"Yeah, and?"

"You told me yesterday that Sara's father banned her from going out with Brian. So, what's he doing at Brian's mother's house?"

"That's not what I said. I don't think he even knew about Brian. Sara just wasn't allowed to go out with anyone on the staff. She still isn't, for that matter." Naomi shrugged. "It makes sense, really. She's the boss's daughter."

Ralf studied the row house. Sheer curtains hung in the front window, but you couldn't see what was going on inside.

"Maybe he was here to talk about work or something," suggested Naomi.

"Work?"

She gestured with her chin at the departing Mercedes. "Emily works in the office at the Horn of Plenty." She frowned. "Doesn't Brian tell you anything?"

"Not about his mother, no."

Naomi got out. She rested her forearm on the door and looked him in the eye. "Are you coming?"

# 5

A woman stepped through the door, a stack of paper in her arms. Solidly built, in her fifties, with a sun-bed tan and bleached-blonde hair pulled back from her face. Helen recognized her instantly: Marjan de Boer from HR.

She flinched when she saw Helen. "Jeez, you scared me to death, Helen! What are you doing here?"

Helen snatched her bag from the floor and tried to look as composed as possible. "Hey—hi, Marjan."

The woman smiled apologetically. "I didn't expect to see anyone here."

*Me neither.* "You OK?"

"Yeah, fine, thanks." Marjan regarded her with slight surprise before looking around the room—perhaps to make sure that Helen was alone.

"I need to get going." Helen pressed her handbag to her side and hurried down the corridor, striding briskly toward the swing doors. She felt Marjan's eyes boring into her back.

It wasn't unusual to run into hospital employees outside their normal departments. Sometimes there were meetings to attend, items to collect or dispose of. But what on earth could explain her presence here? And with the door closed, for that matter? The recovery room had its own refuse containers. She had no business in the waste room whatsoever.

# 6

Emily still didn't look like anybody's mother—not someone Brian's age, anyway. She had large coffee-colored eyes and olive skin, and she wore her thick dark-brown hair in a braid over her right shoulder.

She smiled, exposing a row of white teeth. "Well, if it isn't Naomi! How are you? And Ralf, I haven't seen you in a while." She peered over their shoulders and down the street. "Isn't Brian with you?"

"Um, no. We were wondering whether . . . um . . ." Naomi glanced at Ralf.

Ralf took a step forward. "Well, ma'am—"

"Call me Emily."

"Well, Emily, we were hoping you might know that. Where Brian is."

A shadow fell over her friendly face. "How long has he been missing?"

"Since Friday," said Naomi.

"Come in." Emily walked ahead of them through the narrow hallway and into the living room. The walls were painted blue, and the smell of incense hung in the air. Two skinny Siamese cats were sprawled on the sofa by the window, observing the visitors with interest.

"Take a seat." She gestured toward the sofa.

Naomi plopped down next to the cats, lifted one onto her lap, and began stroking it. Ralf sat down next to her.

"Would you like something to drink?"

"No, thanks."

"Yes, please."

Emily chuckled and looked at Ralf. "I'll bring an extra glass just in case."

Ralf looked around uneasily. He'd visited Emily just a few times before, and only ever very briefly. Her house was small and contained remarkably little furniture: the sofa they were sitting on, a large floor cushion, and a compact wooden dining table by the back window. As his father would say, a blind horse wouldn't do much damage in here.

And yet it was comfortable. There were rugs and paintings on the wall depicting Asian scenes. Ralf noticed a Buddha sculpture on the windowsill, and a pot full of sticks next to it from which smoke was spiraling upward. It was pleasant enough, once you got used to the smell of the incense.

"Here you go, a nice glass of Coke." Emily handed each of them a drink and then sat down on the thick cushion. She rolled up the sleeves of her thin flannel shirt. A serious expression suddenly returned to her face. "So. Friday."

Ralf nodded.

"That was the last time either of you saw him?"

"Yeah, that afternoon," said Ralf.

"Did he say where he was going?"

He shook his head.

"And neither of you have spoken to him since then?"

"No," said Ralf hoarsely. "We can't get ahold of him. I've gone up to his room a few times. His phone is there, on the charger, but as far as I can tell, he hasn't been there himself."

Emily fingered her braid. "And you both thought he was with me?"

"Well, no. But—" Naomi looked to Ralf for support. "We thought maybe someone should go to the police. None of his friends have heard anything from him. Five days is a long time."

Emily nodded and shifted her attention to Ralf. Gave him a penetrating look.

Ralf took a sip of his Coke and examined the nearest wall hanging. It was red, with patches of beige and brown, and showed a mountainous landscape dotted with villages and rice paddies.

"Is there anything I should know?" she asked.

"What do you mean?"

"I think you know what I mean. Did he pick a fight with the wrong people? Does he owe anybody money?" Her dark eyes searched his face.

Ralf didn't move a muscle. "Emily, if I knew what he was up to, I would tell you."

# 7

The brightly painted, high-ceilinged room bustled with activity. Wherever you looked, there were people sitting, talking, and eating; their blue and white lab coats hung loosely over their clothes. Helen wasn't hungry, but to keep up appearances, she poured a little tomato soup into a cup and picked up a cheese sandwich before joining the checkout line.

She had spent the whole morning imagining Marjan carrying out a detailed search of the waste room and ultimately landing on that single, hermetically sealed, blue plastic container—lifting it up, weighing it in her hands, and shaking it from side to side, before slowly realizing that there couldn't be any clinical waste from the OR at that time of the morning. The labor ward was the only place where procedures were conducted twenty-four hours a day, and the waste that came from the delivery rooms was semifluid. The difference would be apparent the instant you picked up a container like that and shook it.

Helen had expected to be called away at any second. She pictured herself sitting in her manager's office opposite a detective, answering questions about the contents of the container.

But the morning passed like any other.

"That's three euros, please."

Startled from her reverie, she opened the front compartment of her bag to hunt for her wallet. "Sorry, new bag," she apologized, pushing a bunch of keys to one side.

"Don't worry, I'll get it."

She looked up. "There's no need."

Lex pretended not to hear her. Helen watched as he pulled his wallet out of his pocket and chatted with the cashier. He radiated a sense of inner calm. She had never seen him look anxious—not even this morning, when he had nearly lost a patient. Against her will, she wondered how he would react if he were in her position. Or in Werner's.

He walked over to a small table with a planter next to it. She sat down opposite him.

Lex unwrapped the paper napkin from his cutlery. "Man, what a morning."

"She made it OK."

"Thanks more to luck than to anything we did. It's rare that people react like that."

"You stayed calm."

He grinned. "It's funny I gave you that impression, because I felt anything but calm."

"I wasn't the only one who thought so."

Helen had the feeling that somebody was watching her. When she looked up, she saw Marjan sitting at a large, round table. She seemed not to be participating in her colleagues' conversation, and was looking directly at her instead.

Helen turned her head away and spooned up a mouthful of soup.

"I shouldn't have called you," he said.

"It's OK. It was sweet that you were worried about me."

"I sometimes forget we're colleagues."

"We're friends too, Lex."

He picked up his sandwich and tore off a piece. "There's no such thing as friendship between men and women. That's what my mother always said. One of the two always wants more."

"And was your mother always right?"

He grinned. "If I'm honest, she did miss the mark from time to time."

"Well then."

## 8

Emily wanted to wait a little longer before she reported Brian missing. "One more day," she had said—but then she had shot Ralf another look and added, "Or is there a reason why we should do it now? Do you know something I don't?"

Ralf had fixed her with a stony expression and had sworn that Friday was the last time he'd seen her son, and that he had no idea where he'd gone after that. He wasn't sure whether she believed him, but she'd stopped asking questions.

After their visit with Emily, he had taken Naomi home. He would have preferred to give her another driving lesson, but she had a mountain of homework to get through.

On his phone, he found a message sent by one of his friends earlier that day. Kevin had written that his parents were away, and asked whether Ralf wanted to come over and hang out. Alex was already there, and Rick and Luuk were coming later. Rick was the motorcycle mechanic—exactly the man he needed to speak to.

I'll be there, he typed, and started up his car.

# 9

It was seven o'clock, and Werner wasn't home yet. Helen wondered if he had finished his task. If it was done. She hadn't seen or spoken to him since she left for the hospital that morning.

She crossed her arms and began to pace up and down. Sara and Thom had gone to visit friends after dinner, and Emma was upstairs, studying for an exam. When the whole family was at home, the house felt different. Less threatening. It made her less conscious of the cold, viscous aura that rose from the basement and seeped into the farthest reaches of her home.

They had to get rid of the body.

As soon as possible.

Two packages down. That left around ten or eleven risky journeys to the waste room still ahead of her. Eleven chances of being caught red-handed.

There had to be another way. One that was quicker, and let her take more at once. But how?

The loud bang of the gate against the house made her jump. She saw Werner walk past the kitchen window toward the back door, his head bent against the rain. Shortly afterward, she heard the door close behind him, followed by the quiet jangle of the metal hangers in the closet.

He didn't kiss her when he came into the room, but walked over to the coffee machine instead. "Well?" he asked.

She looked at his back. "I did it. How about you?"

The appliance hissed and buzzed as he murmured, "It's all packed up."

"All of it? Really—already? How many packages are there?"

He turned to face her. "At least a couple dozen. I didn't count them properly." His mouth took on a grim expression. "The thing is, they aren't all small, unremarkable packages like this morning. Make sure you take that into account."

"Are there any that won't fit in my bag?"

"Yes."

"Why didn't you—"

"There's a limit to what I can cope with," he answered brusquely.

She opened her mouth to ask what he meant, then closed it again.

## 10

Perhaps he shouldn't have had anything to drink. Or not as much, anyway. Alcohol always made him irritable. But even so, he would have felt a lot better if Luuk and Alex hadn't been so goddamn annoying. Luuk was the worst of the two, claiming that Ralf owed him twenty euros when in fact it was the other way around. Ralf had come very close to pounding that smug grin off his face with his fists.

Luckily, Rick had dropped by. Their arrangement for tomorrow was still on. He would make sure he had money at home—cash up front.

Ralf crossed the deserted street, jingling his keys. He didn't mind walking home. He thought of Brian and his DUI. Ralf would go completely nuts if that happened to him. Without his car, he'd be stuck at home with his mother, who always looked at him like he was the biggest mistake of her life.

A bicycle was leaning against the façade of one of the buildings. Plastic flowers hung in a garland from the handlebars, and there was a toddler seat on the back. The bike was fastened to a drainpipe with an expensive lock. Impulsively, Ralf pushed it over. Stamped on the rear wheel and the chain guard, then kicked the rear light until it broke. He cursed under his breath and hurried on.

# 11

"It's eleven o'clock, Sara. Bedtime."

Sara pretended not to hear her, sitting with raised knees on one of the leather armchairs by the kitchen table and watching an American show on her laptop. She wore a thin pair of flannel pajamas that would have been cute when she was twelve, but which now emphasized her curves. None of Sara's clothes were cute anymore, Helen realized. She had become a woman. And it had all happened overnight.

"I'm talking to you."

Sara's tweezed eyebrows shrank into a frown. "Mom, I don't have class until second period tomorrow."

"Then you can read awhile in bed."

Sara rolled her eyes.

Helen opened her mouth in reprimand, but managed to swallow her words just in time.

"What are you guys planning to do on Saturday, anyway?" asked Sara, her eyes still fixed on the screen.

"I don't know yet."

She looked up in alarm. "You aren't staying home, are you?"

"Well, it just so happens to be *our* home, you know. I don't really feel like being kicked out by you and your friends. Your father might have to work, and I—" She stopped halfway through the sentence.

Sara looked at her expectantly.

*Yeah, Helen, what are you going to do when your children throw you out on a Saturday night and your husband is at work, like he always is?* The idea of going for a drink with Lex, just as friends, flashed through her mind. She dismissed it. "I don't have any plans yet," she said finally. "But if you don't go to bed right now, I can guarantee you that you'll find me sitting next to you guys on the sofa on Saturday night. I could do with a nice relaxing evening."

Sara closed her laptop with a sigh and stood up. "You can be so exhausting sometimes, Mom." She looked back over her shoulder at the door. In a bored tone, she added, "Good night."

"Good night, honey."

Helen watched her daughter in silence. No, she wasn't a child anymore. Soon enough, Thom and Emma would go the same way as their big sister, and after that, she would be able to observe her children's lives from the sidelines only.

And yet it still felt like just yesterday that she was pregnant with Sara. She and Werner had been terribly nervous and yet excited at the same time. Soon enough, a baby arrived—*their* baby. A child who would unite all their best qualities: Werner's aristocratic jawline, and her blonde curls; his drive to achieve something in life, and her desire to mean something to other people. In their naïveté, neither of them had stopped to consider that this adorable little pixie who depended on them for everything might one day grow into a teenager with very different standards and ideas from those of her parents.

Helen thought back to May, when she had by chance discovered that Sara was stealing from her. It transpired that she had been sneakily taking a succession of small amounts of money out of her purse. All those small amounts had added up to a substantial sum, which Sara had used to buy makeup, perfume, and a handbag. Helen hadn't confronted her daughter straightaway. She'd wanted to be absolutely certain. So she'd started counting the money in her purse at night. A few bucks had gone missing almost every morning, and very occasionally a bigger note too. And nothing was ever taken when Sara wasn't at home.

Helen had also learned that Sara was regularly getting drunk at parties, though at home she would tell them only about the odd glass of wine. She was going out with boys who were much older than she was and who had no prospects. On top of that, she would lie about where she spent the night—and above all, with whom.

Her kind, clever, promising daughter appeared to have a disturbing dark side.

Together with Werner, she had confronted Sara over her actions and her behavior. That had led to a heated fight, in which Sara had turned the tables and accused her mother of underhanded behavior. She had stormed out of the house that evening, furious and distressed, and only returned two days later. There then followed a dreadful phase during which Helen had barely slept a wink, terrified that she would lose her baby. At times, she'd thought Sara had already slipped beyond reach. Only after many weeks and some long, intense conversations did Helen regain a little hope that things would work out for the best. Sara had apologized and promised to turn her life around.

That was five months ago. Helen had stopped monitoring Sara's movements. The wounds were beginning to heal.

And yet it still gnawed away at her, deep inside.

Helen had missed her own mother terribly during that time, had been so desperate to ask her how she would have reacted, what she would have done. She had mentioned to one or two of her friends that things with Sara were "difficult," but aside from Werner, there was only one other person who knew about all the ins and outs of the situation. Lex had been a rock back then. Much more so than Werner.

*Thursday*

# 1

Werner was right. This was no manageable, unremarkable package. The object inside the gray garbage bag was the size and shape of a rugby ball. It sat imposingly on top of the rest of the packages in the freezer.

"That one's coming with me right now," said Helen.

Werner stood next to her in silence.

A shiver passed through her body. "It has to happen at some point. Then it'll be out of the way."

He nodded at the shopping bag. "In there?"

"It won't fit inside my bag from Rome."

"Won't it be too noticeable?"

"Maybe. But if I only carry a few packages each time, it'll take an eternity. I can't stand this for much longer, Werner. I want to get it over with."

"You and me both." He bent forward and took the package out of the freezer. Placed it in the bag.

Helen lifted it. "Put some more in."

Werner stared at her like he was worried she'd lost her mind. He didn't move.

"I'll be running around with a bright-yellow shopping bag anyway." She thrust her hands into the freezer, hauled out three more packages, and placed them on either side of the head. Then weighed the shopping bag again. It was heavy—very heavy. You could see its weight from the tautness of the handles and the laminated canvas. When she looked away, she could with considerable effort imagine it was filled with bottles of Coke. "It's more stable like that."

"Are you sure?" asked Werner.

"It's doable as long as I don't think about it."

"What will you say if somebody asks you what's in the bag?"

She was silent for a few seconds before answering. "I hope nobody asks."

## 2

Ralf opened his eyes and instantly wanted to close them again. His mother was sitting on the edge of his bed in a T-shirt with the slogan "Sometimes Dreams Come True." Her eyes were free of makeup, and her short bleached-blonde hair was slightly unkempt. She regarded him in silence.

He rolled over, pulling the blanket with him.

"What did I do wrong?" she asked softly.

*Everything,* he thought, but said nothing. He couldn't help recalling the self-satisfied smirk of his old principal as he informed Ralf that he was being expelled—immediately followed by his mother's expression as she sat next to him in that musty office, her disappointment, her anger. She hadn't believed him, even when he shouted it: he hadn't taken anything from those two lockers. She had only grown angrier with him; she had told him that he needed to stop lying, and that the principal wouldn't make an accusation like that for nothing. That was where she had gone wrong, on that October day three years ago. And on ten—twenty—countless other occasions since then too.

Was there anything about him that *was* good enough? Was there anything that he had done well in her eyes? His music was worthless ("ghetto music"); his clothes were unacceptable ("Take that cap off, Ralf; I'm ashamed of you!"); his grades were never good enough. Oh yeah, and his friends were losers. All of them.

*That was how it started, Mom,* he wanted to say, *because you didn't trust me. Because you didn't believe me. Because you rejected everything I thought was important.*

"Ralf? You didn't fill in those forms. I had to order new ones; they were covered in grease."

He threw the covers back and got up to get dressed. It was only seven o'clock, ridiculously early. The light outside was still gloomy.

"Why did you do that?" she continued. "You knew those forms were important."

He briskly pulled on his sneakers. They were a little scuffed on the side, but a new pair was out of the question as long as he wasn't working or going to school. His father had already made that all too clear. *Don't expect anything from us until you finally put your back into something. You can go barefoot for all I care.*

He headed into the bathroom, brushed his teeth, and styled his hair.

His mother stood in the doorway. She talked and talked, but he had stopped listening. He applied his gel carefully; his hair was getting a little long at the sides, but a haircut from a decent barber fell under the same category as a new pair of sneakers as far as his parents were concerned.

A hand clutched his shoulder. Instinctively, he pulled away. "Leave me alone!"

He wriggled past his mother back into his bedroom; grabbed his coat, phone, and charger; and hurried downstairs.

"That's right, run away again," he heard her call from the top of the staircase. "Run away from your responsibilities. You'll never amount to anything, you hear that? Nothing at all!"

He slammed the front door behind him, looked around, and then remembered that his car was still at Kevin's place. Angrily, he started walking in that direction. His vision grew cloudy; the houses and trees blurred into vague gray and green smudges. He sniffed and wiped the moisture from his eyes. The tears kept coming.

Why didn't she understand anything?

Why couldn't she just act normal for one day?

He couldn't go on like this; he had to get out of there. But where could he go? And how? He had no money and no job; his best friend had probably been shot dead; and if he didn't find three grand by Sunday, then Mikey would come not just for him, but for Naomi too. That was only three days from now.

## 3

It was doable as long as she didn't think about the contents of the heavy shopping bag—but at every bump and turn in the road, she felt it shifting around in the small trunk of her car. She drove more and more carefully. Other drivers began to overtake her.

The traffic light turned red at the final intersection. She pulled into the right-hand lane and braked. A white car stopped alongside her, and from the corner of her eye, she noticed the colorful stripes, the lights on its roof. She lifted her chin slightly and looked straight ahead, her clammy hands clamped onto the steering wheel.

When the light turned green, her foot flew off the clutch, and she accelerated a little too hard. From the back of the car came a quiet thud. She smiled nervously at the police officers, corrected herself, and quickly turned onto the hospital premises. To her immense relief, the police car continued straight past.

Her whole body trembled as she drove onto the parking lot and searched for a space as close as possible to the entrance. She didn't want to draw attention to herself by panting as she lugged her bag.

She had spent the entire journey to the hospital desperately trying to think of something to say if anybody asked her what she was carrying, but she still hadn't come up with anything. She parked the Fiat and reviewed her appearance in the rearview mirror. Her cheeks were flushed. She tidied her hair a little; it was damp around her neck. "It'll be OK," she whispered to her reflection. "You can do this."

She got out, hung her handbag over her shoulder, and lifted the shopping bag out of the trunk, placing a blanket over the contents. Then she locked the car and walked toward the entrance. After just a few steps, she swapped hands. The bag was far too heavy; she should have listened to Werner. She did her utmost not to let it show and walked on, greeting acquaintances who also had to start at seven o'clock this morning. Suddenly, a figure appeared beside her, extending his hand toward the bag.

"Let me carry it—I can't bear to watch you."

She looked up in shock. The man taking the bag from her hands was Lex.

# 4

Ralf pulled over in the McDonald's parking lot and walked inside. In the restroom, he splashed water on his face and blew his nose before studying himself in the mirror. His eyes were bloodshot, and the skin around his nose, eyelids, and lips was red and slightly swollen. He could only hope that he looked like he had a cold—and not as if he had spent the last half hour sobbing like a baby.

After ordering some breakfast from the counter, he found a quiet corner to sit in and looked around the restaurant. He had never been here so early in the morning before. The atmosphere was different. Men in suits were sitting on the benches, staring at their laptops, and a few retired folks were drinking coffee at round tables by the window. Almost nobody spoke. He hardly recognized his usual haunt.

Ralf poured three packets of sugar into his coffee, stirred it, and took a bite of his muffin. Then he grabbed his cell phone. Twenty messages from six different people. He scooted to the edge of his seat when he saw that eight of them were from Naomi. The first had been sent just after five in the morning.

5:02

There's a car in front of the house. Is that you?

5:09

It looks like a BMW. Dark-red or brown.

Ralf gnawed the inside of his cheek anxiously. *Mikey?*

She had sent the third message soon after that:

5:11

There's somebody inside it smoking. I don't dare wake my parents up. What if it's Brian?

5:30

I don't think it's Brian, he's still in the car. It's like he's waiting for someone. Brian would have gotten out by now.

5:34

Wouldn't he?

5:49

Shit, this is weird. I don't know anyone with a BMW.

Ralf's heart had started beating faster. Brian must have told Mikey where Naomi lived.

Pure intimidation.

And it was working. Ralf pressed his fist against his mouth and read on.

There were two more messages:

7:34

I fell asleep ☺ The car is gone. Like I dreamed it or something.

8:29

Now the car is at school! Creepy!! It's purple with black rims. I can't tell who's inside.

The last message had been sent four minutes ago.

School should have started by now. She'd be safe in there. Ralf gripped his disposable coffee cup so hard, the base came off. The hot liquid poured over the counter and the remnants of his breakfast. He stood up, leaving everything on the table, and hurried outside.

# 5

"I can carry it myself," she protested.

Lex smiled. "I don't doubt it, but I'd be happy to do it for you." He gave her a friendly nudge.

Helen tried to smile but managed nothing more than a strained grin. Bile rose up in her belly. She was just a few moments away from starting to hyperventilate. Pressing her handbag to her side, she continued walking alongside him.

"What do you have in there, anyway?" Without breaking his stride, Lex peered curiously through the handles. "It weighs a ton."

She felt her heartbeat reverberate through her body like a kettledrum. It felt as if the floor were made of rubber and undulating up and down, like on a cakewalk ride at a fair.

"It's, er . . . stuff from the freez—"

"Lex?"

Lex spun round to face a slim-figured man who had appeared alongside them. He was balding and wore a small pair of rimless glasses. Helen recognized him as one of the cardiologists.

"Hey, Louis. I thought you were sailing on the IJsselmeer today?"

"That's next week. I'm glad I ran into you. Have you heard anything about that patient of Eekman's?"

The men fell into conversation, and all three of them continued at the same pace toward the main entrance. Normally, Helen found it irritating when the specialists talked over her head, but on this occasion, she could have kissed the man on his shiny scalp. The three of them walked through the sliding doors into the hospital.

"Sorry, gentlemen, but I need to give this to Nicole," she murmured as if everybody knew perfectly well who that was.

She took the bag back from Lex. For a moment, she was afraid he might offer to come with her, but he was absorbed in his conversation with Louis.

# 6

The school was one of the biggest in the region, with five yellow-brick buildings, its own playing fields, and two gyms.

Ralf drove slowly past, keeping an eye out for Mikey's BMW. He had no idea which entrance Naomi used. After circling the complex three times, he pulled over. Not a BMW to be seen.

Ralf ran his finger over the inside of his steering wheel. Thought carefully.

What was it that creep had said about Naomi?

*I wouldn't get too attached to that bitch of his either. She's first on my list.*

Ralf was afraid that it was more than just bluster. Brian had told him enough stories about Mikey. That guy was genuinely dangerous. A total lunatic.

He grabbed his phone and sent a message to Naomi:

What time do you get out? I'll pick you up. Wait inside until I get there.

# 7

There was already a sealed container on one of the trolleys. Helen lifted it. The contents were solid and liquid at the same time. They sloshed around a little. It was heavy too—about the same as her packages from the day before.

She quickly placed an empty container next to it and took the blanket out of her shopping bag. Peered inside. She could clearly see the outline of the biggest package. Too clearly. As long as she kept telling herself that it was just a frozen package, she could cope with this. She had to switch off her emotions, that was all. And yet her hands hovered motionless over the bag. Her breath caught.

What if the staff at the waste-processing company gave the containers a shake, just like she had done, and tried to guess what was inside based on the feel, the sound, and the weight? And what if this container stood out from the rest because its contents not only slid from side to side but rolled a little too? Just enough to raise a few questions?

She took a deep breath and sprang into action, wrapping the blanket around the package before placing it in the container. It would move around less that way. She pushed the lid down until she heard a loud click and then grabbed a new container. The remaining packages disappeared inside it. Helen folded up her shopping bag, stuck it under her arm, and walked out of the waste room without looking back.

There was nobody in the hall.

# 8

Naomi's classmates waved to her as they trundled off on their bikes and scooters. She waved back but then scanned her surroundings anxiously. Ralf opened the trunk and took her bike from her.

"He isn't here," he said.

The bike had an inconveniently large handlebar that scraped against the interior of his car. Ralf could almost feel it, as though somebody were scratching a nail over his skin. The trunk wouldn't close properly once the bike was inside, so he tied it down with a length of rope.

"Who is it?" she asked.

He shook his head. Said nothing.

"Someone you know?"

Only then did he notice the tremor in her voice. He glanced across at her. Her dark eyes were flitting back and forth.

"He's gone," he said. "Come on. I'll take you home."

She sat down next to him and locked the door. Clasped her hands together on her lap. Picked at her nails. She was doing her best to act calm, Ralf noticed, but the shock was profound.

"So, it's someone you know?" she asked.

"Not very well."

She drew a deep breath. "Why is he following me?"

"Because he's angry with Brian."

She reflected silently for a moment. "It's not a coincidence, is it? Brian's disappearance, that car . . ."

"This is something different," he said quickly.

"What makes you so sure of that?"

He stared ahead blindly. He would never be able to tell her the whole story, but he had to reveal a small part of it now. "When we went to Brian's place on Monday, that purple BMW was parked next to the entrance. Didn't you notice it?"

She shook her head.

"It belongs to Brian's dealer, Mikey. He lives there too, in the same building."

Naomi's eyes opened wide. "Dealer?"

He nodded. "It seems Brian owes him money. He doesn't believe Brian is missing, and now he wants me to pay him back."

"Why?"

Ralf shrugged. "Because that's how it works with guys like that."

"Do you owe him money too?"

"No." He looked away as he added, "He says he'll do something to you if I don't bring him the cash. It's three grand. I don't have that kind of money."

"We have to tell the police."

He turned his head toward her with a jolt. "No! No cops."

"Jesus, you sound just like Brian with his phobia of the police. It's not like you've done anything wrong."

Ralf rubbed the inside of the steering wheel. A huge weight would lift from his shoulders if only he could confide in somebody. This was too much to cope with on his own. But in the final analysis, he had been an accomplice to robbery, and he couldn't risk Naomi's giving him away.

It was impossible.

On the other hand, did his fear of a criminal record really outweigh Brian's disappearance, the three grand he had to cough up, and the risk of something happening to Naomi? Wasn't he being incredibly selfish?

"Dealer," whispered Naomi beside him.

He didn't respond.

He tried to imagine what might happen if he went to the police with this. They knew him there, at the station. They knew who he was and where he lived. And more important, they hated him. Before he could even drive, the neighborhood officers used to question him about every little goddamn thing that happened. Sometimes multiple times per week. He'd been fined for having a broken taillight, jaywalking, not carrying his ID, and riding a scooter on the sidewalk. One of those creeps had once issued him a hundred-euro penalty for "loitering in a public place as part of a group without a legitimate reason," and not long after that, he'd had to cough up a hundred thirty euros for supposedly having caused a disturbance in the neighborhood. Back then, he earned less than thirty euros a week with his part-time job stacking shelves. They were just picking on him and his friends, plain and simple. And now he was supposed to trust these people?

Fat chance.

"Dealer," he heard Naomi say again. She narrowed her eyes into slits. "Is that really true, Ralf? Does Brian have a *dealer*? A cocaine dealer?"

He shrugged apologetically.

"That stupid asshole!" yelled Naomi suddenly. "I hate him! He told me a hundred times that he'd stopped all that. All those little deals of his, and that stupid blow, and the constant lying, and now—and now that prick has taken off. He ripped off his dealer and left us to face the consequences."

Ralf regarded her inquisitively. So that was what she thought—that Brian had made off with the cash.

"He can drop dead, as far as I'm concerned," she continued. "I mean it. Drop dead!"

## *9*

The morning passed without incident. Two of Helen's patients were currently in surgery—a man having an appendectomy and a boy Thom's age with a knee injury.

Helen rolled up a length of tubing and threw it away. Her thoughts turned to the weekend. Tomorrow and Saturday she had to work, but after that, she had three days off. She'd been looking forward to it for weeks—lounging around on the sofa in her pajamas with an embarrassingly big pack of M&Ms and a stack of DVDs.

Her heart had started beating faster without her realizing. She couldn't do it. She couldn't stay home alone with a dismembered corpse in the basement. The silence would grip her by the throat; it would drive her mad.

Werner had finally counted the packages: there were twenty-five in total. Six had already been disposed of. If she took two shopping bags with her tomorrow, she might be able to carry half a dozen at once. She could do the same on Saturday too. But even then, there would still be six or seven parcels left, which she wouldn't be able to get rid of until Wednesday at the earliest. That was too much. One parcel would be too much. Every scrap, every last hair. It had to go. All of it. The packages, the guns. The chest freezer. The house too, ideally. And her car, which she had used to transport it all. Everything that reminded her of last Friday.

A quiet whimpering emanated from a bed across the way—a heavily pregnant woman waiting for an epidural. She was sitting on the edge of the bed in a hospital gown, leaning forward. Anouk was holding her firmly and comforting her. "It'll all be OK, I promise," she heard Anouk say. "The three of you will be together soon enough. Then you'll have a family."

An uncertain smile appeared on the woman's swollen, sweaty face. "A family . . . That sounds so wonderful."

Anouk's eyes met Helen's over the patient's hunched back. She winked.

Helen did her best to produce a smile, but turned away hurriedly when she felt the corners of her mouth starting to twitch.

# 10

Ralf took Naomi's bike out of his car and closed the trunk.

"Are you up to anything tomorrow night?" she asked as she stuffed her coat under the straps on the pannier rack.

"Not really. Why?"

"Sara's brother is turning sixteen." She blew a strand of hair from her face. "He's a bit of a jerk and his buddies are all idiots, but Sara invited some of her friends who are coming over for the film night on Saturday too. I thought it might be nice for you to get to know them a little earlier."

"Where's the party?"

"In the garage at their place. So it's a date, then?" She gave him a peck on the cheek to say goodbye.

He fought the impulse to pull her toward him and kiss her on the lips. This wasn't the right time. Tomorrow night would be better, and then a repeat on Saturday—or a second chance. He breathed in her scent. "Great," he said hoarsely. "Will you watch out for Mikey?"

She looked at him a little uncertainly.

"If you see him, call me right away. OK?"

"OK."

He watched her as she wheeled her bike away, her schoolbag hanging from her shoulder by one strap. Once she disappeared around the corner, he placed his fingers on the spot where she had just kissed him.

# 11

"I'd prefer to get it over with by Sunday too."

"But how?" asked Helen. "I really can't carry any more at a time. I'm practically dragging the bags as it is." She raised her knees and shifted in her seat. The red leather sofa looked beautiful, but it wasn't designed with comfort in mind. "And it'd be too dangerous to make multiple trips to the car. Everyone in that hospital is so nosy." *And help-ful,* she added silently.

Werner was leaning forward in his armchair, his fingertips pressed together. "The waste room is inside the staff area, you say."

"That's right. You can't get in without a pass."

"Is it far away from the public area?"

"No, it's right next to the access door."

"OK," he said. "What if I bring a couple of bags to the hospital tomorrow? That would save us a day."

Helen made a quick calculation. Her eyes lit up. "Then it'll be gone by Sunday. All of it."

"Exactly." He picked up a notepad and pen from the table. "Where is it exactly, this waste room?"

She felt a sudden burst of energy as she got up and stood behind him. Watched over his shoulder while he drew a map based on her description. He sketched it out in a few quick strokes and then added a cross. "Right here?"

She leaned forward. His hair smelled wonderful, of shampoo and of himself. "Yeah, right there."

"What time?"

"My break starts at around midday."

"Then I'll make sure I'm in the parking lot just before twelve."

She threw her arms around him and pressed her cheek against his temple. "Thank you," she whispered.

He held her hand and planted a kiss on it. "Aren't you going to ask me why I want to get rid of it all by Sunday?"

"Huh? How come?"

"I have a surprise for you," he whispered. His breath tickled the inside of her wrist.

"A surprise?"

He leaned his head back. "I wanted to tell you on Friday night, but something got in the way." He paused. "You and I are driving to England on Sunday. To Sussex."

"What? Really?" Helen ran around the armchair. "That's amazing! We haven't been there since—"

"About a hundred years ago?"

"It was definitely in the last century, anyway."

Smiling, she thought back to the first vacation they had gone on together. All their friends had taken the train to Salou or Malgrat de Mar, but they had borrowed Werner's mother's car and driven to the south of England. There, among the green hills, they'd had the vacation of their lives.

"It was like a fairy tale," she whispered.

"Does it ever rain in fairy tales?" He brushed back a strand of hair from her temple. "It's going to be even better than last time. Just wait until you see the hotel."

## *12*

Ralf lowered himself over the fence into the backyard and unbolted the gate from the inside. It didn't look like the inhabitants were very interested in gardening: the whole thing was covered in mossy paving stones, with weeds growing through the gaps. There was no shed either. He crept over to the back window and peered inside. White floor tiles, a pleather sofa, a dining table with a pile of magazines on it, and a small fish tank. A light was on, but nobody seemed to be home—just like the woman had told him over the phone.

The scooter stood by the back door, propped up against the neighbors' fence. Ralf carefully removed the dark cover. He had a full set of tools in his backpack, but all he needed was his slide hammer: the U-lock was dangling uselessly from the luggage rack, and the key was still inside it. Ralf wasn't surprised. Most people believed their valuables would be safe in their own backyards—even if their only protection was a gate with a simple bolt.

# 13

Helen followed Werner up the stairs. She felt a little flushed from the glass of Bordeaux they had shared.

Werner had thought of everything—even somebody to look after the kids. His parents would stay in the house for a few days to make sure the children's routines weren't disrupted. Ernst would get up with them, and Ria had promised to make a big dish of lasagna—the girls' favorite—as well as the ham with sauerkraut that Thom was so crazy about. It sounded too good to be true—and it was, as Helen knew all too well. Her in-laws would come with a to-do list. They might not have arranged the bookshelves in alphabetical order by the time she got home, but the dish towels would almost certainly be ironed and neatly stacked in the closet. There wasn't a shred of humor, warmth, or pleasure in those people's parenting style—a family was like a company to them. Three days were manageable, but she didn't want to expose her kids to it for any longer than that.

At times like these, she struggled to accept that the children had scarcely known her own mother. Sara and Thom had only vague memories of their dear grandmother who had read *Jip and Janneke* out loud to them, and Emma only knew about her from stories and photos. She'd been six years old when Helen's mother passed away.

"Good night." Werner kissed her on the cheek.

She looked at him in astonishment. "Aren't you coming to bed?"

He avoided her eyes and murmured something in the negative.

"Why not?"

"That bedroom—I can't stand it right now."

She wrapped her arms around his waist. "Then I'll sleep in the guest room too."

He carefully extricated himself from her embrace. "The bed in there is too small."

"We can snuggle."

He held her face in his hands. "Not tonight. I'm in desperate need of some sleep." He brushed her forehead with his lips. "We'll have plenty of time to catch up properly in England."

"OK" was all she said. It came out as a squeak.

His eyes wandered up to the ceiling, as if he were searching for words up there. "Sorry, but . . . the air in here sometimes feels like it's gripping me by the throat. Don't you get that too?"

"A little." *But not so much that I don't want to be with you,* she added silently. Werner wanted to solve everything on his own once again. That had always been his way; he didn't want to burden her with his weaknesses or doubts. It stung now more than ever.

"Night night," he said, and stepped away from her.

She followed him with her eyes. Watched him walk down the long hall, unbuttoning his shirt as he went. He opened the door and disappeared into the guest room. Without looking back.

Helen felt the tears prick her eyes.

# 14

Rick had offered to drive him home, but he'd turned him down. It was only an hour's walk, and it wasn't raining. He wasn't in any hurry to get back either. Ralf stalked through the darkened streets, his hands thrust deep in his jacket pockets. Six fifty-euro notes rustled inside the lining of his coat. He ought to feel good, but the grin that usually covered his face after a successful job failed to appear.

He stared stubbornly at the sidewalk and bit the inside of his cheek so hard, he tasted blood.

*Mother Dear,*

*There was a woman on the ward today having a caesarean. It was her first child. Later on, in the break room, when I heard that she had brought a healthy boy into the world, I got choked up. My own reaction scared me. What touched me most was the expectant look in the woman's eyes. It got under my skin. She couldn't wait to meet her baby, to finally hold that little miracle in her arms. He would undoubtedly be the most beautiful little boy in the world, and he would grow up into a wonderful man who brought together the best qualities of both his mother and his father. He wouldn't have to make the same mistakes as his parents, because they would do all they could to prevent that from happening.*

*Don't we all have towering expectations that our children can't possibly live up to? No woman brings a child into the world and imagines their baby will rob people when they grow up.*

*I can just about manage to stay calm as long as I think about the robber as "the problem," as "packages" and "remains." Abstract words that have nothing to do with a human being. But they're still the remains of a person. A boy, for that matter. One who made bad choices. Choices he never got the chance to put right and that his parents were unable to protect him from.*

*What was his relationship like with his mother? Is she still alive? Looking for her son? Lying awake at night, just like I am?*

*I also wonder what kind of person he was, and if he often carried out robberies like this. Was he the kind of boy you see on news reports, waving a gun around in a gas station? A boy who beat people up on the street at night, just for kicks? Or was he so desperate—so troubled for whatever reason—that a violent robbery seemed like the only way out? I'm pretty sure he'd been using drugs. Cocaine, most likely.*

*Did his mother have any idea what her son was up to?*

*Parents always have a rosier view of their children than the rest of the world, and always stand up for them. You love your children with all your heart—a selfless love that permeates your blood, your DNA, your whole being. Even if they make bad choices and hurt other people in the process. And even if your own baby lies, cheats, and steals.*

*I know that now, after what Sara did.*

*Love persists. The umbilical cord may be cut imme-diately after birth, but there is always another one. You can't see it, but you can definitely feel it. And it tugs at you forever, Mother. Forever.*

*Because of what I did, a mother will never know what happened to her son. She can't even bury him. I took that away from her.*

*Werner says it's pointless to think about it or to talk about it, that it won't change anything. And he's right. It's irreversible. Just like your death, and Father's. I had to get through that, and I'll get through this too.*

*I need to try and sleep now, Mother.*

*I love you.*

*I miss you terribly.*

*Helen*

# Friday

*1*

Ralf took a bite of his grilled ham-and-cheese sandwich. Usually, his mother would have something to say if he didn't eat what she considered a "normal" breakfast, but today she sat with a mug of tea in her hands and stared into the yard through the glass panel in the kitchen door. There wasn't much to see there. The shed, the paving slabs, a few planters. The backyard bordered the neighbors' on all three sides. His father had planted linden trees along the fence to give more privacy, and it had worked: nobody could see you sitting outside. But the trees also kept the sun out. Ralf recalled the yard at Sara's house. They could always find a sunny spot there. And they had that swimming pool, an outdoor kitchen, and a lawn big enough to play soccer on.

Tonight, he would finally see the inside of that house. He hoped the father would be there too.

"There was somebody at the door looking for you last night. A slightly older boy," said his mother.

"Who?"

"He did tell me his name, but I can't remember it."

"What did he look like?"

"Smartly dressed." She gestured to her upper body. "He was wearing slacks and a shirt. And a red cap."

Ralf looked steadily at his mother. He had suddenly lost his appetite. "His face, Mom."

"Pale—a little unhealthy looking. Dark-blond hair. He didn't seem quite with it, but he was very friendly. Very polite."

"What did he say?" He put his sandwich back on his plate.

"He'd lost your phone number and wanted to remind you that you'd arranged to meet up." She frowned. "Sunday, he said."

"What did you do?"

"Well, I gave him your number. Didn't he call?"

He clenched his jaw and turned his face away.

She paused briefly, and then asked softly, "Ralf? That boy isn't a friend of yours, is he?"

He didn't respond.

"Are you in trouble?"

Ralf avoided her eyes. He felt tears welling up, and his body began to tremble. He took a deep breath and sniffed hard, like he had a cold.

"Ralf, if you tell me what's wrong, then I can help you." Then, more gently, "You don't have to figure this out on your own. You know you can always turn to me and your father for help."

"Not for everything."

"You can for this, Son. For exactly this sort of thing." She stood up and walked over, crouched down next to him, and regarded him inquiringly.

For the first time in a very long while, he could see genuine concern on his mother's face in place of the usual horrible suspicion and disappointment. Her expression told him that she was ready to listen to him, to stand by his side. That was how she used to look at him in the past, before it all went wrong. The stupid tears kept coming, flowing down his cheeks one after another. He wiped them away angrily.

"Ralf? Let me help you. Please." She went to lay her hand on his arm, but changed course halfway and leaned against the table instead.

"That guy wants money from me," he said softly.

"Why? Did you borrow from him?"

"I didn't. Brian did."

Her eyes narrowed. "Didn't I tell you that—"

"Brian was my friend, OK?" It came out more sharply than he had intended.

She stopped talking. Stared at the floor in silence, breathing heavily. Finally, she looked back at him. "But why does that boy want money from you?"

"Because Brian has disappeared." He sniffed again.

Suddenly, he felt himself growing flushed. He had spoken about Brian in the past tense—*Brian was my friend*. His mother didn't seem to have noticed.

"Gone?"

"Yeah. A week ago now."

"And you don't have any idea where he might be?"

Ralf scoffed. A scornful voice ran through his mind: *Since he was shot dead by Werner Möhring? For all we know, he might be buried in their backyard. Those people have enough room for an entire cemetery.*

She looked at him tenderly and laid her hand on his arm. It felt good. He instinctively placed his own hand on top of hers. His mother's hands were small and slender, with thin skin. He kept looking at them. Back when he was still in elementary school, he had found it fun to hold his hand against his mother's, palms together. Each time, he had fervently hoped that his fingers would be as long as hers. Now, her hand almost disappeared underneath his.

"How much does this boy want?" she asked.

"Three grand."

Her eyes widened. "And why do you have to pay it?"

"Because that's the sort of guy he is."

"And he wants it on Sunday," she concluded.

He nodded.

"Is he dangerous, Ralf?"

He wiped his nose with the back of his hand. "I think so."

"Then we need to get the police involved."

## 2

At the bottom of Helen's locker lay two folded-up shopping bags. She had distributed their contents over three containers, carefully pressing the lids closed. Nobody had seen her do it.

"Could you give Lex a hand?" she heard Anouk ask.

"I'll be right there." She updated her patient's data and checked his drip. The man was currently asleep, but he'd already woken up and gone to the restroom. He could be sent back to the ward.

*"Whoop, whoop."* A colleague hurried past her to grab an IV bag from the cabinet. "And another one. Where are they all coming from?"

Helen smiled faintly. It was normal for one or two unscheduled operations to be fitted in between the planned ones, but this morning was remarkably busy. All the ORs were in use. Helen had already seen a C-section and an acute hernia go by, and just now, two traffic accident victims had been brought in. She hoped that would be all, but experience taught her that days like this tended to ramp up further and further.

Why now? She felt the tension grow in her neck and massaged the sides of her vertebrae with her fingertips. If it stayed this busy, she could forget about taking a lunch break.

## 3

"Then we'll wait," said Ralf's mother. Her voice rang through the high-ceilinged, almost empty hall. She remained standing in front of the counter.

Behind it sat two officers in uniform. Neither of them looked particularly fit. The man had huge bags under his eyes, and the woman had spider veins on her cheeks. Both were preoccupied with their computers.

Ralf rocked from one foot to the other. It felt wrong to be here voluntarily; if a friend of his were to walk through the door right now, he would die of shame. Then again, Mikey wanted his money the day after tomorrow, and Ralf couldn't offer him more than a 10 percent down payment. What if Mikey saw that as an insult? He wouldn't let it go unpunished. Ralf pulled his cap down over his eyes and looked at the tiles on the floor. As shitty as it felt, his mother was right. This was too big. He couldn't do it on his own.

Of course, he wasn't about to tell them that the last time he'd seen Brian was at Werner Möhring's house. He had his story ready, and he planned to stick to it: They'd spent Friday afternoon hanging out in the shed. Brian had been using a little—maybe slightly too much—and then he'd left without saying where he was going. He hadn't been in his room when Ralf had gone to visit him the following day, and that was when he'd been waylaid by Mikey.

His mother cleared her throat and placed her hand on the counter. "Excuse me, sir?"

The man with the puffy eyes spoke without looking up from his screen. "Please take a seat, ma'am. Someone will be with you directly."

"But I have to go to work soon."

He made very brief eye contact. "We're doing our best."

Ralf shot him a dark look before following his mother across to a row of plastic chairs. She took off her denim jacket. "I Will Survive" was printed on the white fabric of her T-shirt. *An appropriate outfit for a police station,* Ralf thought.

After a few minutes, he broke the silence. "You should just go if you need to, Mom. I can manage things here."

She shook her head resolutely. "I'll just be a little late for work. This takes priority."

He picked at the fabric of his gray hoodie. "They don't give a shit about us."

"They're busy," she said quietly.

Footsteps echoed in the corridor behind the counter. A uniformed officer appeared from the back. Ralf recognized him: Remko van Amersfoort, the neighborhood policeman who had fined him for jaywalking. A bully, plain and simple. Ralf bit the inside of his cheek and looked away.

His mother touched his knee. "Sit still, Son. You're making my chair wobble."

The female officer stood up, and Van Amersfoort took her place. They exchanged a few words, and the man briefly looked in their direction before nodding to the woman.

Ralf studied their movements carefully from the corner of his eye. What exactly was so fucking important that they could leave them sitting here like this? He bit his nails in irritation.

Two officers walked in through the main entrance—an olive-skinned man with a shaven head, and a shorter colleague who spoke loudly with a Rotterdam accent. Their keys jingled.

Ralf looked away and cursed under his breath. More familiar faces: Ahmed Loukili—a.k.a. "the Snitch"—and Rudi Zwart. Those two had spent so long harassing his old group of friends that you could easily call it stalking. Ralf had been fourteen or fifteen back then. At that time, he used to meet his friends in the parking lot of the shopping mall or on the square in front of the church. Sometimes there would be girls there too, but generally it would just be a group of boys standing around, smoking and telling each other tall tales. During one particular period, the police used to drive past three or four times a day—slowing to a crawl—and would question them and check their documents almost daily. As if they were living in occupied territory. Anyone who didn't have their ID on them would be issued an on-the-spot fine, and they'd also give you a ticket if they found even the tiniest thing wrong with your bike or scooter. Those guys never listened to any explanations: that you'd lost your ID card the day before, that the battery for your taillight had gone flat on the way here. Whatever you said, they refused to believe it. They just looked at you with contempt. Smug expressions that said, *Do you really think you're so clever and we're so stupid?*

Back then, Ralf had never stolen anything, had done virtually nothing wrong. All that came later. *If people always blame you, then you might as well deserve it.*

Ralf's mother suddenly stood up and walked over to the two officers.

"Mom, wait."

She didn't hear him.

# 4

I'm here.

The message arrived with an angry buzz. Helen read it and replied:

Five minutes.

She grabbed a white coat from the pile, pulled it on over her uniform, and stuffed her cell phone into her pocket. She tried to head toward the hall, but two colleagues throwing their work clothes into the hamper blocked her path—their shifts were over. Just then, Lex walked into the changing room, followed by Anouk and a new anesthesiologist.

"Are you going to the cafeteria?" Lex took a white coat from the shelf.

"Um, yeah," she muttered.

He winked as he pulled on his coat. "News travels fast, huh?"

"News?"

"Pea soup," he said, looking as though he'd arranged it personally. "No time to lose."

"Oh, right." The soup of the day in the cafeteria was of varying quality. Helen suspected that a lot of it came straight out of a can, but the pea soup was always delicious. Plus, they served it with rye bread.

She walked out of the changing room and tried not to look like she was in too much of a rush. "I just need to do something first. I'll be right there."

Lex walked alongside her. "Can I help?"

"No."

*Don't ask any more questions.*

*Please.*

She didn't know exactly how much time had passed since Werner's message arrived, but she knew she had to hurry.

When they reached an intersection between two corridors, she briefly laid her hand on Lex's arm. "I'll see you in a few minutes. Grab a bowl for me, would you?"

She walked briskly down the hallway. Only at the end did she venture to look back, just in time to see Lex chatting with a group of colleagues as they headed toward the cafeteria.

# 5

"My son and I have been waiting awhile now for somebody to help us. We'd like to file a report."

"The best way to do that is online, ma'am," said Loukili, whose shaven skull and zealous demeanor made him look more like a commando than a police officer. "That way, you won't have to wait."

Ralf stood by his mother's side. "This isn't something we can report online."

"Oh, is that so?" His lips curled into a condescending smile.

"It would be nice if you could take this seriously," Ralf heard his mother say. Her voice trembled slightly.

"I take everything seriously, ma'am. You wouldn't believe the things we have to deal with every day." He looked at Ralf.

The same provocative stare, the same attitude as back then. Ralf felt himself shrinking. The years crumbled away, and from under the dust appeared a little boy trying to hold his own among his older friends. Clammy hands with bitten-off fingernails gripping the handlebars of his bike, its taillight broken.

"You're Ralf Venema, aren't you?" asked the shorter policeman. His eyes narrowed.

Ralf rolled his chewing gum around his mouth. He looked from one to the other, but he couldn't utter a word—he was breathing too hard for that.

"That's right. And I'm his mother. Katja Venema. Nice to meet you."

The officers exchanged a few lukewarm courtesies. Just the right amount of attention so that nobody could accuse them of being out-and-out douchebags, but nowhere enough to make her feel respected and welcome here. They were experts at that, thought Ralf. Belittling people. Subtly, like now—or more obviously, when there weren't any other adults around. Even in front of his mother they had to prove what tough guys they were. Fucking machos. A conversation took place, but he didn't take any of it in—it was drowned out by the pounding of his heart and his rapid breathing.

Maybe, he thought suddenly, it would do more harm than good to report Mikey. A guy like that could talk his way out of a police cell within a day or two, or he might not even be arrested in the first place—and then Ralf would be in truly deep shit, as Mikey would know he'd gone to the police.

"Listen, my shift is over." Zwart looked at Loukili. "Do you have time to deal with this?"

"Sure, I can fit it in."

As his colleague walked away, Loukili turned to face Ralf. His dark eyes glittered, and an amused smile played over his lips. "I haven't seen you at the supermarket in a while, Venema."

Ralf felt his jaw tighten.

The prick was enjoying this. He relished seeing Ralf here in the station with his mother. Two innocent rabbits who had strayed into his filthy wolf's lair. Not a shred of sympathy to be seen on his face. Not a trace of humanity. There never had been.

"Did you move or something?" That humiliating smirk again.

Ralf's hands clenched into fists. Was this actually happening? Did he really have to file a report with Loukili, a neighborhood officer who issued fines on the street to nervous fourteen-year-old boys with broken taillights?

*No way.*

He'd rather eat his own sneakers.

"Screw this," he said sharply. He spun around and marched away.

His mother called after him, but he didn't hear her. He pushed open the glass doors, oblivious to his surroundings. Paced toward his car without breaking his stride. People stepped out of his way and turned to watch him. He wiped the tears from his face angrily.

## 6

This part of the building was remarkably quiet; almost everybody was on their way to get some pea soup. Helen walked through a hall lined with planters before turning left into a dimly lit corridor.

Werner was already there. She saw him in the distance through the glass doors. His arms were folded, and he was feigning interest in some artwork hanging on the wall. There were two yellow shopping bags on the floor next to him.

About fifty paces.

Forty.

Werner looked up and spotted her approaching. His skin was pale, his eyes hollow. The whole situation was affecting him more than he wanted to admit. He bent down to pick up the bags and moved toward the doors.

Helen took her staff pass out of her pocket.

Another twenty paces.

She heard somebody talking—a woman. The voice came from an office on the right-hand side of the hall. The door was ajar.

Straight ahead, she saw Werner look around anxiously, a bag in each hand. There was no going back now—there would be no second chances today.

As she walked past the office, she saw Marjan standing at a desk, talking on the phone. Her platinum-blonde hair was pinned up.

Helen's mouth instantly went dry. She felt a strange sensation—as if she were growing taller, lighter, floating above her own feet.

Fifteen paces.

Marjan must have heard her footsteps—it was unavoidable—but she didn't look up or turn around.

Behind the glass, Werner's face took on a worried expression. He didn't know exactly what was wrong, but he knew things weren't running according to plan.

Ten.

Helen looked back swiftly—Marjan was still on the phone. She sought Werner's eyes and held her index finger to her lips. He nodded to show he understood. Then she held her pass up to the electronic box. The doors swung open almost noiselessly. Helen dropped the pass into the pocket of her white coat and silently took the bags from Werner. They exchanged a brief look of understanding, and then she turned around and hurried into the waste room.

Pulling two containers from a stack, she dropped a full bag into each of them. Pushed down the lids until she heard a click, and placed them on the trolley alongside three others.

She straightened her back and stood still for a moment, her hands folded over her nose and mouth. Her heart felt like it was leaping back and forth behind her ribs.

They'd done it. Early tomorrow morning, she would dispose of the last remaining packages, and then it would be over. Her breathing gradually returned to normal. She gripped the handle and opened the door.

Two pairs of eyes stared back at her in alarm.

# 7

"I'm not going back there, Mom." Ralf flipped on his turn signal and joined the main road. "They won't help me."

"Of course they will. That's their job."

He stared straight ahead gloomily. His mother meant well, but she had no idea. Loukili was a snake, and the rest of them weren't much better. The neighborhood officers could be just as bitter and prejudiced as certain teachers. They had probably started out brimming with idealism, but something had gone very wrong along the way. And they wouldn't pass up any opportunity to take it out on you. "Those guys only look out for themselves. They couldn't give a shit about kids like me."

"But I was there with you, wasn't I?"

"You're nothing but a gullible little mother, as far as they're concerned. They're probably making fun of you behind your back."

She said nothing for a few seconds. Then exclaimed, "How can I go to work now while you're in so much trouble?"

"That's exactly why I never tell you anything. You get too stressed out." He glanced across at her. "I'll take care of it, Mom."

"What on earth have you been doing, anyway?" she asked quietly. "You've been hanging around with all the wrong people."

Until a few days ago, a remark like that from his mother would have made his back go up. Always the same comments. But now he saw that she was right. Even his friends had warned him about Brian; they had started avoiding him as his friendship with Brian had developed.

"That boy is dangerous, you said?"

He nodded, looking straight ahead at the road.

"How dangerous?"

"I don't know."

*8*

Marjan and a nurse Helen vaguely knew—skinny, with short, spiky brown hair that stuck out in all directions—looked at her in shock.

Helen smiled, but her lips were trembling so violently that it was impossible not to notice. She did her utmost to think of a witty remark—something that would dispel the tension—but her head felt like it was filled with molasses.

Marjan broke the silence. "I thought you weren't a surgical assistant anymore."

Helen understood: one of the tasks of a surgical assistant was to dispose of waste, but recovery nurses had no business here. "Not for a while now, no." She coughed a few times, as if she had something stuck in her throat. "Well, I have to—"

"What is it you do nowadays?"

There was no point in lying. "I'm in the recovery room."

Marjan exchanged a knowing look with the woman next to her.

"Sorry, but I have to go. My pea soup is waiting for me." She smiled faintly as she pushed past the women and headed down the corridor.

# 9

Ralf's mother already had one foot out of the car. "Maybe I'll go back to the police station on my own once I get out of work."

"Don't, Mom."

"It can't hurt to talk to them, can it?"

"You'll only get me into even more trouble." He gave her a pleading look. "It's best if I solve this on my own. I mean it."

She hesitated, then reached out and placed her hand on the side of his face. "I love you so much, Ralf. I don't know what I would—"

"I love you too, Mom," he said softly. "You should go; you're already late. It'll be OK."

She stepped out of the car reluctantly. Shut the door and walked toward the mall. At the entrance, she looked back over her shoulder. He smiled at her, gave her a thumbs-up. Then she went inside.

Ralf made no attempt to drive off. He remained sitting behind the wheel, glumly watching the shoppers go by. Bikes and scooters trundled past. There was a group of boys sitting by the fast-food stand. He knew some of them from back when he used to spend all day hanging out here, back when he had no idea what else to do with his life. It turned out he hadn't made much progress since then.

Maybe it'd be better to go away for a while, take Naomi with him. Some of his father's relatives owned a mobile home near Barcelona that was unused in winter. It wasn't exactly luxurious, but it was big enough to live in. Ralf could wait tables, or work as a tour guide for Dutch travelers. He permitted himself to daydream about it for a few moments. Then he took the key out of the ignition, grabbed his backpack from the trunk, and walked out of the parking lot.

A little down the road, he caught a bus to the other end of town. He knew the address by heart. There was nobody home, but with a bit of luck, there would be a red Vespa ripe for the taking.

On Sunday, he would go and talk to Mikey.

He could only hope that he would be happy with a down payment.

# 10

Thom and his friends had emptied the garage and mopped the floor. In the spot formerly occupied by Werner's riding lawn mower, there was now a row of bar tables. Two more folding tables stood against the wall, covered with glasses borrowed from the storeroom of the Horn of Plenty, as well as bags of potato chips and M&Ms. The boys were gathered around a laptop. Hip-hop and rap played from the speakers, along with the occasional dance track.

Helen was attaching a string of lights to the ceiling. Arianne held the stepladder still and passed the fasteners up to her. "My kids never got any big presents like this."

"We don't make a habit of it either," said Helen. "We're paying for the motorbike license, but Thom will have to put his own money toward the scooter, just like his big sister did."

"I imagine you could get something good for seven hundred euros."

"Not the model he wants." Helen got down from the stepladder and pushed the plug into the socket. The lights began to flicker in blue, yellow, and red.

"Whooo!" she heard Thom call in jest.

"All the same, things have gotten a lot easier for you since the old days," said Arianne.

Helen understood what she was referring to. Not very tactful—it bothered her a little. "I'd rather still have my mother with me."

"Yes, of course. Sorry."

"Don't worry about it." She looked at her phone. "Seven o'clock. I'm just about ready for a drink. How about you?"

"I was ready at ten o'clock this morning."

# 11

The Vespa had belonged to a girl. Leather seat, windshield, red paint. It was well looked after. She must have realized by now that her scooter was no longer under the carport. The image of an unhappy teenage girl impressed itself on his mind's eye—staring sadly, her helmet in her hand. If somebody pulled a stunt like that on him, he would completely lose it. But in the final analysis, he thought, he wasn't really stealing from these people. Scooters like this one were always insured, so he was indirectly taking money from the insurance companies—and according to his father, they were the real gangsters in this world. Just like the banks and the multinationals. It was OK to steal from them. But still.

A message appeared on his phone.

Can you pick me up? We're eating at the Drop-In. X

The Drop-In was a fast-food joint on the edge of a small shopping mall, run by a Chinese family. A lot of people Ralf knew went there for something to eat before a night out. He would rather have eaten at home this evening. It felt like the right thing to do after everything that had happened at the police station. Eating at home was also free, and you didn't have to pay for anybody else. He needed every euro he could get.

Ralf picked up a wad of bills from the bed and counted them for the third time. Tens, twenties, fifties. His gas tank was full, and he had a couple of ten-euro notes in his wallet. That left five hundred forty euros for Mikey. It wasn't three thousand, but it was a start. He stuffed the cash inside a magazine, rolled it up, and tucked it between various other items inside a drawer in his desk.

He grabbed his phone and tapped out with his thumbs:

I need to take a shower first. See you in half an hour.

# *12*

"Would you like a Cuarenta y Tres?"

"No, thanks."

Helen grinned. "Straight to the Grand Marnier, then?"

"Sorry, but it'll have to be a glass of wine for me. I'm heading over to the gym after this." Arianne threw her coat over one of the dining room chairs and sat down.

As Helen poured them both a drink, Arianne told her about her elder daughter's sweet sixteen. Helen was barely listening. Only now did it sink in that tonight was her regular gym night, and that the robbery had therefore taken place exactly one week ago. It felt a lot longer than a week—more like a year. An eternity. She also suspected that she was still experiencing some form of shock—as if somebody else had taken control of her body. Her actions, the things she said, even her thoughts sounded like they were whispered by another person—a woman who looked like her from the outside, but whom she had met for the very first time this week. The only thing that felt real was her constant sense of remorse.

Everything had changed since the robbery. That was true of herself—the newly minted murderess who formerly wouldn't have been able to flush a sick goldfish down the toilet because she found it too pitiful and morally objectionable—but the same could undoubtedly be said for Werner too. Down there in the basement, she knew he had forced himself to do things that must have shaken him to the depths of his being. Those sights, sounds, and smells would surely remain with him forever. *What has been seen cannot be unseen.* And they would never be able to discuss it with anybody else, only each other. That might have been romantic if their secret weren't so horrifying—if their deeds weren't so reprehensible.

"Mom? Where did you put the chicken nuggets?" Thom wandered into the kitchen with one of his friends in tow. He continued straight on into the hall. "In the basement freezer, I guess?"

"No!" The wineglasses fell from her hands and shattered on the hard kitchen floor.

Thom froze. Arianne looked up in surprise. For a moment, nobody spoke.

Helen looked at the mess on the floor. "Oh, sorry. I think I've been feeling a little stressed lately."

"I'll say," remarked Thom. "You completely flipped out."

She answered, as calmly as possible, "The chicken nuggets are up here, in the small freezer."

Thom made a quarter turn and went to open the drawer under the refrigerator.

"But, Thom . . ."

He looked at her questioningly.

"Don't go turning on the deep-fat fryer now—that's for tonight, at the party."

"Mom, it's my birthday."

"You heard me."

"Ridiculous!" Thom left the kitchen, protesting loudly, closely followed by his friend. Helen heard the back door slam.

"What was all that about?" asked Arianne.

"Teenagers and their mood swings."

"I was talking about you."

Helen evaded her curious gaze and pulled a few sheets of paper towel from the roll. "Stress."

"What's stressing you out so much?"

She shook her head. "Don't worry about it."

# 13

The closer they got to the Möhrings' house, the more uneasy he felt. Ralf squinted nervously into the rearview mirror. Still no Mikey. He obviously felt he'd made his point and assumed he would get his money on Sunday without any problems. Thankfully, Naomi hadn't even begun to realize how much danger she was in.

She was sitting next to him. Her sleek hair was pinned up, and she was freshening her lipstick in the visor mirror. In the back seat sat Sara; her best friend, Jackie; and Floris—some rich kid who was not only paying serious attention to Sara but also eyeing Naomi far too much for Ralf's liking. He would have gladly let this guy walk all the way to the Möhrings' place, but the girls had been too quick for him and had already dragged Floris into the car.

"Left here, and then another left right away," said Sara.

He obediently followed her instructions, pretending to be unfamiliar with the neighborhood.

"You know what I completely forgot to tell you guys?" Naomi looked over her shoulder at the back seat. "Brian's mother reported him missing today."

"Jeez, that's heavy," said Sara.

"I know, right?"

"What will the police do?" asked Ralf. His voice was pinched.

"No idea."

"They'll probably put out an Amber Alert," said Floris.

"No, that's for kids. Brian is twenty-one."

Floris looked genuinely surprised. "And you all hang out with him? A guy in his twenties?"

"Why not?" growled Sara. "Four years isn't a big difference, you know."

Floris didn't answer, but he clearly disagreed. He stared morosely out the window.

Ralf enjoyed that, somehow.

"Here we are—the house at the end," said Sara. "Just park across the street."

Ralf pulled up next to the bushes and the electrical substation. He got out and looked at the house. A shudder passed through him. He had wanted to get inside this place from the moment he'd heard the shots—but now that he was on the verge of doing it, he had to fight the impulse to run away.

The group walked up the driveway ahead of him. He followed, picking his way through the haphazardly parked bikes, and closed the tall gate behind him. From the garage, he heard voices, laughter, and music that blared for a minute before being turned down. He thrust his hands deep into the pockets of his jacket and surveyed the garden. Right at the back, behind the swimming pool and the lawn, stood the wall he had hidden behind for several hours last Saturday. A good deal closer, between the pool and the deck, was a row of shrubs. That was where he and Brian had spied on Werner Möhring.

"Ralf?" Naomi stood in the doorway. "Hurry up, man. Everyone's already inside."

## 14

"Mom, I want to introduce you to a few friends."

Helen pushed the cushion to one side and stood up. She had no idea how, but she had fallen asleep on the sofa shortly after Arianne had left. She smoothed her hair a little and blinked at the company gathered before her. When Sara said "friends," she apparently meant "boys," and there were two of them standing on the cowhide rug by the fireplace. One was remarkably well dressed, while the other wore a blue cap with a shiny sticker on the brim and looked a little nervous.

"This is Floris."

The well-dressed boy shook her hand. "Nice to meet you, ma'am."

"Floris is studying economics at college," said Sara.

Now she knew for certain that she would be seeing more of Floris: Sara would never share that kind of information if he were just a friend. Helen took another good look at the boy. He was handsome—maybe a little too slick—with well-groomed hair.

"And this is Ralf," Sara continued.

"Ralf," Helen repeated.

The boy with the cap gave her his hand, which felt reassuringly solid. Ralf was a very different sort of person from Floris. Almost the opposite. She looked at his hands—you could often tell more about a person from their hands than from their clothing or demeanor—and saw that he had cuts on his fingers; short, chipped nails; and grazes on the back of his hand. His smile looked forced. Ralf lacked his friend's charm and clearly felt less at ease, but he had a more potent presence. More masculine.

It piqued her curiosity. "How do you all know one another?"

"Through Naomi," said Sara.

A girl with pinned-up, golden-brown hair stepped forward shyly. "Ralf is with me." She had a friendly, open expression.

"Naomi and I met at tennis camp," said Sara.

"Oh really?" Helen wasn't sure if she had already met this girl, but shook her hand to be on the safe side.

## 15

Sara's mother didn't look like the wife of a murderer, or even like somebody who would share her life with one. She had a mild expression and seemed very affectionate, warm, and attentive. An elementary school teacher, or a sales assistant at a florist's, like his mother. He liked her instinctively. And yet she might very well have helped her husband shoot Brian. She had been at home when it happened, so she must at least know about it.

"And what do you study?" she asked.

"I started working right after school, ma'am."

"Call me Helen. 'Ma'am' sounds so old." She glanced down for a moment, smiled apologetically. "So, what is it you do for a living?"

"Um, I'm actually looking for work at the moment."

"I understand. It's not so easy to find a job these days."

"But keeping one is even harder," cut in Floris, before launching into a story about a friend who worked in a restaurant. Floris was making a rather ostentatious attempt to get in well with Sara's mother, and if Ralf wasn't mistaken, his anecdote also contained a job application. It seemed Floris was looking for part-time work waiting tables at the Horn of Plenty.

Ralf lost interest in the conversation. Now that Helen Möhring was talking to Floris, he could study her at leisure. He watched her expressions closely, examined her demeanor and mannerisms. He observed how she spoke and gestured, noted the way she constantly pushed up the sleeves of her top with her elegant hands. His breathing had quickened without his noticing. *That's her, then,* he thought, *the woman who knows what went down.* She was standing just over an arm's length away from him. All he had to do was step forward, grab her by the throat, and yell at her—loudly, deafeningly. Threaten to do terrible things to her so she would panic and tell him everything. In less than a minute, he could find out what had happened to Brian.

"Well, guys, shall we go and get a drink?" Sara led the group away and disappeared into the hall.

Ralf hesitated. He looked at Helen, who nodded back at him with a polite smile. Then he joined the rest of the group.

He studied his surroundings carefully. The house was ridiculously big, and everything inside it looked expensive. There were huge modern paintings on the walls, with spotlights shining on them. The whole place was flooded with light. His parents thought that sort of thing was wasteful. Of course, Sara's father had four successful restaurants—he must earn plenty of money. There was a good chance he had other sources of income besides that too. Cash transactions, for example. There was a reason why Brian had targeted him.

Or had he just been tipped off?

Ralf looked at Sara, with her expensive clothing, her manners, her perfect makeup. She had "rich, cute, and stylish" printed on every inch of her flawless skin. If what Naomi had said was true—that she was into men—then what did she see in Floris, with his baby face and scrawny shoulders?

He sat down in one of the leather dining room chairs and placed his forearms rather awkwardly on the tabletop.

"Coke?" said Naomi, handing him a glass.

He took it from her but didn't take his eyes off Sara.

She was leaning against the kitchen island. Floris whispered something in her ear, and she laughed, baring her teeth. Sara Möhring, he decided, was a girl with two sides: the unapproachable model, and the slut who had let a boy like Brian take her virginity in the kitchen of her father's restaurant. *Was that really her first time?* he wondered. Maybe that was just what she told Brian. Sara and Brian seemed to be cut from the same coarse cloth. Had those two agreed to share the loot from the robbery, or had Brian promised her a reward in exchange for her tip-off—just like Ralf was supposed to get a cut for his services as a driver?

One thing was certain: this family was pretty fucked up.

He poured the Coke down his throat and got up from the table. Walked over to the window and peered out. So much space. So many possibilities. He wondered if there was any disturbed soil out there somewhere.

"Is it OK if I take a look at your backyard?" he asked Sara.

She regarded him with slight surprise. "Yeah, sure. Go ahead."

# *16*

"Sorry I'm so late." Werner took off his coat and scarf. He gestured toward the garage with his chin. A heavy bassline was pounding through the wall. "Nice and busy in there, huh? The driveway looks like a bike park. I left my car on the other side of the street. Who does that old Polo belong to?"

"It's Ralf's."

"Should I know him?"

She shook her head. "A friend of Sara's."

Werner poured out a glass of whiskey and held up the bottle. "Do you want one?"

"Better not. I've already had some wine, and I need to be at work early tomorrow." She glanced at the clock. It was only ten thirty, but given the way she felt now, she could have sworn it was the middle of the night. "I told myself I'd stay up until everyone had gone home, but that's not going to happen."

"You go on up to bed. I'll keep an eye on things down here." He looked at her over the rim of his glass. "Hang in there. On Sunday, we'll be in England. Have you packed yet?"

She smiled wearily. "When was I supposed to find time for that?"

"Well, you don't need to take much with you. As long as you bring a nice dress and a decent pair of walking shoes."

"Thanks for the fashion advice," she laughed.

He lifted one corner of his mouth. "Plus a raincoat, a warm sweater, and a pair of high heels."

"You're making me very curious, Werner. What will we be doing?"

"Everything." He gave her a teasing look.

The bassline from the garage continued undiminished. A low, throbbing *whoom whoom whoom*. Every now and then, the voices and music would grow louder and more distinct as the garage door was opened. Shouts, laughter.

Werner looked out through the kitchen window. "If I catch anybody peeing in the swimming pool, it'll be the last time we throw a party in this house."

"Werner?"

He turned his face toward her.

"I'm dreading tomorrow morning."

"The last packages," he said.

"Not just that. One of the admin staff has caught me in the waste room a couple of times. She suspects something."

"Are you worried?"

"Yes and no. Maybe I'm reading too much into it, but what if she's started keeping track of who throws what away? It wouldn't be much effort for her—the waste room is just across from her office. I've used seven containers over the last few days. Four just today. I have no idea what the normal daily amount would be, or if anybody monitors it."

Werner gave her a serious look. "You think somebody might notice the extra containers?"

"Maybe we should get rid of the last packages somewhere else." She looked up. "What if we took them to England?"

He shook his head resolutely. "Let's stick to the plan. One more trip and we'll be done."

"Do you think so?"

"Of course."

Helen looked at her husband. There wasn't a trace of doubt on his face. Werner seemed completely certain of everything, and that inspired confidence somehow.

## 17

Ralf stood in the garage doorway, his fists clenched in the pockets of his pants. The people behind him were singing loudly and badly along with the music and trying out strange dance moves. The backyard was quiet and peaceful. A misty glow hovered over the swimming pool. Ralf breathed in the cold night air and wandered farther into the garden.

He hadn't noticed anything on his first inspection earlier that evening, but that didn't mean much. For almost the entire length of the yard—along the fence and at the back—the borders were covered with a thick layer of bark cuttings, the ideal material for concealing freshly disturbed soil. There could be ten bodies out there. Thirty, even.

Naomi had come with him. She had seemed to find it odd that he'd withdrawn from the rest of the group, but in the end, had taken his hand and begun chattering away to him happily. She had grown quieter by the swimming pool. That was when he had pulled her toward him and kissed her. Her lips were warm and soft, and her small, smooth hands had disappeared under his hoodie to caress his back. In any other situation, he would have taken her straight back to his car and driven to a quiet spot out in the country. He hadn't done that, and now that the party was drawing to a close, he regretted it.

The garage was full of overgrown toddlers who thought they were something special, showing off to rap tracks by posers like Drake. It was unbearable. Of the few girls present, the only good-looking ones were

Naomi, Sara, and Jackie—with a swarm of losers inevitably circling around them the whole evening.

Ralf tried to keep a level head. He had kept himself slightly apart, drinking only two vodka Red Bulls and grazing on half a bowl of chicken nuggets.

A little before eleven, Werner Möhring had stuck his head around the corner of the garage, brought Sara's little sister indoors, and exchanged a few words with his son. That was nearly two hours ago now. Ralf would have liked to go inside to strike up a conversation with the man, but he would have been the only one to do so. The bathroom was accessible from the garage, and the fryer was outside under the canopy, as was the fridge full of snacks and drinks. Nobody needed to go inside the house.

## 18

"Why can't I stay at the party?"

"Because it's really late."

"What about Thom?"

"Thom is turning sixteen." Helen laid the duvet over Emma and tucked her in. "It'll be your turn soon enough." She yawned. It was one in the morning, and Emma had already gotten out of bed twice.

"I can't sleep because of the music."

"Don't you like it?"

She shook her head. Her skin gleamed under the soft glow of the bedside lamp.

"Me neither, but there's not much we can do about it. It's really late, honey. I was asleep when you came in."

"Where's Dad?"

"Downstairs. He's waiting until everyone goes home, and then he'll come up. Just like Thom."

"Is he going to sleep in the guest room again?"

Helen clenched her jaw. "What makes you say that?"

Emma looked past her at the ceiling. "Kim's father sleeps on the sofa sometimes too. Whenever he argues with Kim's mother." She sought Helen's eyes. "I never hear you two arguing."

"That's because we don't argue."

"Really?"

"No, darling. Your father and I love each other very much."

Emma nodded almost imperceptibly. Helen slipped out of the bedroom. "Should I shut the door or leave it open a crack?"

"Open a crack," answered Emma drowsily.

Helen went to her room and lay down in bed with the lights out. Loud music pounded insistently through the walls, accompanied by laughter and whooping.

*It'll all be over tomorrow,* she thought. She would divide the last packages between two containers, push down the lids, and that would be the end of it. Then she and Werner could put this whole dreadful chapter behind them.

# 19

Werner Möhring walked into the garage. He spoke to his son, who was swaying back and forth, before leaning over the laptop and turning the music off.

Ralf felt a rush of adrenaline course through his veins: he had never seen Sara's father up close before. He wasn't exactly big or muscular, and he looked more prep than perp in his green Gant cardigan and checkered shirt. This was the man who shot Brian? *And then got rid of his body?*

Werner seemed to be used to delegating, Ralf noticed. A natural authority radiated from him, and his voice was deep for a man of his stature. He scarcely had to raise it to be heard.

"OK, guys, if all of you help out a little, then we'll be done in no time."

Was he serious? Ralf had never been to a party where the guests had to clean up after themselves. None of the nerds objected. Chattering drunkenly and unsteady on their feet, they deposited their bottles and glasses on the folding tables. Ralf began to stack a few glasses too, so as not to stand out. He followed Möhring's movements closely from the corner of his eye.

No, he couldn't see even the slightest trace of a murderer or criminal in the man. Werner looked like exactly what he was: a wealthy entrepreneur—albeit one who hid cash in his house. Five thousand euros. Or more. Enough to get rid of Mikey and prevent anything from happening to Naomi. Ralf felt a slight flutter in his stomach and grew a little light-headed. This wasn't the first time he had toyed with the idea. It had occurred to him a few times already over the past week.

The next moment, he noticed Werner Möhring looking at him. He glanced down nervously and stacked a few empty snack bowls.

Werner walked up to him. "I haven't seen you here before."

"That's right," said Ralf, not meeting his eye.

"You look a good deal older than Thom."

"I'm a friend of Naomi's." Ralf gestured with his chin toward Naomi, who had crouched down to sweep up pieces of a broken glass with a dustpan and brush. Sara was standing next to her, holding a garbage bag open.

"And your name is . . . ?"

There was no point in lying. "Ralf Venema."

"Ralf. That your Polo outside?"

"Yeah, that's my car."

Werner nodded thoughtfully. He broke eye contact only after a few long seconds, turning away from Ralf and raising his voice. "All right, guys, that'll do. Thank you for your help. We'll take care of the rest tomorrow." Then he walked out of the garage.

Sara and Naomi came up to Ralf. Floris placed a garbage bag against the wall and joined them.

"Awful, isn't he?" Sara shot an angry look at the garage door, which Werner had just closed behind him.

Ralf shrugged. "He's not so bad."

She shot him a dismissive look. "Oh, come on. He's never at home, always busy with his work . . ." She placed a derisive emphasis on the last two words. "And when he is here, he runs around issuing orders. I mean, take this, for example. Thom throws a party, and my dad treats his friends like employees. It's not right!"

Nobody spoke for a moment.

Jackie broke the silence. "He gives you everything you want, though. Your clothes, that expensive scooter. Remember when your mother wouldn't buy you that coat? He was the one who got it for you."

"Yeah, sure, he can buy us things all right. That's easy enough. But he never actually does anything for us, because he doesn't actually care about us."

"Of course he does."

Sara's face hardened. "He never asks us how we're doing at school, or how we're feeling. It doesn't interest him. He cares more about those restaurants than about his own children. You know, sometimes— sometimes I really wish someone would teach him a lesson. Just give him a good smack in the mouth."

Naomi looked at her in shock. "Jeez, get ahold of yourself! That's your father you're talking about."

She shrugged. "You can have him."

# Saturday

# 1

"You're up early."

"Couldn't sleep," mumbled Werner. He was standing at the kitchen island in a pair of sweatpants and a V-neck T-shirt, buttering bread. "I put the bags in your car and cleaned the freezer."

"Did you get any sleep at all?"

"Not really. I think I might go back to bed in a couple of minutes."

Helen took some yogurt with muesli from the fridge and sat down at the table. On weekday mornings, the kitchen was noisy and chaotic. MTV or Comedy Central would be on, and there would be tablets and phones scattered among the breakfast plates, books, cups, and unzipped schoolbags.

Right now, it was quiet.

Helen took small spoonfuls of her yogurt. She had tried to approach the situation in as businesslike a way as possible over the last few days, suppressing the memories as far as she could—the gun in her hand, the smell of the gunpowder, the saw, the boy in the freezer, those sinister packages. Helen had known plenty of patients who displayed admirable resilience in the wake of an extreme event, whose behavior seemed relatively normal, levelheaded, and even cheerful. *Seemed* that way, at least, since it wasn't unusual to hear about people like that experiencing a nervous breakdown somewhere down the line, at a quieter point in their lives. There was no room for that, she knew. Not now, and not later. She maintained the brittle shell that covered her emotions and allowed her to go about her day-to-day routine. That boy was gone; she could do nothing more for him. But her children were still alive, and they needed her.

"What are we doing this evening, anyway?" she asked.

Werner looked up in confusion. "This evening? What do you mean?"

"Sara is having her movie night."

"Yes—and?"

"They don't want us around."

"Perfect," he said through a mouthful of bread. "I'll be back late tonight anyway." He turned to face the coffee machine and placed his cup under it. Pushed a button. Nothing happened.

"How come?"

Werner leaned forward and studied the machine. "Just checking in at the restaurants. Showing my face."

"That doesn't have to take up the entire evening, does it?"

"I'm afraid it does. I need to train a few people." He glanced at her. "Or you'll have to put up with their calling me constantly while we're in England." He turned back to the machine, thumped the side with his palm, and then tried again. There was a quiet gurgling noise, followed by hissing. "And I need to head over to the bank to deposit the daily takings too."

"What about me?"

He frowned at her. "What do you mean?"

"Weren't you listening to what I just said? They don't want us here."

"Jesus, Helen, you don't have to bend over backward for Sara and her friends."

"Even Emma and Thom are spending the night elsewhere. The kids want privacy."

He raised an eyebrow. "Is that what they call it nowadays? If it's so important for them to be on their own, they can go to a movie theater. Our house, our rules. He who pays the piper calls the tune."

"That's not the point."

"Why don't you go over and see Arianne tonight? Or go out for a drink with your colleagues?"

"That might be slightly short notice on a Saturday." She had a lot more to say, but she swallowed her angry words. This wasn't Werner's fault. She'd assumed that they would go out for dinner or catch a movie, but Werner probably didn't see the need given that they were leaving for England early the next morning.

*High expectations lead to disappointment.*

Maybe she should get that tattooed on herself somewhere. On her forehead, for example. In mirror writing.

# 2

"Ralf . . . Ralf? Wake up."

Ralf opened his eyes. His mother was leaning over his bed. Her cheeks were flushed, and she was breathing heavily.

He was instantly alert, sitting straight up in bed. He wanted to throw off the duvet and stand up, but then he remembered the dream from which he had been so rudely awakened. Naomi. Her tongue circling around his. Her naked body pressed against him, her legs around his hips as she . . . He gripped the duvet and held it down over himself.

"We have visitors," said his mother hurriedly.

"Who?"

"Two police officers."

"What? What do they want?"

"It's about Brian. His mother reported him missing yesterday, and they think you were the last person who saw him."

"Shit," he muttered.

"Ralf?" she whispered, and gave him a searching look. "I'm here for you. Whatever is going on. But you have to be honest with me."

He clenched his jaw. *Great timing, Mom.*

"Could you leave the room?"

"But the officers are downs—"

"I'll be right there, OK? Just give me a minute."

It didn't escape his attention that she glanced at his window. Then sought his eyes again. "Don't do anything silly," she said softly. "I only have one child."

"Come on. It'll be fine. I don't know anything about it."

"And what about that dealer? The man who—"

He pointed at her. "Don't say anything about that, Mom. Not a word! I'm taking care of it." He looked straight at her, breathing rapidly, his mouth half-open. "Do you promise? Mom?"

Ralf saw all kinds of emotions pass over her face. Her voice was hoarse when she said, "I sometimes wonder who you are, Ralf Venema. Or should I say, who you've turned into?"

## 3

Every step seemed to take an eternity. The shopping bags felt heavier than on previous trips. As if she were dragging two millstones around with her. The last pieces—quite literally, as Werner had packed the two guns as well.

Helen was panting quietly. She was constantly aware that her colleagues could see her and that the security cameras were recording everything. Despite her efforts to act calm and look as normal as possible, it was inevitable that she would come across as nervous. From the corner of her eye, she looked up at the nearest camera and pictured the grainy black-and-white images: the enormous central hall, the planters, the plastic benches—and a small, slightly anxious figure walking through it all, struggling under the weight of two shopping bags.

*Don't think about it.*

She had expected this to get easier—that she would get used to it, somehow. If you do something enough, it turns into a routine. Surgical assistants stopped fainting after their second operation, and experienced police officers calmly ate their sandwiches at a bloodstained crime scene. But that rule didn't seem to apply to her. Her hands felt clammy, and her mouth was dry. Helen prayed that nobody would talk to her. She probably wouldn't even be able to get her words out.

Hurrying through the corridors, she turned right and used her pass to open the doors. She didn't waste any time checking whether Marjan was in her office—probably not, on a Saturday. Instead, she went straight to the waste room and stepped inside.

Then froze to the spot.

# 4

It wasn't such a crazy idea that his mother had inadvertently suggested to him—climbing out of the window. He had briefly considered the option but decided to go downstairs after all. There was no point in running away. He had to go through with this.

"What did you and Brian do on Friday?"

The interview had already started before he could even sit down. Two policemen in their thirties. One had a shiny scalp; the other had closely cropped, black, curly hair that was parted on the side and fixed in place with glistening gel. John de Haas, a friend of Loukili's.

Ralf looked over his shoulder and pointed outside. "We were just chilling in the shed."

"Define 'chilling,'" said the bald one.

"Hanging out. Talking. Watching videos online."

De Haas leaned forward. "Hmm . . . Drinking, perhaps? A few lines of coke?"

Ralf looked at him angrily. Said nothing.

"Was it just the two of you?"

He nodded.

"And then?"

"He left," said Ralf.

"On his own?"

"Yeah. I was grounded."

"Did he say where he was going?"

A little voice whispered to him that this would be the perfect time to introduce Mikey into the conversation. With a few well-chosen phrases, he could set the police on the trail of Brian's dealer: *He owed Mikey some money and was supposed to pay him that afternoon . . .* But he held his tongue. If Mikey found out who had ratted on him, there'd be hell to pay.

*Snitches get stitches.*

"No, he didn't."

"What time was that?" asked the other one.

"Around one o'clock, I think."

De Haas wrote something down on a small notepad. "Did you notice anything unusual about Brian?" he asked, without looking up from his paper. "Was he preoccupied, or did he have any plans?"

"No, not that I know of."

"Think carefully."

Ralf looked from one to the other. "I'm telling you I really don't know. We didn't see each other that often."

De Haas leaned forward. "Brian's mother told us you're his best friend."

"Brian didn't have many friends."

The officer cocked his head. "*Didn't* have?"

Ralf's hands began to shake. He folded his arms. "Didn't, doesn't. What difference does it make?"

"I find it very interesting that you're talking about your missing best friend in the past tense," said De Haas.

His colleague joined in. "Aren't you worried about him?"

Ralf looked at his mother. She was standing in the doorway and looked pale.

"Not really," he said.

"And yet you and his girlfriend went over to his mother's house to make inquiries. Because you *aren't* worried."

Ralf scratched his neck. "That was her idea. Naomi's. I went with her as a favor."

"So, you aren't concerned, then?"

He shook his head. "This wouldn't be the first time Brian has dropped off the radar for a while."

De Haas looked him straight in the eye. "One of my colleagues told me you came to the station to file a report. It seems it was a sensitive matter—something that couldn't be reported online."

This was going wrong. Ralf felt a tiny muscle near his eye start to twitch.

"That wouldn't have had anything to do with Brian, would it?"

"No," he said as casually as he could. "As it happens, it didn't."

The officer turned toward Ralf's mother. "Could you confirm that?"

Ralf sought his mother's eyes, but she was looking at the floor. Picking at the hem of her T-shirt. She looked younger, standing there. Like the girl she must once have been.

"It didn't have anything to do with Brian," she replied.

"Are you sure?"

"Yes."

Ralf exhaled inaudibly.

"Would you like to file that report now?"

She lifted her head. "What we came to tell you about—is all settled now."

The officers looked at each other. The bald one stood up, followed by De Haas. "OK. We'll be on our way now. Thanks for the coffee."

De Haas turned around at the door. He lowered his chin, and his eyes met Ralf's for a few seconds. "But we'll be keeping an eye on you, Venema."

"Why don't you go and catch some real crooks?" Ralf heard his mother say. Her voice was trembling. "You've been bullying my son for long enough."

De Haas responded instantly. "You might find you have a rather rose-tinted view of your son."

"I think I know him better than anyone else. Good day to you both."

# 5

Helen felt the blood drain from her face. The trolleys were piled with boxes, and bags of laundry stood next to them. There were stacks of towels inside the open cupboard.

But no waste containers.

Not one.

She looked around in shock. Who was responsible for this? Was it a coincidence?

Or did it mean something?

*Marjan?*

*Was this a trap?*

She felt like she was suffocating. Opened her mouth and sucked in air. And again. It wasn't enough. Her hands remained clamped around the handles of the bags as she greedily gasped for oxygen, her breaths coming more and more rapidly. Still it wasn't enough. It felt like she was breathing through a straw. And then the sudden pressure on her chest as if someone or something were pushing down on it, hard. The pressure intensified, turning into pain. She inhaled desperately—panting, ragged breaths—and staggered forward, backward, as if she were blind drunk. The room revolved around her, and it seemed as if the walls and the ceiling were pulling away—or was it she that was shrinking? Cold. She was suddenly so cold. The bags slipped from her hands, and she slumped to the floor.

## *6*

Ralf sat in silence in the living room. Had he really just heard that? His mother had stood up for him. She'd shown those cops the door with a sarcastic remark. More than that, she had lied to both their faces.

During their meeting with his old principal, his mother had refused to believe that Ralf was innocent—even though he had done nothing wrong. Now it was the other way around. The policemen had been right, of course: she did have a rose-tinted view of him—for now, at least. Not in her worst nightmares would she be able to imagine that he had been Brian's accomplice in an armed robbery. The truth would break her heart. And there was no guarantee that it wouldn't come out, since Brian wasn't just missing—Brian had been murdered. He wasn't coming back. It was only a matter of time before the police opened a serious investigation into his disappearance.

Ralf got up from his chair and stretched. If he was unlucky, he would probably get the blame for Brian's disappearance too. He had a clear motive in the eyes of the law: Naomi. And if he explained—told the truth—then it would fall on deaf ears, just like when he used to hang out at the shopping mall. What was it his father always said? *Being right and being believed are two different things.*

But what should he do, then? Come clean now about what happened? Even if he somehow avoided jail, he'd have a criminal record for robbery. No company would hire someone with a record. He would be doomed to spend the rest of his life stealing scooters, growing weed, and doing sketchy deals with people like Mikey. Or abetting guys like Brian. Because in hindsight, everybody had been right all along. Brian wasn't his friend; he had just been using him. And now Ralf was left with his inheritance: thousands of euros of debt owed to a dangerous moron, and a good chance that the police would soon view him as the suspect in a murder case.

He had to get out of this as quickly as possible. He had to get his life back on track. But first, he had to deal with Mikey. He was due to meet him tomorrow, and he was still twenty-five hundred euros short.

"Are you still here?"

He looked up. "Mom?"

She stood silently in the doorway.

He swallowed. "Mom, I just want to say . . . thank you for—"

She held up her hand. "I don't know what you're up to, Ralf, and maybe I don't want to know. I just hope that one day you understand the path you're currently following leads nowhere." In a softer voice, she added, "And I hope that day comes before it's too late."

Only then did he notice she'd been crying.

# 7

"Helen?"

She knew that voice.

Helen opened her eyes and immediately closed them again. A bright light, directly overhead. She blinked, turned her face away. She was lying flat on her back. The floor was smooth and hard, and around her stood trolleys piled with towels and plastic bags. Close to her head lay a yellow shopping bag. She breathed in the odor of plastic trash-can liners and felt the chill emanating from the packages.

"Helen? Are you OK?" Marjan was looking at her with concern.

"Yeah, I am now." She struggled from the floor and sat upright. Was this a dream? She felt so strange, so light and shivery.

Marjan was hunkered down beside her. A necklace glittered around her neck. "I was just about to go and get help. You fainted."

Helen suddenly remembered what had happened and realized that she had hyperventilated. The pressure on her chest, the pain, the lack of oxygen, light-headedness—it all pointed to a panic attack. The last time she'd had one of those had been during her training, when she'd had to give a presentation in front of a packed auditorium.

"You still look pale."

"I'm feeling much better."

She braced herself against the wall and stood up. Marjan tried to help her, but she fended her off politely. "Thank you, it's OK."

Marjan's eyes went to the shopping bags. "What on earth are you lugging around in there?" She leaned forward and peered inside. "Garbage bags?"

"That's my stuff, not yours," Helen snapped. "Maybe you should stop sticking your nose into other people's business." She snatched the bags from where they stood by Marjan's feet and rushed down the corridor.

There was a clock hanging in the hallway. She had been unconscious for fifteen minutes at most, but even if she headed straight to her ward now, she would still be late. Only she wasn't going to the ward. There was another waste room on the next floor.

## 8

It was a remarkably warm day for October. The terraces of the cafés in town were all packed. Sara and Floris were walking hand in hand ahead of Ralf and Naomi. Two people who had no idea what it was like to be short of money. They stopped in front of the windows of shops that Ralf wouldn't dare set foot in and discussed Moncler and Stone Island jackets as if they already had one in every color hanging in their closets at home. Ralf had seen the prices: just one of those jackets cost as much as two months of minimum wage. And Floris kept bleating on about "genuine goose down" and how wonderfully light it felt. Sara told them she hated designer knockoffs. "*So* pathetic, you know?"

Naomi clung to Ralf's arm. She was remarkably quiet. Ralf didn't know what her parents did for a living—they had never spoken about it—but she lived with her brothers and her little sister in a small row house, just like his.

"My parents drive me totally crazy sometimes," said Sara.

"How come?" asked Floris.

"They had a fight this morning. I heard them in the kitchen."

"What about?"

"About tonight. My father will be working, but my mother thought they'd be going out together."

Ralf pricked up his ears. "Working?" he asked.

Sara turned around. Daylight glittered from her sunglasses. "I thought you knew that already—that we own some restaurants?"

"The Horn of Plenty," explained Floris.

Sara certainly knew how to present it: suddenly the restaurants belonged to the entire family. "Surely your father doesn't have to do the washing up himself on a Saturday night?"

She shrugged. "He just likes to be there on busy evenings. Have a chat with the guests, check that everybody is doing their jobs properly. And he likes to go to the bank with the day's takings himself. It's like I said yesterday—he's married to his work." Her eyes softened. "When we were little, we always used to go to a theme park or the beach on the weekend."

Floris nudged her. "Oh, come on. Like you'd still want to go to Disneyland with your parents."

Ralf felt his body grow tense. As casually as possible, he asked, "Does he work late on Saturdays?"

"Yeah, super late."

"Wow. Until like midnight? Two in the morning?" ventured Ralf.

"He normally gets home around one." She frowned at Ralf for a moment, as if she had just realized that his interest in her father's schedule was a little strange. But then she turned to Floris, who flipped open a pack of Marlboros and offered them around. Naomi declined, as did Ralf.

"Do they fight a lot, your parents?" asked Naomi.

"Not really." Sara put the cigarette between her lips and held it in the flame of Floris's lighter. "Mostly, they just don't talk to each other. My father sleeps in the guest room a lot."

"So does mine. Or he stays on the boat," said Floris.

Ralf dug his phone out of his coat pocket. He quickly tapped out a message.

Are you at home? I need something.

He held the device in his hand and pretended to be interested in the shop window. *Did you really just do that, Venema? Are you in your right mind?*

"Anyway," said Sara, "that means my mother might be at home tonight."

Naomi's eyes widened. "You can't be serious."

"There's not much I can do about it, is there?"

"It's still only the afternoon. We might be OK." Floris threw his head back and puffed out a succession of smoke rings. He was wearing Porsche sunglasses, Ralf noticed. Ralf had on a pair of his own, but they were Ray-Bans. And fake.

Ralf reflected that his own parents had probably never heard of Moncler, and they thought Porsche only made cars. But they slept in the same bed under their Ikea duvet, and they never argued. And he had seen them kissing far more often than he would have liked. Suddenly, it struck him: Was that it, then? Was that how it worked? *You can have a swimming pool and a Mercedes, but an awful marriage.*

Ralf's phone buzzed. He looked at the screen.

I am now, but leaving soon. Back Sunday.

Sara looked at her reflection in the window and freshened up her lipstick. "It's so annoying."

"We can't go to my house tonight either," said Naomi. She sought Ralf's eyes. "What about your place?"

He shook his head absently and tapped out a response:

I'm on my way. Wait for me. It's important.

"Should we go for a drink?" Sara put her lipstick back in her bag and pointed to a large café on the other side of the promenade.

"Sorry, guys, I can't," blurted Ralf. "I have to go."

Naomi looked at him in surprise. "Huh? Already? Aren't we supposed to be going shopping?"

He pulled an apologetic face and held up his phone. "Sorry, I'll explain tonight. I'll come and get you at a quarter to seven." He gave her a quick kiss and hurried away.

Only when he had almost reached his car did he realize that he had just ditched them all in town with no means of transport. He could only hope that Floris and Sara would be obliging enough to split a taxi with Naomi.

## 9

"Are you feeling any better after this morning?" Anouk was standing next to a sleeping patient and nimbly rolling up a length of IV tubing.

"Yeah. It was so weird, though. Never happened to me before."

"Maybe you should get some tests done? People don't just faint for no reason."

"I've been very stressed lately." She rubbed her wrist over her nose.

"Who hasn't been, right?" Anouk hesitated. "Will you be joining us for lunch?"

"Er, no, thank you. I have other plans." That wasn't true, but she didn't want to run into Marjan again today. She would rather lock herself in the restroom.

Helen took over a bed from one of her colleagues and began to check the patient's data.

The man had small light-blue eyes and gave her a searching look. "This is really scary for me. I've never been in a hospital before—not even as a visitor—and now I'm about to have an operation."

"Did the doctor explain what he was going to do?"

He nodded.

"Exploratory knee surgery is genuinely a very minor procedure. One or two quick snips and then you'll be back up and running."

"I doubt I'll be doing any running," he remarked.

She grinned. "In a manner of speaking, anyway. Let me just put in a drip for you."

As she worked, she felt her own anxiety gradually subside. It was over: the last packages had disappeared into two brand-new containers that she had found in the other waste room, one floor up from the old one.

Marjan could say what she liked now—it was her word against Helen's. *It's over. It's in the past.*

All gone.

"Goodness, don't you look happy today?"

"Oh really?"

"You look like you've been on a wonderful date." Saskia stopped for a moment, a clipboard in her hand. She was one of the younger surgical assistants.

"Maybe in my dreams. I haven't been on a real date in eighteen years."

"Too busy spending your evenings on the sofa next to Mr. Right? Doesn't sound very exciting."

"I have a very boring life," she joked.

Saskia walked on, chuckling to herself.

## 10

Ralf walked through the entrance to the apartment block, sprinted up the concrete staircase two steps at a time, and briefly pushed the bell. He looked around nervously, pulling up the collar of his jacket.

Jeffrey opened the door. "What's going on, dude? Why did you want me to wait for you?"

"I need something," said Ralf quietly. He scratched his neck.

Jeffrey stepped over the threshold and looked left and right to make sure that Ralf was alone. "Come in."

Ralf followed him into the living room. It was smoky and it stank. The coffee table was covered in empty beer cans and full ashtrays. The curtains were drawn, and a strip of sunlight illuminated the filthy floor. On Tuesday, the twins had been lying in a crib in the corner of the room; now, an old racing bike was leaning against the wall instead.

"Where's Denise?" he asked purely for form's sake.

"Gone. At her mother's place. Took the kids." Jeffrey plopped down on the leather sofa and started rolling a joint.

"Shit, man."

"She'll be back. What do you need?"

Ralf looked at the floor.

"I don't have any work for you, I already told you," said Jeffrey. "Sorry. There's a lot of—"

"It's not about work."

"What is it about, then?" He picked up his joint like a pen and held it up. "You don't smoke, right?"

Ralf shook his head. Glanced at his sneakers and rubbed the back of his hand over his nose. "I need a gun."

# 11

"How come you were so late this morning?" Lex was walking alongside Helen as she left the hospital.

"I fainted on the way to the ward."

"So I heard. Any idea why?"

"No."

"Of course you know; come on." He put a hand on her shoulder and pulled her to a stop.

"I had a panic attack. It's all getting a bit much for me, I think—everything all at once. The kids, chores, work."

His hands slid down to her arms. Lingered there for a moment. Then he let her go, as if he'd suddenly realized that his touch was too intimate. He kept looking at her. "Why don't you take some time off and rest?"

"I already am. Werner and I are leaving tomorrow for a few days in England."

"A few days," he scoffed. "That's not resting. Resting is doing absolutely nothing for as long as it takes you to get bored."

"Are you saying I should go on sick leave? There's nothing wrong with me."

"If you're fainting at work from stress, that means there's something wrong. You know that as well as I do."

She turned her face aside. "It'll pass."

"When?"

"At some point." It came out as a squeak.

"You look so sad all of a sudden."

"The kids are having a movie night, and Werner has to work." *Why did I say that?*

"And you're getting kicked out."

"So it seems."

Lex's expression shifted. He looked around pensively. Rubbed his forehead. "Helen, I've asked you before if you wanted to come out with me for dinner or a drink." He lifted his hand apologetically. "You didn't want to, and I understand why. You're married, I'm single, people talk . . . But I don't see any harm in it. Really."

She was silent for a moment, allowed his words to sink in. "Maybe you're right," she said softly.

His face brightened. "So you'll come out with me?"

"Just for dinner, OK?"

"Of course. What else did you think we were going to do?"

Despite everything, she had to smile.

# *12*

What was that all about, Ralf?

Such a joke.

Ralf scrolled somberly through the messages Naomi had sent him over the last hour. Floris and Sara hadn't split a taxi with her. After his sudden departure, they'd become totally absorbed with each other and had barely noticed that Naomi was still there. She'd gone home on the bus. Alone.

Ralf liked Sara less and less. But he was the one who had disappeared so abruptly.

Sorry. I mean it. I'll make it up to you.

Ralf laid his phone on the passenger seat next to him and looked through the window. His car was parked on a small shoulder. Diagonally opposite, close to the road and partly concealed behind tall trees and perfectly maintained boxwoods, stood a large, thatched farmhouse. "The Horn of Plenty" was written on the roof in illuminated lettering. This was the biggest of the four restaurants. Brian used to work here. At the front, the building bordered slightly on the road. To its left was a broad driveway, and immediately behind that was a large parking lot surrounded by shrubs and a tall hedge. The office was also at the back, as Ralf knew, with a separate entrance.

It was a gamble, but there was a good chance Werner Möhring would finish his rounds here. And then he would have the daily takings for all four restaurants with him.

Ralf's phone buzzed again.

I'm not that kind of girl.

He immediately tapped out a reply.

I know.

Ralf sat and stared at his phone. No response. His thumbs hovered over the screen as if paralyzed. She had read his message, but she wasn't answering.

He pursed his lips and typed:

I care about you.

He had never said that to a girl before, let alone admitted it in writing. But she wouldn't know that, of course.

Ralf started his car and drove off. As the restaurant shrank in his rearview mirror, Tupac's voice played from the speakers, singing about how all he needed was his girlfriend. Girlfriend was a metaphor, Ralf knew—the song was really an ode to a firearm. Ralf would much rather have a flesh-and-blood girlfriend than the beaten-up piece of crap currently sitting in his glove compartment. He could smell the faint odor of oil and metal. Once he had used it, he would dump it somewhere. Tonight would be the first and also the last time in his life that he would aim a gun at somebody.

# 13

Helen examined her reflection in the bathroom mirror. Foundation, mascara, lip gloss. That should be more than enough: she was just going out for something to eat with a good friend. A friend who saw her every day without a trace of makeup on and wearing a shapeless blue uniform with a stupid cap on her head, for that matter. So why did she feel the need to add a touch of eyeliner now?

She walked back into the bedroom. There were four outfits lying on the bed. She still hadn't made a decision. Jeans or a dress? High heels or suede ankle boots?

*Friends, Helen. You're going out for dinner as friends.*

In the end, she opted for a dress. Green, not too tight, with low heels on her feet. A few bracelets. She spun around in front of the mirror. Perfect. Feminine, but not too feminine.

"Mom, I'm heading out now." Thom stuck his head through the bedroom door.

She walked over to him and gave him a hug. He was getting tall—already taller than she was. She felt his firm shoulders, the emerging strength of his young body. A little while longer and Thom would be a man. It was suddenly all happening so fast. "Have fun tonight. We won't see each other again before I leave for England. Promise you'll do everything your grandma and grandpa say?"

He sighed deeply. "When are we gonna be allowed to stay home on our own? We can totally look after ourselves."

"You're not quite old enough for that yet."

"Mom, we won't do anything stupid."

She stroked his hair. "It's not about whether I trust you. I'm just worried that something might happen if we aren't here."

"Mooom." He rolled his eyes. "Of course nothing will happen."

"There could always—"

"Mom, listen." He looked at her, deadly serious. "You always get overprotective like this. Nothing has ever happened here, and nothing ever will."

"Thom—" She swallowed. "There was a break-in at the neighbors' place last week."

"Yeah, while they were out. And we have an alarm."

*That you always forget to switch on.* "Be patient. Just a few more years," she said.

Helen watched her son as he walked down the hall. Excited voices came from downstairs. Jackie and Floris were already here and had brought a stack of horror movies with them. The oven was on, and the smell of pizza filled the house.

The kids made everything sound so simple, so carefree. It had all been so simple to her too when she was that age. The whole world lay in front of you; everything was still possible.

And now?

Things only got more and more complicated.

She took a deep breath and hung the rejected outfits back in the closet. For the kids, life not only *seemed* easy—it *was* easy. Everything had carried on the same way for the children precisely because she and Werner had chosen to solve this problem together. Werner's decision meant they hadn't been exposed to the media, the courts, or the judgment of their classmates, teachers, neighbors, and strangers at the supermarket. And even more important, not to fathers, uncles, brothers, nephews, or short-tempered friends out for revenge.

She had to hand it to Werner—he'd been right after all.

# 14

On the big flat-screen TV, a girl walked through a dark forest. The camera switched to a lower angle and began to creep toward her. Music swelled, grew louder, sped up. The girl looked around fearfully.

"I can't watch," squeaked Naomi, grabbing hold of him.

She was no longer angry; Ralf had told her that he'd forgotten about an appointment for his course, and she'd believed him.

He felt her breath against his belly. Her long, smooth hair fell over his lap. He looked down. His breath caught, and he immediately turned his face away.

*Don't think about it.*

According to the clock on the mantel, it was ten thirty. Sara and Floris had gone upstairs at the start of the evening. Jackie and her boyfriend were just coming back down. And now it was his turn to make a move. ·

He leaned forward. Whispered, "Should we . . . ?"

She looked up at him, her eyes glittering, and the corners of her mouth curled upward.

He held her hand and led her up the stairs. With each step, he felt the tension ratchet up. Brian had been here eight days ago. Coked-up and still in one piece, he had followed Werner Möhring up this very staircase. Ralf looked around curiously, warily. They reached a large square hallway with a high ceiling. There was a chandelier hanging from it. To the right was a long, narrow corridor lined with doors on either side, and another at the end.

Naomi's slim hands found their way underneath his T-shirt. Her fingertips caressed his belly, explored his back. His body responded automatically, but his mind was elsewhere. He stared down the long hallway, illuminated here and there with wall lamps. The second door on the left was ajar.

"That's Sara's room," whispered Naomi.

"I want to look inside all of them," he heard himself say. His voice was strained. He continued to take in his surroundings. Searching for a clue.

"Huh? You can't do that!"

"It can't hurt to look, can it?"

She followed close behind as he opened door after door. Thom's room was sparsely decorated and had a video-game console. Emma's looked like a bomb had gone off: makeup, clothing, and schoolbooks everywhere. A guest room with a queen-size bed. A black-and-white bathroom, so big that the one at his parents' house would fit inside it four times over. It didn't have a washing machine—he found that in a separate room, behind a door with a sign saying "Laundry." Sara's parents slept at the very end of the hall, it seemed. He flicked the light switch on.

"Wow," whispered Naomi.

The room was spacious and impressive, with a high, white, beamed ceiling that tapered to a point—you could see the ridge of the roof. On the right was a large bed with a chic quilt. There was a patchwork rug on the floor, and on the left stood a few smaller items of furniture beneath an overhanging wall. He walked through the room, poking through the contents, unsure what he was searching for. Had Werner run up here, into this room? Had the shots been fired in here? A good deal of time had passed between the men running upstairs and the gunshots ringing out. They could have been anywhere in the house by then. The kitchen, the living room, the garage . . .

"Should we go to Sara's room?" Naomi insisted.

He pretended not to hear and pushed the closet open.

"What are you doing?"

Men's clothes. Suit jackets, shirts, arranged by color. He crouched down. Drawers full of socks and underwear. To the left of the dresser was a safe with a keypad. The panel was black and the size of a large shoebox. Ralf feverishly tapped in a few obvious codes—0000, the postal code, 1234—but nothing happened.

"Ralf? This is messed up, Ralf. We shouldn't be in here." She sounded panicky, but he barely noticed.

Was this where Werner kept his cash? And the gun that killed Brian? "Stop it!"

He grabbed the safe and tried to lift it. The metal block didn't budge. It was anchored to the floor.

"Are you trying to rob Sara's family or something? You're crazy!" Naomi tugged at his shoulder, then grabbed his arm with both hands and hauled him away from the safe.

He scrambled to his feet. "Calm down, OK? I'm not doing anything."

"You call that nothing? That's private, man. It's their stuff." She looked at him breathlessly, her cheeks flushed with exertion. "What are you looking for?"

"Nothing. I'm just curious."

# *15*

She was so used to her colleagues' baggy uniforms that it had initially felt strange to see Lex sitting opposite her in his normal clothes. He was wearing a pair of dark jeans and a blue cardigan that suited him perfectly. His short brown hair was graying slightly at the temples. In addition to his dark eyes and his surname, he had inherited his hair color from his grandfather—Carlito Melo, a Brazilian sailor who had started a family in the Netherlands, but who hadn't let that stop him from embarking on intimate relationships in other countries too. Lex's father had ended up with half brothers and half sisters all over the world.

Helen used her spoon to break the caramelized sugar on her crème brûlée. "Your childhood sounds very exotic."

"It was completely normal other than that. We mainly kept in touch via letters and photos." He put his dessertspoon down on his plate. "My own father was a good deal less adventurous than my granddad. He thought Belgium was far away. We only ever went on one trip, when we stayed with a half uncle in Italy."

"I always used to be jealous of children from big families."

"They were probably jealous of you, because you had your mother's full attention and you didn't have to share your bedroom. Or wear your sisters' hand-me-downs."

"I never thought of it like that before." Helen had to raise her voice to be heard. The Last Stand was one of the most popular bistros downtown. The food was tasty, and despite the crowds and the chaotic service, it always had a good atmosphere. There had been only one table left when they arrived—tucked away in a dimly lit corner close to the coatracks—but it didn't matter. Lex was great company. There were no awkward silences; one topic of conversation flowed seamlessly into the next. Helen enjoyed listening to him but realized that she perhaps liked looking at him even more. He gestured enthusiastically as he talked about his family, and his open expression made it difficult to suppress the desire to touch him. Her good sense warned her not to compare him with Werner, but she couldn't stop herself from doing so.

"I just don't understand how you can still be single after three years," she suddenly heard herself say.

Most men would have taken that as a compliment, but Lex responded seriously. "Andrea set the bar so high—I find most women aren't fun, interesting, or attractive enough." He looked at her so intensely, she felt bashful.

"Well, you won't meet any of those fun single ladies if you keep spending your Saturday nights with married women," she joked.

"You're the only married woman I spend time with, Helen."

She lowered her chin to her chest. "As friends, right?" She expected him to start laughing so they could dispel the awkwardness. But he didn't laugh.

He regarded her in silence.

When he finally opened his mouth to speak, Helen pushed her chair back and stood up. "I need to go to the restroom."

# *16*

Sara's bedroom looked like something straight out of an American teen movie. It was bigger than her brother's or sister's, with a deep-pile carpet and plenty of pink, white, and red. Her bed was soft and smelled good.

Naomi was lying half underneath Ralf, her clothes still on. She had unhooked her bra, but he hadn't gone near it yet. The moment he put his hands on her breasts, he would lose all track of time. It was difficult enough to keep his head in the game as it was.

"You're an odd one, Ralf," she whispered.

Ralf smiled dreamily. He stroked her hair. Smooth, thick strands slipped through his fingers.

Her hand, which had been resting on his bare stomach, now made its way downward; her fingers disappeared nimbly beneath the taut elastic of his boxer shorts.

He trembled; his breath caught. Swiftly, he grabbed her wrist.

"What's the matter?" she whispered against his lips. She threw her leg over him; her foot ran up his calf. "Don't you want to?"

"Of course I do." He was ready to explode.

"Then why are you stopping me?"

He extricated himself from her. "I care about you. I don't want to do it here—in Sara's room, like this." He looked around as if searching for something. "This just isn't right."

"Should we go to your car? We could leave early."

He closed his eyes briefly. *What do you think? Yes. Of course. Right now.* "No."

"Huh?"

"Not tonight," he whispered. "Not now."

"Why not?"

"Because—" Ralf looked at Naomi regretfully. "I can't stay."

"Hey, you guys! Naomi? Ralf? Do you want some chicken nuggets?" The shouting came from downstairs. Ralf heard Jackie giggling.

"I have to go soon," he murmured.

"Go? I don't understand you at all." She sat up, stiffly rehooked her bra, and dropped her T-shirt back down over it.

When Ralf realized she was about to stand up, he held her back.

"Hey, hello-o?" came from the kitchen. Floris was babbling as if he'd had too much to drink.

"Come and be social, Naomi!" called Sara, before letting out a shriek. "Stop pinching me!"

They looked at each other in the dim light. "Do you remember about that dealer?" asked Ralf.

"Of course I remember. I'm not an idiot."

"I'm meeting him tomorrow."

She looked alarmed. "Why?"

He ran his hand through his hair and rested it on his neck. "I need to make sure I have enough money for him. That's why I have to leave. I'm working on something."

"Why don't you go to the police?"

"You guys are no fun at all!" echoed from downstairs, accompanied by giggling.

She made him look at her. "Ralf, you're having to pay a debt you don't owe. It's bullshit."

Ralf was silent. Her indignation was as genuine as her anger before, in Sara's parents' room. He wondered how close she had been to Brian. Did she really understand whom she'd been dating?

Ralf stood up and helped Naomi to her feet.

"Seriously, why don't you go to the police?" she insisted.

"Because I haven't always played by the rules myself either," he murmured.

# 17

Lex walked beside Helen through the narrow downtown streets, his hands in the pockets of his leather jacket. The closer they came to the dimly lit parking structure, the less either of them spoke.

Inside the structure, he waited while she paid before escorting her up the steps. Halfway between the staircase and her car, he stopped. "OK. I guess I'll be on my way."

Helen turned to face him. "I had fun tonight," she said, but "fun" scarcely covered it. It was the best evening she'd had in years. She had felt loved, attractive, desired—feminine.

"So, you two are leaving for England early tomorrow?" He looked to one side and feigned nonchalance, but his eyes told a different story.

She nodded.

"Looking forward to it?"

*Less than I was yesterday.* "A lot."

"Good." He focused his eyes on a point at the other end of the parking lot. It was as if he still had something important he wanted to say or do, and was carefully considering how to go about it.

For a few seconds, they stood there in silence.

"Good," he repeated. "So I'll see you . . . ?"

"Wednesday at work."

"Until then." He leaned forward and quickly planted a kiss on her cheek, close to her ear. "Good night, Helen. Have fun over the next few days. Enjoy it."

She hurried back to her car and drove toward the exit. When she looked in the rearview mirror, she saw him still standing there in the middle of the parking lot. A tall figure, broad shoulders, his eyes following her car.

She suppressed the impulse to hit the brakes and turn around. As she steered the Fiat through the darkened streets, her vision grew blurred. She dabbed tears from the corners of her eyes with her ring finger. Pointless. They kept coming.

# 18

His balaclava was itchy, and the gun felt heavy in his hand. Once this shit was behind him, he was going to sign those forms and take that course his mother had talked about. Whatever it was.

He was done with all this, at any rate. Playing the criminal was fun when everything was going well, but as soon as things went wrong, there was no end to the misery.

Jeffrey's apartment was a wreck, just like Jeffrey's life. His girlfriend had left him and taken the kids, and all he could think about was blow. Brian had expected to hit the jackpot at Werner Möhring's house, and now Brian was dead. Even an absolute hero like Tupac lived to be only twenty-five.

Ralf didn't want to die.

And he didn't want to go to jail.

It was dark at this end of the parking lot. The fall leaves rustled around him. He looked across at the back of the restaurant. The lights in the dining area had been turned off an hour ago, but the kitchen was still brightly lit. Ralf heard the clink of glasses, the scrape of metal against metal. By the back door stood a few bikes and scooters, along with two small, older cars.

Strangely enough, Werner Möhring's Mercedes was parked all the way over at this end, a good distance away from the rest of the vehicles. Ralf had no idea why.

He peered at the building. On the left was a wired-glass door with an illuminated plastic sign next to it: "The Horn of Plenty Ltd.—Office." The lights behind the yellowish glass were still on. He was banking on Werner's being inside, counting his money—maybe even bundling it up into convenient packages. Ralf couldn't enter the building; there were cameras trained on every door. He had to wait until Werner came out to his car.

Ralf had come up with a rough plan, but a lot could go wrong. He needed to approach him from behind somehow; despite his balaclava, hoodie, and thick coat, he was a little worried that Werner would recognize him.

Behind the wired glass, the light went out. The door swung open, and a dark figure emerged. Immediately followed by another, like a thinner shadow.

Ralf's grip tightened over the gun. He forgot to breathe—every fiber in his body was at maximum tension. He heard the quiet jingle of a key ring, footsteps, then nothing more.

The figures didn't speak but moved quickly toward him. Nervously, almost. The smaller one kept its head down as it trotted after the other. There was something strangely surreptitious about the scene. As they came closer, he saw that the smaller figure was wearing heels. A pencil skirt. Shapely legs underneath it. Once out of range of the security cameras, the man threw his arm around the woman and drew her toward him. They were close now, lit by a small lantern. The man was Werner Möhring. He unlocked his car remotely and the lights flashed, illuminating the couple in front of the vehicle.

Ralf's jaw fell open. The woman walking beside Werner, cooing under his kisses, was Brian's mother.

# Sunday

# 1

A black Anthropologie dress with tights and matching jewelry. Walking boots, a knitted sweater, and sports socks. Makeup bag, phone charger. A scarf. Helen went through the contents of her suitcase and ticked the items off her list. Then checked that the lids of her shampoo and conditioner were properly fastened before packing them in separate bags for safety's sake. Hotel toiletries were all very well, but if she didn't use her own shampoo, she would look like she'd been electrocuted or was wearing a party wig. In a drawer, she found a lace lingerie set that still had the price tag on it, snipped off the label, then laid the underwear in her case. On top of it, she laid an extra cardigan and a woolly hat. She probably wouldn't need them, but it was fall and the English coast could get very windy.

Werner walked into the bedroom. He was already wearing his coat. "Hey, we're only going for two nights!"

She smiled apologetically. "I know."

"What do you think—should we get going?"

"Good idea." She zipped up her case.

Werner picked it up and walked back down the hall. She watched him from where she was kneeling, her hands on her thighs. Last night, she had crept into the house and headed straight to the bedroom. Sara and her friends had still been in the living room, laughing and chattering. Once in bed, she had sent her daughter a message saying she was back and that she didn't want to disturb them. Luckily, she had fallen asleep before Werner got home. He hadn't seen her tear-stained eyes, was oblivious to all her emotions.

What she had done last night was wrong. And unbelievably stupid. It had been a date, plain and simple, and it could so easily have gotten out of hand. Lex's mother had been right in her assertion that there was no such thing as a platonic friendship between a man and a woman because one of the two always wanted more. In this case, it was even worse: both of them wanted more. That made everything a thousand times more complicated. She resolved to keep Lex at arm's length from now on.

Helen entered Sara's room. Jackie and Naomi were sprawled on the air mattress, fast asleep. She tiptoed around them and squatted down next to Sara. "Honey, your father and I are leaving now."

Sara rolled over drowsily. "What about Grandma and Grandpa?"

"They're coming this afternoon. Sophie's father will bring Emma home soon, and Thom will be back as soon as he wakes up."

Sara held out her arms toward her. "I'll miss you."

Helen gave her daughter a hug. "I'll miss you too," she whispered. "But we'll be back on Tuesday night."


When Werner saw her coming downstairs, he turned off the TV and grabbed his scarf from the kitchen island. "Let's go!" he exclaimed playfully in his best English.

She put on her coat and stepped out into the cold, dark morning. Werner locked the back door.

The sun hadn't risen yet, and not much could be seen in the garden other than the black silhouettes of the bushes and conifers and the sinister glow of the swimming pool. Leaves rustled quietly. "Aren't you worried, Werner?"

He stopped. "What about?"

"I feel so terrible leaving the girls alone in the house. You never know if—"

He cut her off. "It's over."

"But it could happen again, couldn't it? You'd already been worried for a long time, and with good reason. That's why you bought a gun. Where did you get that from, anyway?"

"I work in the restaurant business, honey. You get all kinds of customers coming through the door. Including people who can help you out with that sort of thing."

She stared past him into the garden. "Maybe it was naive of me, but I never thought something like that could happen to us. I mean, we never keep cash in the house." She looked at him. "Do we?"

He shook his head. "No, of course not. Not much, anyway."

## 2

Ralf tossed and turned in bed. He was trying to unpack exactly what he had seen last night—and what it might mean. Sara's father was sleeping with Brian's mother. That explained why he had seen him at her house last week. Was she aware that her lover had shot and killed her son? He didn't think so—they seemed to be enjoying each other's company.

He rolled over and stared at the wall. Could it be Emily, not Sara, who had encouraged Brian to rob Werner? She worked in the office at the Horn of Plenty, so she would know how much money Werner took home with him, and when. Or had Brian's mother inadvertently let it slip that Werner kept money at home, and had Brian then used Sara to find out the best time to strike? That sounded plausible. If Brian had gone about it the right way—and he was perfectly capable of that—then neither Sara nor Emily would have suspected a thing.

Ralf stretched and rubbed his face. Really, he shouldn't be concerning himself with other people's problems. He had more than enough of his own.

Mikey would be expecting his money in exactly five hours' time. Of the sum that Ralf had set aside for the down payment, there were now only three hundred euros left after his purchase of the gun. There was no way he would be able to get hold of the remaining cash today without going to extreme lengths.

But what if he could borrow it from somebody? Ralf grabbed his phone and sat up in bed. It was Sunday, and early in the morning. With a bit of luck, his friends might still be awake.

# 3

"Not even four hours from home, and a whole other world." Helen gripped the railing and drew a deep breath of sea air. Seagulls circled around the boat. The metal deck hummed with the pistons of the engines; she could feel the vibrations under her feet. Slowly, the dock disappeared from view; diesel fumes rose into the sky.

Werner stood beside her and looked out pensively over the Strait of Dover. The sea was gray green, with white foam capping the waves. "We could have taken the tunnel instead, and it would have been much quicker, but I think this is more fun. More of a view."

"Good choice. Though the other passengers aren't quite what I expected."

He looked around. The early sailing from Calais to Dover seemed to be particularly popular with stocky men in leather jackets. Gruff-faced, smoking, most of them alone. The hold was full of vans and trucks with Eastern European license plates. "You're right, I don't remember it being like this last time either."

"Well, that was twenty years ago now. Isn't it strange that we haven't been back in all that time? It's so close."

He shrugged. "Bad weather, no euro. All the fuss and expense of crossing the channel. Driving on the left."

"Fuss? The kids would love this. They've never been on a boat before."

"They've already been enough places with us—we need to leave them a few things to look forward to."

"True." She pulled her coat tighter. From the corner of her eye, she could see the men staring at her. "I think I might be the only woman on board."

"Lucky me." Werner moved behind her and threw his arms around her.

Helen expected him to let go at any moment. Her intimate moments with Werner had all been so brief over the last few months—or was it years? They lasted exactly as long as he thought necessary to placate her.

But he didn't let go. Their fingers locked together, and she felt his cheek lightly brush against hers.

"Wonderful," he sighed. "Nothing to do. No kids, no work."

Helen looked out dreamily at a container ship in the distance. The fall sun sparkled over the waves. "Are you finally going to tell me what we'll be doing?"

"You'll find out soon enough."

She turned her head slightly to look at him. "Not the same bed-and-breakfast as last time?"

He grinned. "No way. Remember that dining room? The three different kinds of carpet joined together with duct tape?"

"And the breakfast with the homemade black pudding? That woman watching from the doorway with her arms folded and asking us what we thought of it the whole time?"

"Yeah," said Werner. "And she kept shooing that dog out of the dining room, even though we kept telling her, 'No, don't worry, he isn't bothering us!'"

She burst into laughter, and Werner joined in. A warm glow flooded her body. It was glorious—the salty sea air and the wind, and Werner so close to her.

Suddenly, out of nowhere, she was seized by the feeling that she was doing something wrong—a deep sense of shame.

"Is something the matter?" asked Werner. "You got so stiff."

"I was thinking about that boy. We're here on vacation, and he—"

He turned her around and embraced her, holding her head against his chest. "No more of that now," he whispered. "It's over. OK?"

She nodded, but it didn't feel over.

# 4

He had managed to drum up two hundred five euros—not even 10 percent of what he needed. The fruits of an entire morning of phone calls and text messages. Some friends he had. *Laugh with many, but don't trust any.* A few of them hadn't bothered to reply, and the rest were either unable or unwilling to help. Rick was the only one who had been honest with him, telling him to his face, "I don't lend money to friends—all you get is grief." Ralf had hung up angrily.

After that, he had shaved, gotten dressed, and eaten breakfast, and he now found himself pacing back and forth in the kitchen. His parents were still in bed. He heard the muffled sound of their TV, and from time to time, his father's voice carried through the wall.

Ralf looked at the clock on the microwave. Quarter past eleven. In forty-five minutes, he would have to report to Mikey. He caught his reflection in the shiny door of the appliance. His jaw muscles were taut, and his eyes seemed deeper in their sockets than usual. He had hardly slept. Time after time, his thoughts had led back to the same place: strangely enough, it wasn't Mikey who scared him most. Ralf was more afraid of himself. Of what he might be capable of if things got out of hand. Jeffrey's gun was in the drawer of his bedside table, stuffed behind a stack of car magazines. It was fully loaded. He didn't have to take any more crap from Mikey.

His phone started to buzz. He pulled it out of his pocket and looked at the screen. A message from Naomi. She'd slept at Sara's last night. Looked like a photo was coming through. Maybe a cute selfie, or a picture of the girls having breakfast? Curious, he tapped at the screen to load it. A few moments passed before he fully understood what he was looking at. He felt the blood drain from his face.

# 5

They were driving through a lovely village filled with old houses. The streets were narrow, the sidewalks even narrower, and a lot of the shop fronts had small-paned bay windows and hand-painted signs. The whole place was like something from a fairy tale.

"It looks like a film set for *Midsomer Murders*," said Helen. There was so much to take in.

Werner had pulled off the freeway barely an hour ago, and since then, the view had changed constantly. At first, the landscape had been flat, then increasingly hilly. Helen had seen white outcrops of chalk, as well as thick woodland and rolling fields dotted with sheep.

"This bit is more like *Top Gear*," joked Werner as he drove out of the village. He stepped on the gas and took obvious pleasure in the curves and undulations of the road.

Helen tried to catch a glimpse of the landscape behind the tall, untidy hedges that grew almost directly alongside the asphalt. According to the GPS, they had only another two miles to go before they reached their destination. "Can you tell me where we're going yet?"

Werner glanced at her. "I'll give you a clue: it came highly recommended by Serge."

Serge was someone Werner knew well—a top chef whom the kitchen staff at the Horn of Plenty would visit each year for inspiration.

They drove past a large brown-varnished sign that alerted passing motorists to a five-star hotel farther down the road. Their view of the landscape was still blocked by the tall hedges, but through occasional gaps in the vegetation, Helen saw flashes of hills, meadows bordered by hedgerows, and here and there, an enormous tree.

She caught a glimpse of a building standing high up on a hill. It was half castle, half manor house, and it looked historic. "That can't be it. Can it?"

Werner said nothing. He took his foot off the gas and turned onto a driveway, which meandered through a carefully maintained patch of woodland. On either side grew the biggest rhododendrons Helen had ever seen. At a bend in the road stood a small stone wall bearing an elegant sign, "South Down Hotel." There were five stars printed below it, as well as the name of a restaurant and the logo of the Michelin Guide.

"Are you serious? Here?" Helen felt like a child on an unexpected outing to a theme park. She and Werner had always kept their vacations simple. Camping in France—"cramping," Sara called it—or cute little guesthouses on the Adriatic coast. They hardly ever stayed in fancy hotels.

The driveway crossed a neatly mowed lawn and curved around in front of the portico of the impressive building. A uniformed older man stepped out through the entrance.

Werner pulled up and turned off the engine. A second man, also in uniform, hurried over. The two employees greeted them politely, and one of them took the car keys from Werner while the other placed their suitcases on a trolley and escorted them inside.

The entrance hall was magnificent. On the floor lay gleaming marble in a complex pattern. The white walls were lined with wood paneling, and chandeliers hung from the high ceiling. Richly upholstered sofas, enormous Persian carpets. Grandfather clocks with gold detailing.

"Werner, pinch me."

He put his arm around her waist. "Good choice?"

"Wonderful," she replied, almost breathlessly.

# 6

It was a selfie, taken from slightly overhead. Naomi looked frightened. The man next to her was holding the camera; he had bent his knees slightly to be at the same height as Naomi, and his cheek was pressed against hers. It looked like they knew each other intimately. The man's crossed eyes were fixed directly on the camera, and his stubby teeth were bared in a mocking grin.

Ralf forgot to breathe.

Mikey.

Naomi was with Mikey.

Below the photo, it said:

*See you soon. Looking forward to it!*

Ralf could feel a vein throbbing in his temple. A monotonous buzz filled his ears. The photo didn't show much of their surroundings—all he could see was a gray carpet, a radiator, and the bottom of a curtain. Dusky pink. He recognized that curtain.

They were in Brian's room.

Ralf stuffed his phone into his pocket and sprinted up the stairs—two, three steps at a time. In his bedroom, he hauled the stack of magazines out of his nightstand, grabbed the gun, and tucked it under his waistband. He pulled his jacket on over it and zipped it up.

On the landing, he ran into his father, who had just emerged from his bedroom and was yawning as he tied the belt of his bathrobe. "You're up early. That's not like you."

"I have to go out," muttered Ralf, ducking past his father and heading for the staircase.

"Ralf?"

Their eyes met, long enough for him to see the open, contented expression on his father's face give way to concern.

"Is everything OK, Son?"

Ralf opened his mouth to answer, then closed it again. He turned his back on his father, hurried down the stairs, and sprinted down the street. Flustered, he put the key in the ignition. By the time he hit the road, all his doubts had vanished, and his fear had been replaced by a sharp and clear image of what he had to do.

# 7

Mr. Hawtrey wore a neat suit and a waistcoat. He had a big, friendly face, and short legs that propped up a significantly oversized torso. Maybe that explained why he walked in such a strange way—waddling slightly, like a character from a fantasy movie. Helen guessed he was around seventy.

"Here we serve our breakfast," announced Mr. Hawtrey proudly. He took a step back so that Werner and Helen could peer inside.

There were roughly twenty round tables decked with white linen and surrounded by upholstered chairs. Eggplant-colored carpet, wood paneling running up to the ceiling.

"How beautiful," answered Helen in her best English.

Mr. Hawtrey took obvious pleasure in her remark. He was the fourth generation of his family to work at the hotel, and he went on to tell them about the manor house's walled gardens, where the chefs grew fruit and vegetables for use in the hotel kitchens. "You'll look back very fondly on our jam."

The tour continued. Mr. Hawtrey led them into a long corridor with a Persian carpet running the full length of the parquet floor. Everywhere you looked, there were oil paintings and side tables laden with sculptures, bouquets of dried flowers, and ornamental dishes. They wandered up and down staircases, passed through hallways lined with antique clocks and yet more art. In one softly lit room, they encountered a handful of respectably dressed guests drinking tea. Helen saw tiered cake stands covered with petits fours, and somebody was playing a grand piano. A large staircase led to the oldest part of the building.

"This wing dates back to the fifteenth century," said Mr. Hawtrey.

The floor of the corridor was creaky and slightly crooked.

"Your room." Mr. Hawtrey opened the door and ushered Helen and Werner inside.

Their suitcases were already there, standing at the foot of the enormous four-poster bed. Mr. Hawtrey pointed out the TV, "the coffee- and tea-making facilities," the iPad and docking station on top of the walnut desk—all of which clashed somewhat with the antique furniture. The adjoining bathroom was set a few steps down from the bedroom; resembling a chapel, it was laid out in gleaming travertine with brass faucets. The bath was built into a niche and had a small Gothic-style window above it. According to Mr. Hawtrey, the stone windowsill was nearly six centuries old, though the lead-lined stained glass had been installed at a later date. After concluding his explanation, he vanished noiselessly.

"This place is like a fairy tale," said Helen. "That man!"

"Straight out of *Alice in Wonderland*."

A picture frame standing on the marble mantelpiece drew Helen's attention. She picked it up. Behind the glass lay a sheet of paper with text printed on it. She read:

*Our hotel is set in ninety-three acres of garden and parkland, which were created by Frederick DuCane Godman, an eminent nineteenth-century botanist. Please feel welcome, when taking a stroll around the gardens, to pick flowers for your room and place them in the vase provided.*

"Amazing! You need to hear this." She read it out loud to Werner.

"What a great idea." Werner's eyes twinkled. "Get your guests to pick their own flowers and tell them it's a privilege. Genius."

Grinning, she walked over to the window. The view was just as breathtaking as the hotel itself. Rolling fields ringed by woodland. In the distance, she could see ridges ranging in color from diffuse violet to blue gray. She heard somebody laughing nearby.

"Wow, Werner, look at this!"

Directly below the window, on one of the exterior staircases, stood around fifteen women and girls in cocktail dresses, drinking champagne. Beyond them, on the lawn, a group of men were playing cricket—in dinner jackets.

"A wedding party." Werner came and stood next to her, his hands in his pockets. "I was warned about them when I made the reservation, but they assured me the inconvenience would be minimal."

"Inconvenience? But this is wonderful!" Helen folded her arms and took in the scene. "It's just like a movie. Some kind of aristocratic wedding, I suppose."

"A family with money, at any rate. They've booked dinner for one hundred people in the hotel restaurant tonight. But that doesn't affect our plans, as I've arranged something different for us."

"Let me guess: another recommendation from Serge?"

"Bingo."

She threw her arms around him and planted a kiss on his lips. "It's so sweet of you. I mean it—you've exceeded all my expectations. I feel like a twenty-year-old again."

## 8

Ralf's whole body was shaking. His hoodie was plastered to his back, but he didn't notice. After leaving his car in the parking lot, he had sprinted into the building, his pace gradually slackening until he found himself standing before Brian's door. Panting for breath, vibrating with anxiety. He ran his hand over his jacket and felt the gun underneath his waistband. The door was slightly ajar, and the room behind it ominously quiet. Ralf felt light-headed—for a moment, it felt like he was hovering just above the ground. He swallowed and nudged the door with his foot, causing it to slowly swing open.

"Brian's little helper." Mikey grabbed his arm and pulled him inside forcefully.

Ralf was pitched into the room but remained standing. He saw Naomi cowering on the bed. She was deathly pale, and her mascara had run.

"Are you OK?" His heart thumped behind his ribs.

She nodded. Looked anxiously at Mikey as he closed the door behind him.

"What did he do to you?"

"Nothing," she said. It came out as a sob.

"Goddamnit—you call that nothing?" He spun around to face Mikey. "You'd better—"

Mikey lunged at him, but Ralf was on his guard this time. Ducking to one side, he rammed his fist upward and caught him directly on the jaw. Mikey's face twisted in pain, but he recovered almost instantly and narrowed his reptilian eyes into slits. "Dumb move, Ralf."

Ralf was beside himself with fear and rage. "You keep your filthy hands off her!"

"I don't take orders from you." Mikey slowly rubbed his jaw. His eyes ran inquiringly over Ralf's clothing. "Where's the money?"

Naomi made herself even smaller behind Mikey, lifting her knees up to her chest.

Ralf wondered how she had gotten here. Had Mikey dragged her off her bike? Run her off the road?

*What the fuck has he done to her?*

"I'm asking you a question."

"I heard you." Ralf's voice sounded pinched—like it belonged to somebody else. He could feel the gun behind his waistband; the clammy skin underneath it; the smooth, dense metal. "I don't have any on me."

Mikey's expression shifted. He raised his eyebrows, then narrowed his eyes once more.

"You want Brian. Not me," continued Ralf. His eyes flickered back and forth between Mikey's eyes and his hands, alert to the slightest movement. "And you'd better leave Naomi alone. She has nothing to do with this."

Mikey slowly began to move. He made a half circle around Ralf, like a predator encountering a rival on the edge of its territory, staring at him all the while. A butterfly knife appeared in his hand, the metal clinking between his fingers. "Think you're tough, do you?"

Naomi shrieked.

Ralf took a step backward and simultaneously pulled the gun out from under his jacket. Aimed it at Mikey. His hands were trembling uncontrollably; the grip was slippery with sweat. The room went blurry. Ralf could only see Mikey, his crooked eyes. The knife.

*There's no going back.*

# 9

"Would you like one?" asked Helen. She held up a packet of instant cocoa she had found in the box next to the kettle.

Werner was standing by the window, looking at the brilliant-blue sky. "We should drive over to Brighton for a drink and then go for a stroll along the beach. What do you think?"

She put the packet right back down. Brighton had made a big impression during their first visit. It had an enormous palace festooned with white minarets and cupolas—the Royal Pavilion—and the city center was overflowing with cafés and small theaters. Not to mention the shingle beach and the esplanade full of fairground rides and slot machines. "Will the pier still be there?" she wondered out loud.

"It must be."

Helen grabbed her coat and hung it over her arm. "OK, let's go," she said, smiling.

Werner didn't move.

At the door, she looked over her shoulder. "You did mean now, didn't you?"

"Sure." He looked pensive for a moment before adding, "Don't you want to take any photos for back home first? So they know where we are?"

"Oh yeah, of course."

She was a little shocked at herself. All these new impressions had absorbed her attention so thoroughly that she hadn't thought about the children at all. Hastily, she pulled her phone out of her purse, but there were no missed calls or messages. She began taking pictures of the view and the wedding party, as well as the four-poster bed and the bathroom, then sat down and sent the images to Sara, Thom, and Emma, adding:

> We're at the South Down Hotel and it's fabulous here, just like a museum! Your father and I are about to head off to Brighton. Is everything OK at home? Are Grandma and Grandpa already there? Lots of love (and hello to Jackie and Naomi), Mom

She remained on the bed, staring expectantly at her phone. The texts had been received, and Sara was already typing an answer.

"What are you waiting for?" asked Werner.

"I just want to make sure everything is OK at home."

"Why wouldn't it be?"

She looked up. "Have you forgotten already?"

"Jesus, Helen, are you still worrying about that?"

She frowned. Was he serious? "What do you mean, 'still'? It only happened nine days ago."

Her phone began to buzz. Sara sent a selfie with Jackie and Emma in the kitchen. Below it, she had written:

> OMG! Have fun over there! I'm so jealous!

Emma's message was longer and more informative:

> Are you really going to sleep there, Mom? It looks like a haunted house. We made pancakes. They turned out really good! Naomi already went home. X E

Thom's reply came immediately after:

Nice, Mom. Grandma and Grandpa are on their way (they just called).

"They made pancakes." Helen smiled up at Werner. "And Emma thinks this place looks like a haunted house."

"Wonderful. Shall we?" He was standing by the door, holding his coat demonstratively in his hand. Despite the smile on his face, he had a cool, nonchalant look in his eyes.

Why was he acting like this? she wondered. Or was he completely unaware that he was putting distance between them?

She stood up and followed him out of the bedroom. Said nothing. She didn't want a fight, least of all now.

# 10

"Stop!" Naomi leapt up from the bed.

"Get out of here!" bellowed Ralf. "Run!"

Naomi looked from Ralf to Mikey, her eyes wide. "You're crazy, both of you!" She sprinted toward the door.

Mikey was quicker. He grabbed her hair and pulled her back against himself. With a fluid movement, he placed the knife on her throat.

"Let her go," said Ralf. "I don't want to shoot."

Mikey held Naomi in front of himself like a shield. His eyes glittered. "Come on, Ralf. This is too much for you. Put that thing on the floor and kick it over to me."

Naomi stood stock-still, her eyes squeezed shut. Ralf didn't dare pull the trigger. The risk of hitting Naomi was too great. He had never fired a real pistol before, and besides, he was shaking uncontrollably.

But he knew one thing for certain: whatever happened, he wasn't going to hand his gun over to Mikey. No fucking way. The moment he did that, he would lose all control of the situation. Then they would both be at Mikey's mercy.

"I don't have all day, buddy." Mikey tightened his grip on Naomi's hair. She was panting through clenched jaws, her eyes squeezed shut.

Ralf locked eyes with Mikey, concentrating as hard as he could. He could see or hear nothing else.

"I won't ask you again."

Was he imagining it, or did Mikey's voice sound more uncertain? His demeanor seemed to be shifting too; he was moving away from Ralf, very slowly, as if he wanted to back out of the situation altogether. Ralf's hand gradually ceased its trembling.

"You're asking for it," growled Mikey. The razor-sharp tip of the knife pressed against the soft, thin skin of Naomi's throat. Pushed down harder. Her eyes shot open.

"Don't!" exclaimed Ralf. "I swear it, I'll—" He stretched out his arm, stared tensely down the barrel of the gun. His finger on the trigger.

Mikey pulled Naomi closer and shrank, hiding behind her body. Then he swore and took the knife from her throat, pointing it toward Ralf and pouring a torrent of abuse at him. At that exact moment, Naomi sprang into action, bringing her heel down forcefully on Mikey's foot and swinging her arm downward. Her fist landed squarely on Mikey's crotch. He emitted a muffled squeal and struggled to stay upright as Naomi fought her way free.

Ralf leapt forward, grabbed Mikey's wrist, and lashed out with the pistol. The heavy metal collided with Mikey's temple. He struck him again, and again, as hard as he could, holding Mikey's wrist in an iron grip. The knife fell to the carpet with a faint jingling sound as Mikey tottered over, pulling Ralf with him.

Ralf heard a loud bang, followed by the sound of breaking glass. A dull pain ran up the side of his body. The panels of the coffee table had been forced apart under their combined weight, and the black glass tabletop had shattered into countless shards. Amid the fragments of glass and particleboard lay flat white packages, wrapped in transparent plastic.

Mikey saw them first and emitted a shriek.

Ralf instantly understood. "There's your fucking three thousand euros," he panted. He crawled away through the shards of glass toward his gun, which had been knocked from his hand and was lying by the wall, underneath the radiator.

Naomi got there first. Holding the butterfly knife between her thumb and her index finger, like it was something dirty, she pushed the window open and threw it outside. Then she snatched up the gun.

"Give it to me," Ralf said.

She shook her head, gripping the pistol clumsily with both hands. "Don't point it at me—are you crazy? It's loaded!"

She glared at him. "I thought you were nice, Ralf Venema, but you're just as big a sicko as the rest of them."

Mikey was frantically gathering up the packages of cocaine behind Ralf. Occasionally, he glanced at Ralf and Naomi, but he didn't seem particularly concerned by their presence, or by the gun. He was counting under his breath, stopping now and then to wipe the blood from his face, and stuffing the packages into his pockets.

## 11

"It's so wonderful here!" Helen wanted to spread her arms wide and run in circles. It had been a long time since she had felt so light, so free.

She had taken off her shoes and was running with Werner across the expansive beach. The fine shingle crunched under their feet. The wind was up, but it was warm for the time of year, and the fall sun flooded the entire coastline with a yellow glow. Helen held her arm up to her forehead and looked at the colorful amusements lining the esplanade—the Ferris wheel, the fairground rides, the ice-cream and candy stalls—and the stately Victorian buildings that formed a gleaming white backdrop. For a moment, it felt like they had landed not just in a different country but in a different dimension.

Werner came and stood next to her. "Come on; let's take a photo." He pulled his phone out of his inside pocket and put his arm around her.

She looked at him with pleasant surprise. Werner wasn't a fan of photos. He viewed the selfie trend as an affliction—a sign that half the world was suffering from a form of viral narcissism.

"Say 'cheese'!" he shouted.

The wind swept back Werner's hair, exposing a slight widow's peak. Helen's was hidden under a scarf.

They smiled at the camera.

"Well?"

Helen cupped her hand over the screen. The device had captured two ecstatically happy people; she and Werner both looked years younger. Even the sky looked bluer in the photo. "It almost looks real," she joked.

He frowned. "What do you mean? It is real."

"Oh, lighten up. I was kidding!"

He held the phone in his hand as if weighing it. Then his thumb raced back and forth over the keypad. He sent the photo to his mother.

Helen saw him type:

Brighton is glorious. We're having the time of our lives. It's very windy, though ☺ Is everything OK at home? Werner

He put his phone away. "Shall we head downtown? See if it's changed much?"

They walked back. The wind tugged at their clothes, and Werner had his arm over her shoulders.

She didn't know if it was the weather, the fairy-tale surroundings, or Werner's cheerful mood, but she hadn't felt such an intense connection with him in a very long time. Who knew? Maybe this would work out; maybe they really would find each other again.

## *12*

Ralf felt himself slowly growing calmer. Occasional shudders continued to run through his limbs. His throat was raw, and there was a dull pain in his side from when he had fallen onto the table, but his head felt clear and calm. It was over; he no longer had to worry about money or about Naomi.

Mikey had his coke.

And Naomi was sitting next to him in the car, her fingers knitted together on her lap.

"What did you do to him back there?" asked Ralf.

"I punched him in the balls."

"You're a real—" He raised his hand and shook his head.

"It was a reflex. I have two older brothers, remember."

He gnawed on the inside of his cheek. "Yeah, I know. It was still pretty dumb, though."

She was putting on a brave face, Ralf could see. But it was all fake. Behind the bluffing was a good deal of fear and uncertainty. He could see it in her eyes, in the faint movements she was making, in the minuscule twitch by her mouth. She had been scared to death, and it would take her a good while to get over it.

And it was all his fault.

"Well." She sighed and placed her fingers on the door handle. "I should go."

"Naomi—"

She turned her magnificent eyes on him. They were the most beautiful he had ever seen, but now they were red and puffy from crying.

He licked his thumb and wiped a trail of mascara from under her eye. "What will you tell your parents?"

"Nothing."

He raised his eyebrows. "Nothing?"

"I'll tell them I had a fight with Sara or something. They'd never let me leave the house again if they knew what happened. Seriously. They're superprotective. And my brothers are even worse."

"They've got a point."

She looked at him thoughtfully and slowly shook her head. "It's insane. What you did back there . . . Seriously, man, a *gun* . . . That was totally—"

"Shh." He held her face, moved his own closer to hers. "I'm sorry," he said softly. "I mean it, Naomi. I'm so ashamed of myself. Go home, OK? Go back to your parents and your brothers and your little sister. Keep your distance from me. Keep away from boys like me and Brian. You deserve better."

She bit her lower lip. He saw tears well up in her eyes again. "I don't know what I should do."

"Just do what I say," he said sternly. Then he kissed her gently on the mouth. Her lips parted in response, but he pulled his head back and gave her a friendly peck on the top of her head. "I mean it. And I'll be watching. If I ever see you around town with a son of a bitch like me, I swear I'll kick his kneecaps in."

"So romantic," she said cynically.

"Go on, get going."

Hesitantly, she opened the door and got out. He watched her go. She turned around at the corner, and her hair wafted behind her, speckled with gold.

He stepped on the gas and drove off without looking back.

At the intersection, he turned right. Back toward Brian's building. He had seen something in his room that didn't quite seem right. The packages of coke weren't the only things that had emerged from the base of the coffee table. Ralf had also seen an envelope with sheets of handwritten paper sticking out of it. If he wasn't mistaken, there had been photos too. Initially, he'd paid little attention. But the more he thought about it, the more mysterious it seemed. Why would Brian hide an envelope full of notes and photos in his room? An envelope bearing the logo of the Horn of Plenty?

# 13

Brighton had changed. Helen was almost certain the Ferris wheel hadn't been there last time. The esplanade seemed busier, noisier; but up here in the city center, there were still the same narrow, bustling streets packed with small theaters, galleries, and cafés.

Werner and Helen had ensconced themselves on a glassed-in terrace. They were surrounded by tourists speaking all manner of languages—everything but English. Helen heard a young couple speaking German, and behind them sat a group of girls who probably came from Sweden. A street musician was singing on the promenade and accompanying himself on a guitar.

Helen lifted her face toward the sun and closed her eyes. It was unseasonably warm—and yet she struggled to enjoy it as much as she should. Her smile gradually faded from her face. A treacherous voice kept whispering in the back of her mind, ever louder and more insistently, until she was unable to ignore it any longer.

"What's up?"

"I don't know. I can't stop thinking about that boy. Do you know what his name was? He used to work for you, didn't he?"

Werner took a swig of his beer. He said nothing, merely fixed her with a reproachful look.

"I don't have any right to ask, of course. I know that. But—"

"I'll say it one more time: you need to let this go."

Helen took a sip of her wine. And then another. It smelled of rotten grapes, and the taste wasn't much better, but the alcohol rising out of the glass was welcome.

"It didn't happen," he said, as if talking to himself. A mantra. "It simply didn't happen."

"I can't think like that."

"It's not a question of trying. You have to just do it. Flip the switch."

"I know that's how it works with you, but is it really so strange that I want to talk about it? Who else am I supposed to discuss it with?"

He looked at her in silence, almost pained. Sometimes she didn't understand him at all.

She leaned toward him and put her hand on his wrist. "What we've done, Werner—we can't share it with anybody else. Never. You're my partner. Don't shut me out."

# 14

Brian's room still looked the same as an hour ago. Fragments of glass lay all over the floor. They sparkled against the synthetic carpet and crunched under Ralf's sneakers. The white envelope lay half-concealed under a black panel, with sheets of paper protruding from it that were covered in blue handwriting. Photos too. Something that looked like a map. Ralf sat down on Brian's bed and shook the contents out of the envelope. The map was a printout from the internet. It took a moment for him to realize that it was the district where Sara lived. Close to the edge of the neighborhood, next to one of the main roads, was an *X*. The number "23" had been scribbled next to it. Ralf cocked his head and rotated the map slightly. There was no mistaking it: Sara's parents' house.

Next, he picked up the notes. On a sheet of square-ruled notepaper stood a list of abbreviations. The letters W, H, S, T, and E seemed clear enough to him: Werner, Helen, Sara, Thom, and Emma. Next to these were times—all in the evening—and yet more abbreviations. TC must be tennis club; those letters were written next to Thom and Emma. Ralf pursed his lips. Brian had used this sheet of paper to plan the robbery. It described where the members of the family would be that evening, and when.

Another sheet of paper, written on in pencil, described the route that he and Brian had taken: along the embankment where he had parked the Polo, over the wall and past the swimming pool. It was all planned out. Ralf grabbed the photos from the bed. There were two, both of Helen Möhring. One of them was a passport photo, enlarged and printed on glossy paper. The other had been taken at the Möhrings' home: a full-length image of Helen in jeans and a white blouse. She was standing in the kitchen, raising a glass and smiling at the camera. Ralf furrowed his brow and held his fist to his lips. He studied the images carefully, turning them over, but there was no other information. What was Brian doing with photos of Sara's mother? He felt his heart throbbing in his throat. This was weird. Really weird. He looked inside the envelope, but it was empty. Then he gathered together all the notes, spread them out over the bed, and set about deciphering them with renewed interest.

*Inside 7:30 p.m., up to B -> find P*

*B,* he thought. Bram, Brigitte, Bastiaan? Or Brian himself? And then P. Who was P? The second sentence was easier to work out:

*Tie up + hit W, wait for H (about 8:00 p.m.), H 2 shots (chest)—Done!*

Ralf forgot to breathe. Did it really say what he thought it said? He read through the sentences again and recalled how Brian had cursed Werner from behind the shrubbery before entering the house. Werner had fled upstairs, and Brian had followed. Ralf rubbed his neck. Werner's face had looked beaten up for a few days after the robbery. *Tie up and hit Werner.* So these cryptic fragments amounted to a plan? In other words, Brian had tied Werner up and beaten him, and then waited for Helen Möhring. *Two shots in the chest . . .*

She was supposed to die.

He shook his head, his mouth slightly ajar. He could hardly believe it. Brian hadn't entered the house to rob Werner Möhring. It was merely intended to look like a robbery that had gotten out of hand with the husband bound and roughed up, the woman killed.

But it wasn't a robbery.

It was a cold-blooded murder, planned in detail.

Ralf recalled the moments leading up to the robbery—the things Brian had said and done. He had been extremely jumpy and had fortified himself with a good deal of blow—much more than usual. He'd been snorting coke all day, in fact, having already started using in Ralf's shed that afternoon. Maybe because he was about to do something he didn't want to do? Something he needed to suppress his emotions for?

Ralf chewed on his thumbnail. Had this been Brian's idea, or had he been hired to do it? But by whom? And what about the five thousand euros Brian had expected to make from the robbery—had that actually been his fee for the murder? Or had Brian simply made it up to persuade Ralf to be his chauffeur?

Ralf's head spun. He looked at the photos of Helen—a woman he barely knew, but whom he had liked from the moment he met her. She was unaware of any danger. Smiling trustingly at the camera.

"You were supposed to die," whispered Ralf. "But you didn't. Brian did."

# 15

"Bye-bye, Brighton," said Helen softly.

They left the coast behind them and drove north, heading inland. On their way out of the city, they had driven down streets lined with small antiques shops, fashion boutiques, and stores selling Asian goods. It was so different from home, where the shopping streets all looked the same in every town and every village.

"Are we coming back to Brighton tomorrow? Or maybe on our last day?"

"You don't want to go shopping, do you?"

"Just quickly. To buy something nice for the kids."

"No way." He laid his hand on her knee. "It's a waste of time. We're only here for two nights."

"Yes, but—"

"You can always buy something on the ferry."

Helen recalled the shop on the boat. It mainly sold perfume, liquor, and tourist trash. Not an amazing selection, but he was right—they were here for such a short time, and if she did go shopping, they would easily lose half a day.

Reaching for her bag, she noticed that the zipper was open. Strange—she was normally very careful about that. She opened it farther and peered inside. That was lucky: her wallet was still there. The only thing she didn't see was her phone. She searched the main compartment, opened the zippers on the side, and felt around with the flat of her hand. To the left. To the right. No phone.

"Huh?" she said out loud. Had she left it at the café? No, she was positive she'd put it in her bag.

"What's up?"

"I can't find my phone." She took her jacket from the back seat and searched the pockets. Empty. "It's definitely gone, Werner."

# 16

A gentle rain had begun to fall. The drops fell onto the weed-choked parking lot outside Brian's place. Ralf pulled up the collar of his jacket and hurried over to his car. He wondered who had put Brian up to it. Who wanted Helen Möhring dead?

Sara hated her father, but he'd never heard her say anything negative about her mother. So, what reason could she have for getting her ex-boyfriend to—no. It made no sense. On the other hand, the image of Brian's mother was still fresh in his memory: intimately entwined with Werner as they left the Horn of Plenty. Was she behind this? Maybe she was tired of playing second fiddle and thought it was her turn to live in a house with a swimming pool. Had Emily encouraged her son to eliminate her rival? Ralf gnawed on his cheek, slowing his pace. *Or did the two of them cook this up together?* He didn't know Emily well, but she seemed like a spiritual type with her Buddhas, her cats, and her incense. He couldn't see her coming up with a murder plot on her own. Then again, he had never imagined Brian would be willing to murder somebody for money. A mother of three children, at that.

The heartless piece of shit.

Maybe Emily knew nothing about any of this, and Brian had planned and executed the whole thing himself out of love for his mother—or more likely, because he thought he would be better off himself with a wealthy stepfather like Werner.

But in that case, how had Brian come by all this information? By staking out the Möhrings' house for weeks on end? No. That wasn't his style.

As Ralf got into his car, he realized with a flash that Brian hadn't had a pistol with him. The gun he'd been carrying was fake. A replica.

Ralf plopped down behind the wheel, pulled the envelope out from under his jacket, and took another look at the notes.

*Inside 7:30 p.m., up to B -> find P*

*Go inside at half past seven. Head up to the bedroom. Find pistol.* That was it: the gun he was supposed to use to shoot Helen had been waiting for him in the bedroom. That meant there had to be a second person involved. Somebody who had access to the house, and who had either offered him help or put him up to it. Or both.

Ralf suddenly felt cold, as if ice water were flowing through his veins. It couldn't be Emily. That left only Sara and Werner. Werner had a girlfriend, and thus a motive. He wanted to share his life with Emily, so he had to get the current Mrs. Möhring out of the way. That would definitely save him a hefty chunk of alimony, what with those restaurants of his. But then why hadn't he let Brian finish the job? He'd ended up protecting his wife and killing Brian. Ralf stared at the paper. The letters danced before his eyes as he strove to understand what it all meant. Sara could have planted a gun. She could have provided Brian with all this information. But what was her motive? He was missing something. Ralf held his face in his hands and thought carefully. Sara was a money-grubber; maybe she wanted to raid her inheritance. But then both her parents, not just her mother, would have to die. *Is this part of a bigger plan? Is this . . . step one?*

He started the car and drove out of the parking lot. Shivering, he reached for the heat and turned it up. The cold had seeped into his bones.

# 17

"I think it's been stolen."

Werner raised an eyebrow. "How come?"

"The zipper on my bag was open."

"When did you realize?"

"Just now, right here in the car. Shit, it's definitely gone." Helen zipped up her bag and put it on the floor by her feet. Her sunny image of Brighton had just been severely dimmed. "I want the kids to be able to get ahold of me."

"They still can." Werner dug his iPhone out of his pocket and held it in the air. "Just give yourself a quick call, to make sure."

Helen selected her own number and listened intently. "Voice mail," she said. "It isn't even ringing. That's weird, isn't it?"

"It must be switched off. That means it's been stolen." Werner took the phone back from her.

"Should we report it?"

He shook his head. "Waste of time. They probably won't be able to do anything more about it than the police in the Netherlands would." He glanced at her briefly before looking back at the road. "I'll tell you what: when we get to the hotel, I'll ask them to call that café. Maybe your phone fell out of your bag there, or you left it on the table, and a waitress found it. It happens all the time at the Horn of Plenty."

She nodded, but she wasn't optimistic. A waitress wouldn't turn off a phone she had just found. A thief would.

He put his hand on her thigh and gave it a friendly squeeze. "It happened, honey. We can't do anything about it now. But I refuse to let it ruin my vacation, and nor should you."

Helen mumbled a reply and looked outside. They were driving past a bright-blue-painted building that was home to a fishing tackle shop. Immediately next to it was a little church with a small cemetery full of lichen-covered headstones. It looked as though the last resident of the village had been buried there at least two centuries ago. Southern England was one big fairy tale, but she couldn't enjoy it right now.

Werner rubbed her leg. "Don't worry. I'm sure I can put a smile on your face this evening."

# 18

Ralf parked his car directly opposite number 23. Werner's Mercedes wasn't there. On the driveway next to Helen's light-blue hatchback stood a gray BMW 5 Series. He recognized the car: the grandparents were here.

He crossed the street with the envelope in his hand. Just now, he had been on the verge of shoving it through the mailbox at the police station—but then he had stopped to reflect. What would the police do with these notes? Investigate them, of course. And Helen was still alive, but Brian had disappeared. So, if they managed to figure it out, they would end up back at his door—and he didn't know if he would be able to keep his cool when they did. Too much had happened for that.

Ralf rang the bell. Brian, Mikey, the police, Sara—they'd all underestimated him. Mikey had already learned his lesson. And now Sara was about to meet a whole other Ralf.

She opened the door herself. Behind her in the hallway stood a dignified, gray-haired man who looked him up and down.

"Hey, Ralf." Sara smiled, then peered ostentatiously over his shoulder. "Where's Naomi?"

"I'm on my own."

"Oh?"

"I need to talk to you."

She gave him a questioning look, but said nothing and opened the door wider.

The gray-haired man hadn't moved from his spot. Ralf greeted him with a forced smile. The man gave a brief nod.

"This is a friend of mine," said Sara to her grandpa, before turning back to Ralf. "Come on upstairs."

# 19

"I'm sorry." The receptionist put down the phone and looked at Helen apologetically. "I wish I had better news for you. But they said they'd keep an eye out for your phone."

"Thank you." Helen wasn't particularly disappointed; she hadn't expected any other outcome.

Werner walked up to her. "Nothing?" He had been standing at the other end of the lobby, calling her provider to have her number blocked.

"No. I'm so upset about this."

"Me too." He gave her a kiss on the forehead. "But we can always replace it."

"There were photos and videos of the kids on it too." *More than a thousand,* she thought. Unique moments she would never get back. For a long time, she had been meaning to transfer them to her computer—it'd only take a moment—but she had never gotten around to it. And now everything was gone.

"We'll buy a new one when we get back."

She just nodded. Werner was still focused on the device, not the sentimental value. It was irrelevant to him; he never looked at photos of himself or the children.

"Now it's time for a good old English tradition," he said.

"What's that?"

He put his arm around her and led her away from the lobby. "We're going to stuff ourselves with tea and super-sugary cakes."

# 20

"Why did you want your mother dead?"

Ralf almost vomited the words out. He had spent the entire journey here thinking about it—his opening question. That was the most important one. It was the sole way of taking Sara by surprise. She would give him an honest answer only if he could shock her into it.

Her reaction was disappointing. She looked at him uncomprehendingly. "I'm sorry?"

"I was here on that Friday," he said. "I was standing right there, watching." His voice shook as he pointed toward the embankment through the wall of Sara's bedroom.

"What do you mean, Friday? What are you talking about?"

Ralf launched forward and grabbed her by the arm. Pushed the envelope into her face. "I'm talking about *this*, bitch. The sick plan you and Brian came up with to kill your mother. What the fuck made you do it? And where's Brian?"

She shoved him back. "Get a grip, man. Are you crazy? Killing my mother—that's insane."

"Brian came in here; I watched him. Your father was in the kitchen, and your mother—" He stumbled over his words. "I saw her come home. Three shots, Sara. Then nothing. Brian didn't come back out." He was panting, his mouth half-open. "It was supposed to be your mother, but it was Brian."

Sara stared at him as if he had suddenly sprouted tentacles out of his ears. Then her face hardened. "When?"

"As if you don't know. The Friday before last, in the evening."

"That's when I play tennis."

Ralf had to restrain himself from wrapping his hands around her throat. "Stop it, Sara. You make me want to puke." He waved the envelope. "Of course you were at tennis. It says so here. Along with who goes where and when, what time everyone gets home. And where you put the gun." He narrowed his eyes, then added in a quieter but more menacing tone, "You came up with it all, and you wrote it all down, together with your sick boyfriend, Brian."

"Brian isn't my boyfriend. He never has been, and he never will be. And I never wrote anything down with him. This conversation is over." She pushed him on the chest. "Now, get the hell out of here, idiot."

He leaned forward and whispered, "Do you know what I've been wondering all this time? Did you choose Brian especially for this? Did you think, *Hey, look, a bad boy, exactly what I need?* Had you already made up your mind to use him when you let him bang you at the Horn of Plenty?"

She lifted her hands to her mouth. Froze.

"I'll take that as a yes," crowed Ralf. He took a step back and folded his arms.

"That piece of shit."

Until now, Ralf had been wondering if she had taken acting lessons or if she was just a natural liar, but from the way she was looking at him now, he could detect nothing but shame. It confused him.

"He promised he wouldn't tell anybody," she said quietly.

"Well," he sneered, "you probably could have guessed in advance that he wasn't very trustworthy, couldn't you?" He was fed up with this whole charade, so he pulled the notes out of the envelope. Held them in front of her nose. "Recognize these?"

She ducked backward and started to read them. Her eyes flitted from left to right. Ralf watched her expression change—her eyes growing wider and wider. "Oh my God. Do you know whose handwriting that is?" She tried to snatch the paper from his hand, but he pulled it back and held it out of her reach.

"Whose?"

Her shocked expression had given way to complete bewilderment. "But that can't be right," she whispered. "It can't be."

"Whose?" he repeated.

"Let me see the rest." She grabbed the envelope from his other hand and pulled out the rest of the notes. Fell back onto the bed and examined the photos. "Am I going crazy?" she whispered.

# 21

"This will be the death of me," laughed Helen.

The waiter had already brought them some tea, and he now returned with a stand laden with sweet treats. He cleared a space for it on the round table between Werner and Helen, put it down, and disappeared with a bow.

Helen could smell how sweet they were. "These cakes must be six hundred calories each."

"No way," replied Werner.

"How much, then? Seven hundred?"

"Wait; let me check." Werner picked up a cake from the bottom of the stand and took a bite. "At least a thousand," he said with his mouth full.

"Jeez. And we're going to dinner after this."

"Don't think about it." He passed Helen a petit four.

It tasted divine. Cream, caramel. A little salt too. Sweet, rich, and gooey. "Goodness," she said once she'd finished. She had an immediate hankering for a second.

Werner also took another. There was a dab of cream on it, and gold-colored pearls. Miniature masterpieces, made with great care.

A British couple sitting opposite Helen had already polished off at least six. The woman was slim and chic. Her husband had a slight paunch, but none of the guests in the lounge had the sort of figure you would expect to see on somebody who regularly overindulged in these calorie bombs.

Werner followed her gaze. "Once they've finished their afternoon tea, I'm sure they'll both spend hours running around the *ninety-three acres of garden and parkland*, looking for flowers for their room."

The woman heard Werner's overly affected English pronunciation and shot him an irritated look.

"You're being told off." Helen kept her head still, but pointed the woman out with her eyes.

Werner raised his hand and winked at the guest, who turned away. "That must be because I don't know what 'the done thing' is. *Nouveaux riches, madame*—my apologies."

Helen almost choked on a mouthful of cake and held her hand over her nose and mouth, coughing.

Werner grinned at her over the rim of his china cup. There he was again, thought Helen: Werner as she used to know him, the boy she had fallen in love with. He was still there, then, hidden under his pragmatic and irritable exterior. She leaned forward to take his hand, but he pulled his phone out of his pocket.

"The light in here is really nice." Werner stood up. "Come on. Let's take a photo for the folks at home."

# 22

"Why would your father want to murder your mother?" asked Ralf. "Because of the alimony?"

Sara had leapt up from her bed and was standing in the middle of her lavishly furnished room, staring at the wall. "Alimony?"

Ralf tried to imagine how he would feel if somebody told him that one of his ex-girlfriends had conspired with his father to murder his mother. He couldn't—he didn't know where to start. It was totally insane.

Sara's phone buzzed. Just once, discreetly. She paid it no attention. "Alimony?" she repeated. Her eyes were moist.

Ralf wanted to tell her what he had seen. Compared to what Sara had just learned about her father, the news that he also had a girl-friend on the side didn't seem particularly shocking. It was like telling someone who'd severed an artery that they'd also grazed their knee. But when he saw how hurt Sara already was—how disillusioned and deeply betrayed—he decided to keep it to himself for the time being. "Yeah, I don't know. Obviously he wants to get rid of her. He must be afraid that he'd have to pay her too much money if they got a divorce."

"The business doesn't belong to my father."

He hadn't seen that one coming. "What do you mean?"

"When Grandmother died, she left her money to Mom. She used it to buy our house. At the time, my father was still working as a manager at the Horn of Plenty, and the inheritance meant he could take over the company. Or rather, my mom could. Everything is in her name."

"When was that?"

"Seven years ago. I was ten."

"So your mother is rich?"

She nodded.

"Why does she still work, then?"

"Because she likes her job."

Ralf scratched his neck. Thought carefully. "So, if your father wanted to get a divorce—"

"Then he'd lose his restaurants," Sara said, finishing his thought.

Ralf recalled hearing about rich celebrities who'd had to pay out millions to their exes. "Wouldn't he be entitled to half of everything?"

Sara shook her head decisively. She seemed to be growing calmer. "I don't think Grandmother liked my father very much. At any rate, she arranged things so he wouldn't get any of the money if they ever divorced. My parents had a few fights about that at first." She frowned. "They thought I couldn't hear them. Dad was really angry about it."

Ralf tried again. "But would he be able to get his hands on the money if your mother died?"

"Yeah—in that case, he would. Because then he'd have to look after us, I guess."

"How do you know all this?"

"Dad told me. We often talk about finances." She said it casually, as if it were the most normal thing in the world.

Nobody ever talked about money at Ralf's house. He had no idea what his parents earned, except that it couldn't be much. And he knew nothing at all about their financial arrangements.

"There's still one thing I don't understand," he said.

"What?"

"If your father wanted to murder your mother, and he asked Brian to do it for him, then why did he kill Brian?"

"Did he do that?"

"Yeah," Ralf said softly.

"Did you see him do it?"

He shook his head. "I heard the shots. Three. I mean—"

"Heard."

"Yeah."

"Not saw."

He stared at her in silence.

"So how do you know it was my father?"

*I don't,* he thought.

He had simply assumed.

It hadn't occurred to him for a second that a mother would be capable of something like that.

He let it sink in for a moment, then asked, "Your parents are on vacation?"

She nodded. "In England. They left early this morning."

"London?"

"No, southern England. Sussex, I think it's called. On the coast. My parents went there on their first vacation, back when they met." Her eyes glazed over, and her voice sounded dull. "It was Dad's idea. A present. Mom sent us photos of the hotel this morning. Super fancy. Wait . . ." She pushed a strand of hair from her face and took out her phone. "He just sent me a message." She read it out loud. "'Your mother has lost her phone. If you need us, use this number.'"

"Lost her phone," repeated Ralf.

Sara leapt up from the bed. "We need to go to the police."

"And then what?"

"I don't know. If all this is true, they need to stop my father."

"What will you tell them? That your mother shot somebody? That I helped Brian with a robbery that turned out to be a contract killing?" He had raised his voice. "And anyway, do you really think they'll jump into a helicopter and fly over to England? No way. First they'll do some paperwork, open an investigation, in their own good time. Get in touch with their colleagues—"

"That would lose us a few days."

"Everything OK up there?" The male voice calling from downstairs had an unmistakable German accent.

Sara put her finger to her lips and walked over to the door. Opened it a crack. "Yes, Grandpa," she called. She sounded like butter wouldn't melt in her mouth. "Ralf is just about to head home."

She closed the door and turned to face him. "We have to do *something*, don't we?" she whispered. "If this is true—" She shook her head in disbelief. "Please tell me I'm dreaming this, Ralf."

He looked at her with a strained expression. "I'm afraid—"

Sara's phone started to buzz. She started so violently that she almost dropped it. Looked at the screen. "My parents."

Ralf looked over her shoulder at the photo that Werner had sent. Helen Möhring was sitting in a dark-red leather armchair and smiling as she lifted up a cup of tea. Next to her stood a stand laden with tiny cakes.

This is your mother. Dad and I are putting on weight! Tonight we're eating at a fancy restaurant that belongs to the hotel ☺ Everything OK at home? Love, Mom

"I want to warn her," she said.

"You can't. This is from your father's phone. He'll see it."

"Yeah, but—"

"Send something like 'Sounds great, have fun.' Something normal." She shook her head. "I could just call?"

"But then—"

"I'll tell my dad it's about women's problems or something, and that I want to speak to my mom in private."

"Sara, I don't think that's a good idea. Maybe—" He swallowed. "Maybe it would be better to call the police after all?"

She shot him a furious glare. "You said it yourself. I'd have to report my own mother. And you too. And it would take too long. What if my father . . . ? These are my parents we're talking about, Ralf. Who says it's even true? I can't believe it."

"Yeah, but—"

"Shh." She raised her hand and looked up her father's number, but her thumb hovered motionlessly over his photo. "Fuck." She bit her lower lip. "What should I tell her?"

"That she needs to get away from your father because he probably took her to England to kill her, or to have her killed?"

Sara stood frozen in the middle of her bedroom, holding her phone in her trembling hand. Slowly, her shoulders sagged. "I just can't believe it," she whispered. "That this is happening. But that handwriting—" Her breath caught. She turned her face toward him. "Ralf? We need to go there."

"What?"

"We need to go where my parents are. If it's really true that my father . . . then I need to stop him myself."

"I don't know if—"

She grabbed his arms and looked up at him. "I want to look him in the eyes, Ralf. He's my *father*. You have a car."

"Hey, I only got my license five months ago. They drive on the left over there."

"It can't be that hard, can it? We'll just go to, what's it called, Calais, and then it'll be clear enough from there."

"Don't you need to book the crossing in advance?"

She shook her head.

"Are you sure?"

"Yeah. A friend of mine just got back from England. They have ferries there, plus a railroad tunnel. All sorts of options. You can travel around the clock."

Ralf was unconvinced. "What about your grandparents? You're supposed to go to school tomorrow."

"Jackie will cover for me. I'll tell them I'm staying with her, and I'll park my scooter at her house."

"And what will you tell her parents?"

"I'll come up with something. Come on. You need to get going. Pick me up from Jackie's in half an hour. Oh, wait." She stopped him. "Do you have ID?"

He patted the inside pocket of his jacket.

"Perfect. I'll see you soon."

## 23

"The way that woman reacted!" The tears rolled down Helen's cheeks, and her stomach muscles ached.

Werner put on his poshest English accent. "Not. Amused. At. All." He threw his cardigan into the corner of the hotel room and pulled Helen toward him.

She put her arms around his neck. "I haven't laughed like that in a long time."

"Me neither."

"You know the waiter saw you, right? Those silly faces you were making. They'll ban us from that restaurant tonight if we're not careful."

"I'm more worried about something else." His face took on a serious expression.

She grew alarmed. "What?"

"What if those two end up sitting right next to us at dinner?"

She burst into laughter once more. "Oh, stop it! Honestly, if that happens, then you'll have to carry me out of there."

"It's her husband I feel sorry for. She had him perfectly trained."

"Not entirely. He kept staring at my cleavage."

"I don't blame him." His hand cupped her right breast. "Scandalous, the way you carry on."

"Since when are Anthropologie dresses scandalous? They're very tasteful, don't you know."

His fingers brushed teasingly over her nipple. "Not with your gorgeous body squeezed into them, they aren't. Then they're positively outrageous."

Helen gasped. Her whole body responded to his touch.

"Especially in a respectable hotel like this," he murmured as his other hand disappeared under her dress. "Full of such respectable people."

# 24

The drive had gone well until they reached the Antwerp ring road, where an overturned truck had delayed them by a full hour. Shortly after that, they had filled up the gas tank—Sara had paid—and they were now crossing the French border. The voices on the radio were incomprehensible.

Ralf was dazed by the lights of the oncoming traffic. He narrowed his eyes to slits and pretended that he had everything under control. The imminent prospect of driving on the left in England filled him with anxiety, but it wasn't half as terrifying as the knowledge that he would be coming face-to-face with Sara's parents once he got there. And yet he had to do this. Not for Sara or her mother, but for himself.

Sara obviously wasn't feeling her best either. She had her face turned away from him and was pretending to look out of the window, but he could see her shoulders shaking. Every now and then, he heard a sob.

"How much farther do we have?"

Sara wiped her nose with the back of her hand and looked at her phone. "Another hour and a half or so. Just follow this road." Her voice was nasal.

"Wouldn't it have been better to book tickets in advance?"

"How could I? I don't even have a credit card."

"What if—"

"It's a regular service. Trains go back and forth all the time. It won't be a problem—it's not like we have a big truck or anything. They always have room for a car."

He paused briefly. "How many times have you been to England?"

"Never. But I've heard enough about it." She kept looking at him. "Why were you there that night, Ralf?"

"I already told you." His eyelids fluttered. These oncoming head-lights were driving him crazy. He was afraid to drive as fast as he normally did. "Brian needed a ride. He'd lost his license. All I had to do was wait for him outside. I only found out later whose house it was."

"Do you do things like that a lot? Break into people's houses?"

"No, that was the first time." A muscle twitched in his cheek. "And the last."

"You're a good liar."

"I'm not lying."

"Maybe not right now. But we talked about Brian at the party, and about his mother—how she'd reported him missing, and stuff. You didn't give anything away."

"I'm not proud of it" was all he said.

For a long time, there was silence; they were both lost in their own thoughts. Ralf focused on the road and listened with half an ear to Tupac. The volume was low, but it didn't matter. He knew all the lyrics by heart.

"Why are you helping me?" asked Sara.

"I don't know."

He did know, but he wasn't about to tell her. He was sick to death of people belittling him, constantly being underestimated. Year after year, he had been mistreated by frustrated teachers, by the neighbor-hood police, even by Brian. He wasn't going to let anybody else push him around or put him down. The first step had been standing up to Mikey. Now it was everybody else's turn. When he found Werner and Helen, he would make the two of them tell him everything they knew about what happened to Brian. Then it would be up to Sara to figure things out with her parents. They could murder each other or fall sobbing into each other's arms—whatever they wanted, as long as they left him out of it. That said, Sara's mother had seemed like a good person. She was cut from a very different cloth from Sara and her father.

But that wasn't his problem.

He had enough to worry about with his own mother.

Less than three hours ago, he had gone home to pick up his things and had pulled the wool over her eyes—telling her he had found work on a construction site up in the north, in Groningen. A project that would last a few days. He would stay with a friend. Previously, she would have looked at him with suspicion and asked for names and numbers, but after everything that had happened last week, she'd trusted him. She'd been genuinely happy for him. The look on her face . . . Shame cut through him like a knife. He was her only child. She deserved better.

His parents both deserved better.

# 25

Helen was glad that the romantic part of their first day of vacation had taken place before dinner, as the atmosphere in the Michelin-starred restaurant the Boss was like the inside of a refrigerator. The same went for the temperature. Her bare legs were covered in goose bumps, and she regretted not bringing a cardigan. Or maybe a parka. The concept was doubtlessly very trendy, but it was lost on her. A raised, diner-style bench had been installed along the wall of a large industrial kitchen, with a step to help you get onto it. There were smooth, square tables lined up against the bench, with barstools opposite. The furniture was arranged in one long row, with hard, white lighting overhead. It felt uncomfortable to sit so high up, with your legs dangling into space, although you did have a good view of the chefs as they went about their work. There was barely any privacy for the guests either, as the tables were positioned very close together.

Fortunately, their neighbors were speaking English.

Werner didn't seem to notice her discomfort. He examined every course with interest and ate with dainty bites. "Molecular gastronomy," he called it, but it felt more like a chemistry lesson to Helen. Or a guessing game. Something that looked like a vegetable could easily turn out to be fish or a piece of meat. White chocolate crumbled into powder when you touched it and tasted of rose petals.

The courses were brought out in quick succession, accompanied by mumbled explanations delivered in incomprehensible dialect, and so the conversation never had a chance to get going. The chefs delivered their creations to the table personally, the sommelier served wine after wine—each with its own explanation too—and a waitress topped off their water glasses so often, it felt intrusive.

It all put Helen on edge. "It's awfully expensive, isn't it?" she remarked when she realized that this little dinner would cost more than six hundred euros.

"Even so, I don't think they make much money here." Werner surveyed his surroundings calculatingly. "Not many covers compared to the size of the kitchen staff."

There were eight or nine chefs hard at work in the kitchen, and every one of them looked young, toned, and hip. It was clear that they hadn't just been hired for their cooking skills. A black woman was mopping the kitchen floor, while two of the chefs leaned against a counter and chatted.

The memory of her evening with Lex sprang to Helen's mind. A snug little table in a warm, noisy, dimly lit eatery, with recognizable food that tasted the way it looked. And a dinner partner who had looked at her as if she were the most beautiful woman he had seen in years. Werner was mainly preoccupied with his food. After they'd had sex—which had admittedly been very good—he had withdrawn into himself once more. That was nothing new, she realized. He had been like that from the very beginning, though it had bothered her less back then. After all, she had changed over the years just as much as Werner had. Maybe even more. Originally, she had fallen for his pragmatism—his cool, rational way of looking at the world. She had mistaken it for strength. But since meeting Lex, she had realized that strength could also go with warmth and friendliness—and that those things might even be a better combination.

# 26

"Shit. Look at this."

The Eurotunnel was closed. Electronic signposts above the road displayed alternate routes.

"How is this possible?" asked Sara. "They can't do that, can they? Just close the entire tunnel like that?"

"They can if there's a bomb threat."

She looked at him in alarm.

"Or a fire, or whatever." Ralf looked at his dashboard. It was just after nine, but it felt like midnight. He yawned and rubbed his eyes.

"There are ferries too," she said. "Let's try those instead." She pointed to a line of cars following the signs toward a ferry terminal.

He pulled out of the line, moved into the outside lane, and joined the traffic.

# 27

"Did you understand what he said?"

"Not a word. But this"—he lifted his glass and examined the liquid inside—"is definitely white wine."

Helen took a sip. The wine tasted good, but she still didn't feel at ease. Her feet were resting on a metal bar positioned halfway between her seat and the floor. She felt like a toddler. Or a dwarf. She had hoped she would adopt a more positive view of the evening after a few drinks, but she was struggling to enjoy herself.

"What's on the program for tomorrow?"

She noticed his jaw clench. "Something very different."

"Like what?"

He picked up a piece of bread and tore it down the middle. "Do you want any?"

"No, thanks. Will it be something fun?"

"We're going to walk off all the calories we consumed today."

"Oh really? On the hotel grounds?"

He shook his head. "An hour's drive away. It's a tough hike, I've been told. But well worth the effort."

"What is there to see?"

He pinched the bread, plucked a piece off. "You'll find out tomorrow."

She gave up. There was no point asking questions when he was in this mood. And why should she, anyway? He had arranged everything perfectly so far, and a little mystery made everything more fun. More exciting. Although she would have much preferred to eat a burger at a local pub this evening.

"It's interesting, I'll grant you, but it's not exactly homey, is it?" she said, looking around demonstratively. The room was now flooded with sharply dressed people, but it was still as brightly lit as the freezer aisle in a supermarket.

"Not everything has to be," answered Werner. "It's a trendy concept, and they've executed it without making any concessions. Kind of fun to experience something like that. They say it's the best restaurant in the region."

"It must just be me, then."

"Sometimes it's good to step outside your comfort zone," he said.

Course number six was brought to the table by a young chef with a South Asian background who listed the ingredients one by one. He had a friendly smile, but his explanation—delivered in brisk English—was lost amid the noise from the kitchen and the background buzz of the restaurant.

Helen peered at her plate. Its contents resembled a collage made of bath foam, flower petals—purple and yellow, were they violets?—and a few cubes of a glistening substance.

"Looks amazing, doesn't it?" asked Werner.

"Very interesting. But is it edible?"

"Of course. Why wouldn't it be?"

She picked up a petal from her plate and placed it on her tongue. It tasted of petal.

# 28

Ralf drove away from the terminal building, which had the words "Port de Calais" painted on it in black lettering. There were still long lines of stranded travelers waiting inside. Truck drivers, businesspeople, students. Everybody was hoping to buy tickets for the next crossing, but the ferry companies had all sold out. The later sailings were all full too. Ralf was relieved that they'd managed to get hold of some tickets, even though the boat wasn't departing for eight and a half hours. At least their place on board was guaranteed.

"Are there any potato chips left?"

Sara shook her head. "They're all gone."

Ralf looked around. Nothing but cars, tall fences, barbed wire, concrete. Not a KFC or a McDonald's to be seen.

"I think we have to go through customs first," said Sara. "After that, I'm sure there'll be a café somewhere selling sandwiches and stuff."

Ralf followed the signs for the ferries. The word "customs" made him uneasy. It had felt like such a good plan when he'd been packing his things at home, but now that he was confronted with all these grim fences, cameras, and uniforms, it suddenly seemed a lot less clever. Naive, even.

At home, whenever he was unsure whether to take a scarf or hat out with him, his father would always say, *Better safe than sorry.* But that saying wasn't always true, he realized now.

Or maybe it only applied to hats and scarves. Not to the item lying at the bottom of his duffel bag.

# 29

Dessert consisted of small morsels that looked like pieces of summer fruit. Helen bit into a blueberry and lifted her eyebrows in surprise. No powder. No chocolate or ginger. It was a berry. A real one. She nearly burst out laughing.

Squinting at the menu on the table between them, she mentally ticked off the dishes that had already been served. This was the final course. Just a little longer in this noisy kitchen and then the whole exercise would be over.

"Shame—a bit basic, this one." Werner laid his spoon on his empty plate.

"I like it. The Bavarian cream is good."

"True, but I'd been hoping for ice cream."

Helen wanted to remark that the events of the past week had left her with an immense aversion to frozen food, but she held her tongue.

"Are you looking forward to tomorrow?" he asked.

"I think so."

He looked straight at her for a moment, then lowered his eyes to the tabletop. Wiped a crumb from the surface. "We're going to do something exciting. Something you've never done before. Me neither, for that matter." He smiled. "I don't even think it's allowed. But we're going to do it anyway."

"You're making me very curious now."

His face tightened. He gave no other response, so she summarized: "It's about an hour away. A tough hike, you said. And it might not be allowed. Something I've never done before, and you haven't either." It couldn't be a ride in a hot-air balloon, as that wouldn't involve a long walk. And it was legal, of course—even in England. At least, she assumed so.

"Do you think the kids are in bed already?" she wondered out loud.

"Are you really thinking about the kids right now?"

She opened her bag out of habit and went to take out her phone. Then remembered she'd lost it. Was everything OK at home? It was nearly midnight, and all three of the children had school tomorrow, so it was too late to call. A sad feeling welled up inside her. Homesickness, she realized. "I wanted to wish them good night."

"Then send them a message. They'll see it first thing in the morning."

He picked up his phone but didn't pass it to her. Instead, he held it out in front of him with both hands. "Say 'cheese.'"

Automatically, she raised her wineglass and smiled.

Werner looked at the photo and then handed her his phone. "Now, write something to go with it."

Underneath a photo in which she looked much happier than she felt, she typed:

Everything OK there? The food here is very interesting: clove-flavored foam with flower petals. Thom would love it, haha ☺

We're getting up early tomorrow and packing our sandwiches for an exciting day hiking along the cliffs!

Do your best at school and say hi to Grandma and Grandpa for us.

Love, Mom

"What did you write? Can I see?"

"I haven't sent it—"

Werner snatched the phone out of her hand.

"Yet."

His expression was slightly anxious at first, but then he began to read, and a smile broke out on his face. "Perfect—that's great. I'll send it, OK?" He pressed the button and then tucked the phone away again.

There was something strange about how he was handling that phone—and all their communication with home, for that matter. "Why are you being so—"

"More water?" The waitress appeared at the table with a carafe. She looked at them both in turn, clutching her decanter clumsily.

"No, thanks," answered Werner, and then looked at Helen. "How about coffee?"

# 30

A short, balding customs officer stepped away from his colleagues and waved them through with a bored expression.

"That was easy." Ralf accelerated past the tall fence topped with barbed wire. He smiled but could feel his eye twitching.

Past a curve in the road was another barrier. More men in uniforms—but this group looked a good deal more active. An officer raised his hand and waved them over to the side.

Ralf stopped underneath the canopy. The checkpoint was flooded with bright fluorescent light and felt like a space station.

Ralf opened his window.

"Passports, please."

The man sounded very English. A little snobby.

"I think this is the British border," he heard Sara say from the passenger seat. She took her ID out of her bag and handed it to Ralf, who passed it to the man along with his own. "Back there was the French one."

Another customs officer walked around the car. He looked at Sara, made eye contact with Ralf. Walked to the back of the Polo and peered in through the windows.

Ralf tried to swallow but couldn't.

"Where are you from?"

"Holland." Why did the man ask that? Couldn't he tell from their IDs and license plate? Ralf coughed to cover a nervous shudder.

The officer asked them what they were planning to do in England.

"Romantic weekend," answered Sara, leaning across Ralf's lap and smiling as her eyes met the officer's. She placed her hand on Ralf's leg.

The customs officer took another look at their IDs and asked them how long they intended to stay.

Ralf opened his mouth, but Sara beat him to it.

"Two nights."

"And where are you staying?" He looked at Ralf as if he had already decided in advance not to take his answer seriously.

Ralf fought the impulse to react. He didn't think he would ever be able to get along with anyone in uniform. "What's the place called again?" he asked Sara in Dutch.

She addressed herself to the man and gave him the name and location of the hotel. Her voice had a proud note, as if to say, *You weren't expecting that, were you? Two teenagers in a fancy place like that.* Ralf wondered whether the customs officers knew every hotel in the country, or if they only asked questions like that to see how you reacted. Maybe it was suspicious if you looked like you'd memorized the answers, or if you took slightly too long to think about it.

"My parents are already there," she continued, before complaining in fluent English about the closure of the Eurotunnel and the ensuing delay. She asked him whether he knew what was going on.

The customs officer told her there was a technical problem. He still had their IDs in his hands and looked like he was mulling something over.

Ralf could feel himself sweating. His T-shirt was clammy and tight. What if the man called the hotel to check Sara's story?

The second officer had apparently been unable to find anything suspicious. He took another look over his colleague's shoulder for the sake of form before walking off.

"Have a nice stay." The man handed the IDs back to Ralf, who gave him a friendly nod and tried to drive off without any screeching tires.

Sara fell back into her seat. "Jeez, what a bunch of paper pushers."

She had a lot more to say, but he was only half listening. He knew he had just dodged a bullet. If the officer had searched his bag . . .

*Don't think about it.*

Was that it? he wondered. Would there be no more checkpoints? Or could they expect to go through the same thing again tomorrow in England?

He didn't feel confident.

## 31

Werner lay down next to her in bed. "I thought that was a very enjoyable evening. How about you?"

"It was very interesting."

"I know, right? Good tip from Serge. The contrast is pretty great too—this historic hotel, and then that restaurant."

"Yes, very different. Like day and night."

"Speaking of which . . ." There was a cord hanging over the bed. Werner gave it a tug, and the light went out. "Good night," he said, and turned his back on her.

# 32

Ralf and Sara were in agreement: a hotel was a waste of money. And anyway, all the cheap hotels nearby would be full thanks to the disruption in the tunnel. The car had a lock, the seats were fully reclinable, and the entire terminal site was under so much surveillance, it felt like an open-air prison.

And yet Ralf still couldn't sleep. He stared at the roof of the Polo and listened to the cars and trucks as they trundled in long lines toward the ferries, ready for boarding.

Next to him, Sara was sitting cross-legged and finishing off the last piece of a limp baguette. Her phone buzzed. "My mother."

Ralf sat up. "What does it say?"

"Read it yourself."

Ralf read the message. Looked at Sara. She was thinking the same thing.

"Cliffs," she whispered.

"How far do we have to go from Dover?"

Back in the Netherlands, Sara had mapped out the route to the hotel and saved countless screenshots. She looked them up and swiped through the images. "About an hour and forty-five minutes, I think."

"What if we don't make it in time?"

"It might be OK. They're on vacation, and my father isn't really a morning person."

Ralf gnawed on his cheek. "The boat docks in England at seven thirty, but it could easily take us half an hour to disembark. And then we might have to go through customs again."

"I want to call them, Ralf."

"I wouldn't."

"Why? I could just ask for my mom—tell her I miss her and ask if everything is OK. That way at least I'd have spoken to her."

He looked at the clock on the dashboard. "Would you normally do that after midnight?"

She shook her head.

"Then I definitely wouldn't do it now."

Sara stared at the phone for a long time and then pressed it to her breast.

Ralf was worried that she would start crying again, but she didn't make a sound and remained sitting motionlessly. Like a statue. Her voice sounded small, almost childlike, when she spoke again. "This is a dumb idea, isn't it? Should we call the police after all?"

"Sara, suppose it's true. That your mother did kill Brian—"

She fixed him with a troubled expression.

"In that case, they'll arrest both your parents. Remember?" His face fell. "And me too. Sara? Are you listening to me?"

She nodded. It almost hurt to look at her. "Could it all be a mistake? I really hope so."

*I've been hoping so too, ever since I heard the shots. Every single day.* "I don't know," he answered.

From the way she was sitting there—her phone cradled against her chest like an injured pet, her eyes damp—he had the impression that he was seeing the real Sara for the very first time. The little girl behind the glossy exterior. He began to feel sorry for her.

"We'll get there in time," he said.

She looked up. "You think so?"

"Yeah. Absolutely. I promise."

*Monday*

# 1

"Shit," said Sara.

The car that had driven off the ferry immediately ahead of them was being directed to the side by a pair of customs officers. Another glanced in their direction and raised his hand to indicate that Ralf should wait.

"It looks like there's something going on," said Sara. "Like they're searching for someone or something."

Ralf glanced nervously at the dog handlers. If those were sniffer dogs they had with them, then he was in trouble. There would inevitably be traces of cocaine or weed on the mats and upholstery in his car. Then the customs officers would search his entire car, and though they wouldn't find any drugs, there was something else they'd unearth instead.

An officer walked up to the car and asked him to roll down his window.

"Fuck," muttered Ralf.

"Chill out—it's not like we're doing anything wrong."

Ralf didn't answer. He did as he was told and took his ID out. When he looked up to hand it over, the officer turned away from him and spoke into his walkie-talkie. His colleague stepped forward and instructed Ralf to keep driving.

"Huh?" said Sara.

Ralf hesitated, lifting his eyebrows inquiringly. The man nodded at him. *That's right, drive on.*

He continued anxiously, leaving customs and heading for the open road. *Drive on the left.* The words rang in his ears like a mantra. *Left, left.*

"It's so different here," he heard Sara say. "Those houses. And the white cliffs." She smoothed her hair down. It had gone a little frizzy overnight.

"Sara, do you think you could concentrate for a moment? Where do we need to go?"

"Oh yeah." She reached for her phone and looked up the pictures of the route. "You want the M20, toward London."

"Are you sure?"

She pointed. "There, on that roundabout. First exit."

"Third," he corrected her.

He turned left onto the roundabout, closely following a car with a British license plate. It felt incredibly strange—almost as if he were driving a car for the first time in his life.

As he turned jerkily onto the M20, he realized that getting to the hotel in time was by no means his biggest concern. They'd be lucky if he didn't crash into a guardrail on the way.

## 2

Helen spread some of the hotel's specialty jam on a slice of Brie and took a bite. "That really is incredible. Do you think they sell this stuff for guests to take home with them?"

"It's never the same at home. Different ambience."

That felt improbable—the breakfast already tasted better to her than the Michelin-starred menu from the night before, and they had only just sat down to eat. But maybe Werner was right that it was partly due to the atmosphere in the breakfast room: instead of screeching appliances and bright lighting, there were thick carpets, wood paneling, and huge windows offering cinematic views of the estate.

Outside, men in overalls were hard at work, pruning shrubs, raking, and sweeping.

"They'd be welcome to spend a weekend at our place," she remarked.

Werner cut a piece off his toast. "When I'm back in the Netherlands, I'm going to see about hiring a gardener."

Helen wanted to say that she'd rather call a real estate agent, but she held her tongue. The mood was good; she didn't want to ruin it.

## 3

"How far do we have to go?"

"Forty-five minutes, an hour. Something like that."

They were halfway there. Ralf hadn't driven on the wrong side of the road or crashed into the railing. Actually, it was perfectly doable, he thought, driving on the left. He'd really gotten the hang of the round-abouts, and he also had merging on and off the freeway fully under control. Half an hour ago, they had stopped to call Sara's school. He did a decent impression of Sara's father. "Well, there is a bug going around at the moment," they'd replied. "Please give her our best, Mr. Möhring." It had put a faint smile on Sara's pallid face.

Ralf began to drive a little faster. He wanted to catch Werner and Helen before they set out on their hike, since it would be impossible to find them otherwise. Besides, he thought it would be more sensible for Sara to confront her father inside the hotel where there were people, phones, cameras. It was safer there. The man was planning to murder his wife, so why not his daughter too? And the friend she'd brought with her?

"Do you know what you're going to say to him?" he asked.

"No idea. I still can't believe it." She looked across at him. "I mean, I know I'm sitting here talking to you, but I sometimes think, *Am I dreaming this?* It feels like a nightmare. So surreal, you know? The whole thing—including this. I've never slept in a car before. And I should be at school right now." She turned away from him and stared at the landscape as it rushed past.

"You need a plan for what you're going to say. And what you're going to do." He paused for a moment. "Just assume that it is true."

She turned her face back toward him. "That Brian and my father staged a botched break-in so they could murder my mother? *That's* what I should assume is true?"

"Yeah, that."

# 4

"Here you are." The waitress placed their plates on the white tablecloth.

On each plate lay an enormous mushroom, as thick as a finger.

"Nice—portobello," murmured Werner.

The mushrooms were surrounded by grilled tomatoes, a heap of scrambled egg, fried bacon, a piece of white fish, and two sausages that glistened with fat.

"It's only eight thirty," said Helen once the waitress had disappeared. "I already had all that Brie with jam. And we'll be having lunch soon. Plus dinner tonight!"

"You're forgetting afternoon tea," he remarked drily.

"Bizarre. What a country."

"We'll walk it all off soon enough," he said, and began to eat.

Helen's eyes lingered on him. His elegant hands, the fine hairs on his wrists, and that aristocratic face she knew so well. The gray morning light streamed through the window and cast shadows, deepening his laugh lines and making the grooves on his cheeks look harsher. It was the same Werner as ever, and yet there was something about him. She couldn't put her finger on it. He talked, listened, ate, smiled, but his actions didn't quite seem to match up with his mood, somehow.

Tension.

That was it; that was what she felt when she looked at him. Tension. Distance.

# 5

"I didn't know your parents were *this* rich."

"Me neither."

Ralf expected somebody to step out of the perfectly maintained shrubbery and escort him off the premises. His sixteen-year-old Polo would almost certainly spoil the view for the chic hotel guests. The place was enormous, and looked distinguished and very old—it was like they had just driven onto a film set.

"They only ever take us camping," said Sara. "Or to Grandma and Grandpa's rickety old witch's house in France."

He drove slower and slower, unsure where to go. Everything here was so big.

"There." Sara pointed to a neatly painted sign standing in a flower bed. Ralf followed the arrow and drove down a wide gravel path onto a parking lot, which was divided into sections by hedges and shrubs. Each section had room for around ten cars. The fine gravel crunched beneath his wheels.

"This is for the guests, right?" he asked.

"I think so."

"Then your father's car must be here somewhere."

"If they haven't left yet," added Sara softly.

He drove slowly down each of the rows, looking for the gray Mercedes. On another day, he could have easily spent an hour or two here gawking. The parking lot was like the showroom of a luxury car dealership, and the Aston Martins, Range Rovers, and Porsches on display must have been worth a fortune. But they all had British license plates.

Not a single Dutch car.

"We're too late," he said.

"Try over there."

He drove off the path again as a favor to Sara, and then back up to the entrance. She slumped in her seat in disappointment.

Ralf turned off the engine and took his key out of the ignition. "What now?"

"We can go and ask inside. Maybe the staff will know where they went."

"Sure, like they'd tell us that."

"They will. I'm their daughter, remember?"

They got out and walked down a perfectly maintained footpath to the main entrance. Ralf was intimidated. His red Adidas hoodie suited him and was nice and warm, but in this setting, it was just as out of place as his car. He glanced at his sneakers as they walked. Colorful, but thankfully clean. Next to him, Sara was frantically tying her unruly hair into a tight bun, making him suspect that she wasn't entirely confident of being taken seriously either.

They passed under a portico and entered the building. Ralf did his utmost not to be distracted by the lavish décor. The hall was enormous, with chandeliers on which every lamp was lit. Gleaming stone floors, Persian carpets. In one corner stood a grand piano.

Ralf and Sara received a friendly welcome from an elderly man behind the reception desk. If he thought they didn't belong here, he certainly didn't show it. His arms and legs were short, Ralf noticed, and his hips were broad. It had probably taken him many decades to grow that impressive belly. Ralf had never met anybody before who physically resembled a spinning top. A huge, live spinning top.

"We're looking for Werner and Helen Möhring," said Ralf.

The man raised his hand. "I'm afraid that—"

Sara stepped forward. "They're my parents. It's an emergency."

He looked at her, his head slightly cocked. "I see it now. You're the spitting image of your mother. Your parents have just left."

"Do you know where they were going?"

"I'm afraid not."

Sara's phone began to buzz inside her bag. She unzipped it and retrieved the device. "My dad," she said breathlessly. "A photo."

Ralf looked over her shoulder at the screen. Helen was standing with her thumbs up, smiling at the camera. She had a scarf wrapped around her head. It was obviously very windy.

Your mother and I are ready to take on the Seven Sisters!

"Seven Sisters?"

Ralf took the phone from Sara's hand and showed it to the man. "Do you know where this is?"

He took a pair of reading glasses from his breast pocket and placed them carefully on his nose. "Not precisely, but you can see Beachy Head quite clearly in the background."

"Does that have anything to do with 'Seven Sisters'?" he asked.

*6*

"What are we doing here?" asked Helen.

They were standing on a footpath up the coast from a place called Eastbourne, which looked chic and expensive. White Victorian houses, golf clubs, and a marina.

"Do you see those cliffs up there?" Werner pointed to some chalky crags emerging from the gray North Sea. They were very imposing. Steep and vertical, almost perfectly white. Above them lay a green and undulating landscape. Pasture, by the looks of it. The transition between it and the sea—at least three hundred feet below—was abrupt: as if a mythical sea monster had bitten an enormous chunk out of the hills. On the ferry, Helen had already seen the coastline for which the south of England was famous—but the White Cliffs of Dover had nothing on these.

"Impressive," she said. The wind tugged at her hair. She tried in vain to smooth it down, and in the end simply wrapped it with a scarf.

"That's where we're going," said Werner.

"Can you get up there, to the top?"

"On foot, yes."

She squinted. "I can't see anybody."

"I doubt there will be many people up there right now. The one you're looking at is Beachy Head." He pointed to the undulations in the rolling landscape. "There are more cliffs and hills behind it. They call that area the Seven Sisters because there are seven hills. It takes two hours to hike from the first sister to the seventh."

They gazed together at the chalk cliffs. The slopes didn't look that steep, but it was difficult to tell from this distance. Her eye caught a minuscule black speck on the vast, green, undulating carpet. She held a hand over her eyes.

It was a person.

"Man, I feel dizzy already. It's so high up there."

"Photo!" cried Werner with a smile. "It'll make a great backdrop." He told her where to stand. "Come forward a little. That's it—perfect. Thumbs-up. Say 'cheese.'" Werner cupped his hand over the screen and examined the results. "Fantastic. I'll send it to the kids."

Helen observed his movements. The sudden strain in his voice hadn't escaped her notice. What was making him so agitated? And why was he so obsessed with sending photos to the family? It was almost a compulsion. When they first arrived in the hotel room, on the beach in Brighton, at afternoon tea . . . Over dinner last night, he had even wanted to check exactly what she was writing to the kids. And now they were here, in Eastbourne, not even ten steps away from their parked car. The sole reason they had pulled over was for this view of the cliffs, to take a photo. With any other man, a photo op like this might make sense—but not with Werner.

She had grown accustomed to how he could be cool and distant at times, only to suddenly become affectionate and take an interest in her once again. Nobody was perfect. But this was new.

And a little unsettling.

"What's with all the photos?" she asked.

"What do you mean?"

"You're never interested in taking pictures."

His face fell. "All these years, you've been complaining that you never appear in any vacation photos because you're always the one who has to take them. This time, I try to be considerate for once, and it still isn't good enough." Werner took her by the elbow and pulled her toward him. He threw his arms around her and kissed her forehead. Gave her a slight shake. "Come on, Helen. Lighten up a little. Today is a special day."

# 7

"There! There it is."

Ralf spotted Werner's Mercedes before Sara. It stood in a sandy parking lot next to a building that served as a visitor center.

Anxiously, he drove his Polo into the lot and pulled up alongside an old Land Rover—the only other car there.

He got out and walked up to the Mercedes. The visitor center looked closed. A stream gurgled somewhere nearby.

"What now?" asked Sara, peering into her parents' car.

Ralf put his hand on the hood. It was still warm. He looked around and hurried over to an information board. "Seven Sisters Country Park" was written at the top. This part of the site was a large forest full of mountain-bike trails, while the cliffs were on the other side of the road and were accessible only on foot. The first route led through a valley and along a small stream, with a steep climb at the other end. The second was shorter and ran straight across the hills.

"'For less experienced walkers,'" read Sara, who had appeared next to him. She looked at Ralf. "I don't think my parents do much hiking."

"The second route, then?" Ralf didn't wait for her to respond, quickly walking back to his car. He opened the trunk, unzipped his bag, and rummaged through his things. He turned his body slightly to conceal his actions from Sara and placed the gun under his waistband.

# 8

The wind whipped around them. The gray clouds constantly changed shape and hue. A pale sun cast its diffuse light over the hills. The shifting illumination produced a threatening atmosphere, as if the scenery had been filmed through a dark lens. And yet there was also something romantic, Helen thought, about being swept up in this immense landscape. From a distance, she and Werner would look like slowly moving dots on an endless green stage. There was nobody else here, as far as the eye could see.

Helen was in decent shape, but she was still panting a little. There was almost no level ground; each step took them higher and higher. Sometimes Werner walked ahead of her, sometimes alongside her, avoiding rocks, his hands in his jacket pockets. He was wearing a scarf, and his hair was tucked underneath a knitted gray hat.

"Werner?"

He looked at her.

"Maybe we should move," she said.

"Where to?"

"Closer to downtown. I drove past those new condo developments the other day. The more expensive ones look like they're a decent size—big enough for the five of us. And they have video surveillance."

"You'll have to convince the kids first. They won't want to give up their swimming pool."

"I think they'd rather live close to school and downtown. Thom and Emma complain every day about how far they have to bike."

"Thom will be riding a scooter soon enough." Werner bent over to pick up a stick. "Honestly, it's no safer downtown than where we live now. I think the reverse might even be true." He weighed the stick, tried to bend it, and leaned on it briefly. Snapped off various twigs. "The idea that you would be safe in any particular place is wishful thinking. Nowhere is truly safe."

Helen stood still. "Maybe it's more of a feeling. Our house is out in the farthest corner of the neighborhood; the yard is so big. And then those woods all around it. That gloomy embankment."

"You used to think all those things were advantages."

"I know. Now I've realized they also make us vulnerable."

"We were just unlucky," he said, and continued walking.

Unlucky. So that was his view of the matter. Werner wasn't very sensitive to atmosphere. Never had been. In the immediate aftermath of the robbery, he had found it hard to spend time in the bedroom—perhaps more than anything because of the feeling of powerlessness he had experienced in there. But that had only been a brief phase. For her, though, the house was tainted forever. The walls of the bedroom, the kitchen, and the basement were stained with ghastly memories. Quite literally. Even if she redecorated the entire house, she would still know what was hidden underneath. It would remain there for all eternity, like a bricked-up corpse.

They had approached a flock of sheep on the hillside. Yellowy white, with long tails and swiveling ears perched on top of their heads. Some of them interrupted their grazing and watched them, still chewing, their ears pricked up like rabbits.

"Are you sure we're in the right place?" she asked.

"Of course we are—take a look for yourself." He pointed to a section higher up, where a wooden signpost was standing in the grass. The trail up to and along the Seven Sisters was marked out with these signposts, but the path itself was almost invisible. It was nothing more than a tendril winding across the landscape, scarcely a hand's width across, on which the grass looked slightly shorter—or maybe it was just growing at a different angle.

Werner stopped for a moment and turned to face her, leaning on his stick. "Listen, Helen—if it would make you feel better, then maybe we should give some serious thought to selling the house."

She could scarcely conceal her surprise. "Do you mean it?"

He looked at her blankly. "Absolutely. Let's talk about it with the kids at some point." Then he turned around and continued walking uphill.

The higher they got, the harder the wind blew. It tore at their clothes. Werner didn't look back once, and Helen did her utmost not to fall behind. She had to place her feet carefully. There were rocks, potholes, and patches of uneven ground hidden beneath the grass and weeds. One false step and she would sprain her ankle, or worse. Every now and then, she looked up at Werner's back—his stooped posture, his fist clenched around the stick, the knuckles white.

There was something strange about this hike—it felt more like a military drill. She caught occasional glimpses of Werner's face. Grim, determined. Werner looked as though he were in pain, as if they weren't doing this for fun but were undertaking this harsh exercise out of necessity. His temperamental behavior unsettled her. One moment, he was the Werner who cracked jokes and treated her kindly, and the next, it felt like he was looking right through her.

Werner stopped abruptly. He lifted his chin and looked into the distance. Strands of hair poking out from under his hat flapped back and forth, then pressed flat against his temples.

Helen followed Werner's gaze out to sea. The curve of the hill seemed to fade into nothingness. As if the land suddenly vanished into the now iron-gray sky. She recalled the signs at the visitor center warning hikers that the cliff edges crumbled more and more each year. That was how they remained so beautifully white. She looked at her feet. Then straight ahead. She felt a shudder that seemed to emanate from deep in her belly.

"Werner?" Her scarf whipped against her shoulder.

"This is the first 'sister,'" he shouted over the wind. He slowly turned to face her. "The highest of the seven."

When her eyes met his, it was like she was looking at a stranger.

*9*

"I can't go on."

Ralf pretended not to hear Sara. Stabs of pain shot through his side and his lungs were on fire, but he refused to give in. He felt his fury toward Brian and Werner mount with each step. If everything had gone according to plan that Friday evening, then Sara would have had to bury her mother last week. For Möhring, it had been about the money—but also about Emily. It wouldn't have been long before she was introduced to the family as "Dad's new girlfriend." And, of course, Emily would have come with Brian in tow. The new stepbrother. And their mother's murderer. How fucked up was that? How cold, sick, and heartless did you even have to be to come up with something like that, let alone carry it out?

It was impossible to imagine a greater betrayal.

# 10

"We're going to do something exciting." Werner had to yell to make himself heard. The wind threatened to carry them away.

Helen recalled what he had said to her last night: that they were going to do something that wasn't allowed. They were alone up here—not even the sheep would come this far—but Werner didn't seem to be talking about sex. Quite the opposite. He looked at her tensely. His jaws were clenched, his eyes narrowed. He tapped his stick on the ground.

"What?" she shouted back.

He gestured at the precipice with his chin. "We're going to lie down on the edge."

"*What?*"

"The edge," he yelled. "We're going to lie down on the edge."

Instinctively, she took a step backward. Shook her head.

He grabbed her by the arm and pulled her against him. "The fear is something to savor, Helen. Looking into the abyss—it's an incredible kick, by all accounts."

"I can't."

"Of course you can. Nothing will happen. You just stick your head over the edge. Only a very little bit."

"Werner, you're scaring me." She tried to free herself, but he held her with a firm grip.

He grinned. "Scaring you? Don't you think experiences like this make life more interesting? Doing something every now and then that you've never done before? Sometimes you just need a little push in the right direction."

"Is that supposed to be a joke? I don't think it's funny." She gasped for air and kept shaking her head. "Not funny at all."

They were standing just a dozen steps from the edge. No grass grew this close to the precipice. The hills rolled onward into the distance: the second, third, and fourth sisters, with cliffs as far as the eye could see, and pale sunlight reflecting off the waves of the English Channel at their feet.

"If you're so desperate to do it," she shouted, "then go ahead. But I'm not coming with you. I'm terrified enough as it is." Her whole body was trembling.

He gave her a piercing look. "I want you to do it, Helen. Go and lie down over there. I'll hold on to your ankles."

"Have you lost your mind?" Her voice cracked. "I said no."

"Don't you trust me?"

"That's not the point."

A sinister gleam appeared in his eyes. "That's exactly the point, for Christ's sake. You've spent your entire life coloring inside the lines. You're such a fucking Goody Two-Shoes, it makes me sick, did you know that? Even when we have sex, it always has to be by the book." His voice suddenly went high and shrill. *"No, Werner, I don't want to; that hurts. It's too weird."* He pinched her arm and shook her. "All the constant bullshit about your work, like you're Mother fucking Teresa herself. Monopolizing the children, as if I don't count for anything—" He resumed his mocking tone. *"No, Werner, they didn't mean it that way. Don't interfere."* His face was red with fury.

"What are you talking about? Werner, you're not yourself."

Fragments of chalk crunched under their feet.

"Oh really, *I'm* not myself? What about you, then? The wild child who turned into the most uptight bitch I know."

"Will you—"

"I found your book, Helen. I read all those pathetic little letters you wrote to your mother. Does that shock you? I thought you meant for me to read them, since you weren't exactly discreet about it. Very enlightening to learn that you've been through with me for years now, but that you still keep up appearances"—that mocking tone again—*"because it's better for the children."*

She looked at him in horror, unable to move. All she could see was his contorted face, the revulsion and contempt. The seething hatred in his eyes. She suddenly understood that he wouldn't let her leave this place. He had planned all this.

She wouldn't get out of here alive.

The realization spread over her body like an ice-cold shiver, seeped through her veins, chilled her to her bones and beyond, to the depths of her heart.

"You disgust me, Helen. I've spent far too long trapped in this fucking sham of a marriage. I want to move on, for Christ's sake. I want to *live.*"

"Werner, no!" She tore herself from his grasp and tried to run. A sudden, sharp pain exploded through her lower back. She pitched forward and fell face-first onto the ground.

"I'm sick to death of you," he panted, gripping the stick in his hands.

# *11*

Ralf plowed uphill through the grass. He saw Werner Möhring standing by the edge of the cliff. First his head, then his shoulders. There was nobody with him. He was alone.

Ralf's eyes widened; he gasped.

*I'm too late.*

*Too late.*

*Too—*

Werner raised a stick and brought it down onto a figure sprawled on the ground in front of him.

"No!" bellowed Ralf, drawing his pistol.

Werner looked up. His eyes were bloodshot; his lips thin, pale and retracted; his teeth clenched in a horrible grimace. He no longer resembled a human, but a rabid animal.

"Mom!" Sara ran toward Helen, stumbling over the uneven ground.

Werner froze. His rage gave way to complete bewilderment when he saw his daughter.

Sara fell to her knees and drew her mother's head onto her lap. "Mom?"

Werner remained still, taking in the tableau of his wife with his elder daughter. His shoulders sagged. The stick slid from his fingers and fell to the ground. Slowly, jerkily, he sank to his knees and bent forward, holding his hands over his face.

Ralf kept the pistol trained on Werner. All he could hear was his heartbeat growing louder and more insistent, like a kettledrum in his head. The gun felt cold and heavy in his hand.

"Ralf? Give that to me." Helen was suddenly standing next to him. Her eyes were bloodshot and her hat was askew, but her voice was strangely calm. "We aren't going to shoot anybody here." She gently pushed his arm down and took the pistol from his hand.

He watched her tuck it into the pocket of her coat. Behind her, Werner had scarcely stirred. Sitting there like that—huddled on the edge of the cliff, his face in his hands—he suddenly looked so small and vulnerable. All energy and aggression seemed to have drained out of him.

"Come on; we're leaving," said Helen. She put a hand on Ralf's arm.

Ralf hesitated. He looked at Werner again. His back was hunched, his body shuddering. He might have been crying, but the wind carried the sound out to sea.

*Broken,* thought Ralf. *A broken man.*

"Ralf, are you coming?"

He looked up and saw Helen and Sara walking down the hill. Hurried after them, without looking back.

The fall sun hung low over the hills and cast long shadows on the fields. The rolling landscape seemed friendly, gentle. All the villages in this region had complicated names and lay remarkably far apart. Between them, the landscape was dominated by rugged wilderness and farmland, with just the occasional house dotted here and there—at the end of a long, muddy driveway leading through a thick coniferous wood, or on top of a freshly plowed hill and surrounded by open barns full of farm equipment being stored until spring. Settlements that looked like they had been built in the Middle Ages, assembled from large red or sand-colored stones, with shutters over the windows and a well in the yard.

The surroundings made a great contrast to the congestion on the freeway. A whole other world—a silent world, seemingly outside time. Ralf hadn't seen a single person in the last twenty minutes, although he had spotted packs of long-eared hunting dogs. They were scavenging by the side of the road, their noses sniffing along the ground. Just now, a deer had jumped out of the path of the Mercedes.

Ralf tapped his fingers on the leather steering wheel. The latex operating gloves had felt unfamiliar and uncomfortable when he put them on this morning in the Netherlands. He had grown used to them by now—just like the brand-new coveralls and work boots that he was wearing, and the disposable cap covering his hair. Not that you could see it—he was wearing a new knitted beanie on top, pulled down firmly over his ears.

He looked like an employee at a garage delivering a car, or somebody who had borrowed his boss's Mercedes. That was the exact intention. He had had to get out only once to refuel, but there were often cameras in places like that.

Invisible speakers were playing "Dear Mama," Tupac's ode to his mother. He hadn't listened to this song in a long time. The slow tempo suited the landscape and the thoughts running through his mind—memories and resolutions—while the music and the lyrics fed emotions that he couldn't quite put into words. Tupac's mother had outlived her son, he realized. All she had left was his music.

Ralf pushed up his sunglasses. Outside it was hot, but the climate control kept the temperature inside the car perfectly comfortable. Next to him, on the beige leather seat, lay a Montblanc laptop bag that didn't belong to him. It contained items that weren't his either: an iPhone, a MacBook, a passport, a wallet full of cash, bank cards, and a gleaming golden credit card. He had used the latter item to pay the toll—more than one hundred euros. The receipts were tucked underneath the sun visor.

Ahead of him stood a signpost announcing a village. The name was long and full of abbreviations. He couldn't pronounce it, but that didn't matter. The GPS would take him where he needed to go. Just before he reached the sleepy French hamlet, he turned off the main road and followed a narrower lane that took him deeper into the countryside. Forested plots, empty meadows. Not a house to be seen. Crows hopped across the stubble-covered fields, and hawks swooped high above them in the azure-blue sky.

Ralf slowed down. Following the instructions from the GPS, he steered the Mercedes onto a forest trail. It was bumpy and poorly maintained, exactly as Helen had described.

Just a few minutes later, he emerged onto a clearing. There was a small house with a pointed roof and a wooden shed next to it. A small round yard covered with dusty gravel.

Ralf got out and looked around. Listened. No noise from a nearby highway; no voices or music. Only birdsong. Earthy odors: soil, vegetation, decay. An animal smell too. A shudder ran through him. Who would want to live in such a remote place? He would go crazy after just one day here.

He opened the rear door and took a suitcase from the back seat. Tucked the laptop bag under his arm and walked up to the front door of the house.

The key fit the lock.

"Helen? It's Ria. Sorry to be so direct, but Ernst and I are worried about Werner."

"Why? Is something the matter?" Helen braked for a red light. It was early in the evening, and the roads were busy; most people were on their way home for dinner. Her workday was only just beginning.

"We've been trying to get ahold of him for a week, but he isn't answering his phone."

"The signal in the Gers isn't great," said Helen as the traffic started moving again.

"That's not the reason. At first, his phone rang when we called it, but it hasn't done that for a few days now. Instead, we hear a sort of cut-off tone."

"Werner wanted some peace and quiet. He probably just turned his phone off."

"Have you heard from him in the last week?"

"No. The last time I saw him was when he came over to pick up his things last Thursday."

"Did he say anything? Did you talk to each other at all?"

"Barely. He collected what he wanted to take with him and then left for France."

Her mother-in-law sighed and was silent for a moment. "I might as well tell you that Ernst and I think it's a real shame you two are fighting.

So unexpectedly too. It was such a shock when you came back from England separately."

"I'm just glad he was able to stay at your place," she remarked.

Ria sighed again. "Werner told us that you two had been having problems for a while now. He'd expected your trip to turn out very differently."

"Oh yes, I'm sure he did. You could say the same for me, of course."

"He kept saying there was no way to patch things up."

"I don't know what else he told you, but it wasn't a real fight, Ria. If you ask me, he's struggling with his own feelings more than anything else. He's been working far too hard over the last few years. But it'll all blow over, I think. We've been together for such a long time." Helen drove onto the hospital parking lot and looked around for a good spot, as close to the staff entrance as possible.

"Well, Helen, there's something else."

Helen felt her eyelid twitch. "What?"

"I asked the neighbors to pop over and take a look at the house. They said his car is parked in the yard, and the bed has been slept in. The lights were on, but Werner himself is nowhere to be seen."

"Huh. You're right; that is strange. Maybe he went hiking? Or camping? He did take the tent with him."

"Oh, I didn't know that."

"I really wouldn't worry, Ria. Werner was looking for peace and quiet. He didn't want to be bothered by work calls when he was in England either. Anyway, speaking of work, I have to go. I got to the hospital a few minutes ago, and my shift is about to start. As soon as I hear anything from Werner, I'll let you know. But honestly, Ria, there's no reason to be worried. I'm not."

Helen got out of the car. Two colleagues walked past, greeting her. She smiled, then pretended that an important message had just arrived on her phone. For appearance's sake, she reread one of the messages that she and Lex had exchanged over the past few days. She felt tense, but she still couldn't help smiling.

Only once her colleagues were out of sight did she walk to the back of her Fiat and open the trunk. She took a deep breath.

"Well, here we go," she whispered, before lifting out two heavy yellow shopping bags. As she walked toward the staff entrance, she felt the chill emanating from them through the thick fabric of her jeans.

*Mother Dear,*

*This summer, it will have been eight years since you passed away. Your absence feels different now from how it felt in the beginning. Different, but not less. What I didn't fully understand back then was that, when you died, I lost the last person in the world who loved me selflessly. Somebody who would always take my side, whatever I did. You once said to me, "Mothers love their children more than their children love them. That's natural, and it's how things should be." You were probably right, just as you were right with so many other things.*

*I wasn't always very understanding toward you, Mother. I regret that. When I remember our arguments, I cringe with shame. I was always so critical of you.*

*I often blamed you for splitting up with Father. I was jealous of friends who had a normal family life, and I focused on what I didn't have instead of all the things you gave me. Only now can I see that it's sometimes better to grow up without a father. And that your feelings about Werner were correct—though you could never have*

*predicted any of this. Who could? It's pure luck that I'm
still alive.*

*I would rather have had him locked up, Mother. That
would have been far preferable. But if I'd followed the
official route, then Sara, Thom, and Emma would have
lost both their parents. They would have been left depen-
dent on one another, brought up by Werner's parents, or
drifting from one foster family to another. The thought of
it tore me up inside. The alternative was just as horrible:
Should I have held my tongue and continued to expose my
children to the man who tried to kill their mother? Should
I have suffered in silence while they spent their weekends
with him? A mother's duty is to protect her children. So
that's what I've done.*

*Yes, Mother, I know—I'm just as worried about Sara
as you are. She's seen and heard too much. But she's strong
too. She has her pragmatic father's genes. I think I've managed to gloss over most of it. Justify it, even. And as far as
she knows, Werner went to France to work on himself.*

*His body was never found. Ultimately, she'll be better
off without him.*

*We all will.*

*I've been thinking a lot about Emily and Ria lately.
Emily was on TV just now. Her son has been missing
for six months, and she thinks the police aren't doing
enough to investigate. She wept; she looked straight at the
camera. I was so close to picking up the phone. It's eating
away at me, Mother. More and more. I don't know if
I can stay quiet, if I can keep the truth from her. Then
again, I'll never know if she and Werner were partners*

*in crime, or if she knew that Werner wanted to remove me from his life so drastically.*

*Maybe I'll still do it; maybe I'll confess what I've done to Ria and Emily. Not now, but in the future. When my kids no longer need me.*

# *Acknowledgments*

Berry
&
Annelies

Sally
Sabrine
Sabine
Renate
Nini
Monique
José
J. and L.
Debby
&
Carola

Thank you to Jozef van der Voort, Liza Darnton, the copyeditor, the proofreader, and the teams in the US and UK for all the work, effort, knowledge, and love you have put into this translation. I could not have asked for a better team.

# *About the Author*

*Photo © Noortje Dalhuijsen*

Nova Lee Maier is a pseudonym of Dutch bestselling author Esther Verhoef, whose psychological thrillers and novels have sold more than 2.5 million copies in the Netherlands. Esther is the recipient of numerous awards, including the NS Publieksprijs (NS Audience Award/ Prix Public); the Hebban Crimezone Award; the Diamanten Kogel (Diamond Bullet); and for *Mother Dear*, the prestigious Gouden Strop (Golden Noose) Award for best crime thriller of the year. She is also the author of *Close-Up* and *Rendezvous*, both available in English. For more information, visit www.novaleemaier.com and www.estherverhoef.com.

# About the Translator

Jozef van der Voort is a professional translator adapting Dutch, German, and French into English. A Dutch-British dual national, he grew up in southeast England and studied literature and languages in Durham and Sheffield. He has lived and worked in Austria, France, Luxembourg, Germany, and Belgium. As a literary translator, he took part in the Emerging Translators Programme run by New Books in German and was also named runner-up in the 2014 Harvill Secker Young Translators' Prize. *Mother Dear* is his first translated novel.

Printed in Great Britain
by Amazon